THE HARDEST HIT

by

Bethany Maines

This book is a work of fiction. Names, characters, and incidents are products of the author's imagination or are used fictitiously. Any resemblance to actual events or persons living or dead is entirely coincidental.

Cover art by **LILTdesign.com**.

ISBN-13: 978-1-7332813-5-5

Dedicated to my writer's group—
Brittney Noble, J.M. Phillippe, and Karen Harris Tully.
Thank you for your endless encouragement
and helpful criticism.

CONTENTS

THE HARDEST HIT

Olivia Rose West

Olivia West stared at the door of the hospital exam room and tried to decide what to do if the cops didn't get a warrant.

"Are you sure?" asked the doctor, perusing Olivia's test results.

Olivia West looked up at him from her spot on the crinkly paper. It had seemed safe to leave her purse, phone, and jacket in Glen's apartment while they went to his neighbor's Halloween party. If they left her purse in the possession of Glen, what would she do? Glen had tried to rape her. And the cops thought that she should just, what? Leave the keys to her entire life with him?

"Am I sure about what?" she asked the doctor. She knew her Georgia accent made people here think she was stupid, but the doctor's aura of condescension seemed beyond even what she was used to.

"Well, I mean, it is easy to be mistaken about these kinds of things. Maybe you saw something, you didn't really see?"

"Excuse me?"

"I'm just saying the results from your blood test are so minimal that it could be a false positive."

"Yes," said the nurse, looking as though she was barely holding her temper, "because she made herself puke on the instruction of the 911 operator. The test of the glass showed it was enough to knock out someone three times her weight. See?" The nurse flipped the page in the doctor's chart and pointed forcefully.

"Oh. Right. Well. As I said, the results are minimal, so you're going to be fine and there shouldn't be any after-effects."

"The cops said I need to submit the test results," said Olivia. "Can I have two copies please?"

"Sure," said the doctor. "The nurses at the desk can take care of that."

He turned and left without saying goodbye.

Olivia stared at the nurse. "I'll make sure they're waiting for you at the desk," said the nurse. "You go ahead and get dressed. I love your costume, by the way."

"Thanks," said Olivia, already beginning to pull off the medical gown.

Being a comic book character for Halloween had seemed like such a good idea. She knew she looked amazing in her Dark Phoenix costume, but she hadn't counted on having to get her arm out of the lycra bodysuit for blood tests to prove that her date had tried to put a roofie in her drink.

She pulled the top half of her suit back on and zipped herself up, trying to figure out how to handle the cops. Her only ally was the nice guy who'd come sprinting across the party to yank the drink out of her hand. Evan, last name not specified, had dialed 911. He'd gotten her into the bathroom and when Glen had tried to put up a fuss, Evan had called him a *fucking rapist* and punched him in the face. Something she would have appreciated more if she hadn't been trying to force herself to puke up half a cocktail. Then, Evan had gotten the glass and cocktail put into a plastic bag for testing. He'd even driven her to the hospital when she didn't want to ride in the ambulance. But while Evan might be the bright spot in her evening, what could he do about the cops?

Taking a deep breath, she went out to the lobby. There was now only one cop, and Evan was staring at him, arms folded across his chest. Evan was wearing a suit. If it was a costume, then he was dressed as an investment banker. A good-looking, six-foot-two investment banker in an expensive suit. She didn't think it was a costume.

"Hi," said Olivia, approaching the pair.

"Hi," said Evan, his face stretching into a smile that even she could tell was fake. "Good news. Officer James has gone to collect the warrant. Officer Sanchez is going to go wait for it outside Glen's apartment."

"Oh, thank God," said Olivia, relief sweeping over her. "Thank you so much," she said. She reached out and touched Officer Sanchez on the arm. Officer Sanchez's face flashed with expression Olivia didn't quite catch, but then he seemed to straighten up.

"Of course. Just doing my job. You can wait at the police station while we collect your things."

"At the police station?" repeated Olivia, doubtful. This was going down as the worst night of her life, or at minimum the worst night she'd had since arriving in this city.

"No," said Evan, his voice hard. "She is not a criminal. She will wait at my place. I'm in the same building, number 803."

"OK," agreed the cop, barely looking up at Evan. "I'll go now."

"Great," said Evan.

Olivia considered herself socially slow. Not stupid. Just slow. She could never recognize things in the moment they happened, so it wasn't until Officer Sanchez was walking away that she realized his look had been the same expression as the hound dog who stole her grandmother's pie off a windowsill. *Hangdog* didn't begin to express the amount of guilt on Officer Sanchez's face. But why? What had he done?

"I'll go get the car," said Evan. "You wait here."

Olivia found herself nodding out of habit, but paused to question the decision as Evan left the lobby. Did she want to wait here? She decided that she *did* want to wait. She wanted someone to bring her a car and take care of her. She was feeling particularly genteel and not at all interested in doing things for herself at the moment.

So Olivia pretended that she was a princess and stood right where she was and waited for Evan to come back and do all the appropriate pampering things that befit a princess. The TV screen in the waiting room was playing CNN. The woman senator her grandfather hated was making a speech.

"The scourge of white nationalism must be pushed back. We cannot allow those who push for hatred to rule us. But neither can we turn to hate ourselves. I believe that the best way to fight nationalism, misogyny, and violence is to raise the standard of living for all, to make sure that the opportunities available to the rich are also available to the poor. Science and education are not dirty words. It's what brought us success after World War II. They are what make America great. If we want to bring back the good old days, then let's start with the things we know that worked—education, taxation of the one percent, and refutation of all that those Nazi scum stand for."

Olivia didn't follow politics—mostly on purpose. All she knew about the woman speaking was that her grandfather hated her. It was the first time she'd actually heard "Evil Eleanor" speak. Now that she had, it was crystal clear where the hate was coming from. Inclusion, science, taxation, and using the word misogyny in all seriousness were all forbidden in her grandfather's house. Hell, words with more than one syllable were apt to get someone a talking to. At any other time, Olivia probably would have whipped out her phone, figured out Evil Eleanor's campaign website, and made a five-dollar donation. Since leaving Georgia, she'd made dozens of five-dollar donations to anyone and everything that promised to fight everything that she had left behind. But at the moment, she just wanted Evan to come back with the car and drive her home, even if it wasn't her home.

The nurse from the desk came around and handed her a clipboard and a pile of papers.

"This is your discharge form," she said pointing out where to sign. "And these are your reports. We already gave one to the cops." She glanced out the sliding glass doors at Evan. "How well do you know your friend there?"

Olivia looked after Evan, his red-gold hair glinting in the street lights as he crossed into the parking garage.

"I just met him tonight. Why?"

"Well, while you were in getting your blood drawn, he tore those two cops a new one, and then he called up their boss and did it again. I haven't heard anything that feminist since I listened to the Gloria Steinem biography audiobook. The only reason they're going to get that warrant and get your stuff is that he made them. If I were you, I'd keep that guy around."

Olivia didn't know how to respond to that. At the moment, Evan was indeed the only person she wanted to keep around. This evening had been a nightmare.

The nurse put all the papers into an envelope for her and then Evan returned for her and held open her door and put her in the car. Olivia felt pleased to be pampered but found herself trying to sort through the events of the evening in a coherent manner.

Evan drove in silence and Olivia wasn't sure what to make of that. She should probably thank him. But he so clearly hadn't wanted her to know about what he'd said to the cops.

"I know I did the right thing," she said at last. "Right? It's what everyone said we should do."

"Yeah," he agreed, glancing over at her.

"Then I'm not sure why I feel so... embarrassed. Those cops, that doctor… It was like they thought I'd made it all up. Even with what you said, and the damn evidence right in front of them, they were still skeptical. They were supposed to be the ones helping me."

"That's why I hate hospitals," he said. "The doctors take one look at you, make a decision, and then write it down for the next doctor to say the same damn thing. Getting them to write down anything different is like trying to turn a train. And even when they're nice, they steal every little bit of control you ever had and reduce you down to an idiot."

"Yes! Yes. It's humiliating."

"Yes," he agreed. "Sorry you had to go through that."

She pondered that for another moment. Or at least she tried to ponder it.

"I suppose tomorrow I'll wake up and I will be pissed as hell."

"You'll have a right to be."

"But right now all I can think is how damn hungry I am and how much I want a drink."

"Well, that I can help you with," said Evan glancing away from the road, a smile flitting across his face.

"Oh, well there's a shocker, said no one," she blurted out.

"What does that mean?" He looked halfway annoyed. She wanted to palm her own forehead. She had just meant it to be funny.

"Evan, you held my hair while I puked. If that didn't polish up your official Knight in Shining Armor plaque then punching my would-be rapist in the face certainly did. The fact that you can also offer me sustenance and an alcoholic beverage is really, at this point, simply showing off." She added a smile to show she was joking.

He laughed and relaxed, but shook his head. "No. I'm not that guy. I'm not the knight guy."

"Really?" She looked at him in surprise. How could he not

think he'd ridden to the rescue? "You're going to try and argue with me on this?"

"It's not arguing," he said. "I'm just trying to point out the truth. I'm not that guy. Those guys don't argue about it, for one thing."

He parked the car in the garage under the building. The condo building was ridiculously expensive. She guessed that the parking space alone cost about as much as the annual rent on her apartment. Olivia looked at him across the emergency brake. He really was breathtakingly good-looking. She usually wasn't attracted to those of her own kind. It was her general belief that gingers should not get together with other gingers, but his hair was on the gold side of red, and those pale gray eyes over a square jaw and lips that looked made for kissing, made her re-think the theory.

"And how many of those guys have you met?" she demanded.

"None. Maybe one," he amended.

"Then how would you know? Maybe all you knights are extremely argumentative."

"No," he said firmly and got out of the car.

Evan Alexander Deveraux

Evan Deveraux was at the end of the car and she still hadn't gotten out. He had even stopped at the trunk to pull out the box he'd driven out to Jersey to retrieve from DevEntier Industries and she was still in the car. He rolled his eyes. His Dark Phoenix was far more Rogue than Jean Grey and if she insisted on proceeding down the Knight in Shining Armor path he wasn't sure how much he could take. He had just been mad at the cops, not wanting to take her home. And now he was stuck with Olivia, last name unknown, for the evening. Admittedly, she seemed shockingly funny for someone in her situation, but there had been a lot of talking, and he had been looking forward to being able to crash at home and switch his brain off. He waited another second, but she still hadn't moved from the car. He heaved a sigh and went to open her door.

"Sorry," he said yanking open the passenger side door. "I forgot you were Southern and can't open doors on your own."

She looked up at him, one hand pressed to the side of her head, eyes slightly teary, and he felt a moment of panic. He'd been trying for funny. Well, snarky anyway.

"I wasn't waiting for you to open the door. My hair got sucked into the seatbelt retractor and I couldn't get out."

He knew he shouldn't, but the laugh was expelled out of him in an uncontrolled gust. His own idiocy and inability to be suave on any level was just the perfect capper on a ridiculous evening of dealing with the most traumatic shit.

"It's not funny," she said, climbing out of the car, but a smile was twitching out of the corners of her mouth. "It hurt."

He straightened up, tried to rein it back in, and realized he couldn't. He laughed again, his shoulders shaking.

"Ya'll need to take a lap and walk it off?" she demanded.

He pressed a hand into his eye socket, trying to quell the laughter.

"No, no. I got this." He took a deep breath and tried to look her in the eye, almost made it, but then started to laugh again. He took another deep breath and managed to make eye contact this time.

"So glad my pain can amuse you."

He didn't respond—wasn't sure that he *could* respond—and gestured toward the elevators.

"This does prove my point," he said, as the metal doors closed behind them. "I'm not that guy. The knight guy does not laugh at a lady who can't exit a vehicle."

"I could have gone bald. I could have a giant bald spot right now and you'd still be laughing," she sounded torn between annoyance and amusement.

"So hard," he agreed—might as well put the knight thing to rest right now.

"What's in the box?" she asked scrutinizing the faded white box.

"Oh, stuff from my dad and uncle's old company," he said, wishing he could hide it. "Cleaning out some old files and junk," he lied.

"Why didn't your dad go get it?" she asked, and Evan froze. Almost no one asked about his father anymore.

"Um. He's dead." Might as well put that out there—he was pretty sure it would send her running for the nearest exit. No one wanted to date family trauma in a suit. "Plane crash. My uncle and aunt too." He added the last bit, just for good measure.

"Oh." Her lips twisted unhappily. "So is my mom," she offered. "Suicide. It's always so awkward to explain death, let alone early death, in social situations. It makes other people uncomfortable."

Evan breathed out a sigh of shocked relief. "It really does and then things just get weird. You can see they want to ask about it, but then they don't, and then they're mad at you for bringing the party down and all you really wanted was a drink and to make it through the next thirty minutes without having to use someone's name because you already forgot all of them."

Olivia burst out in a peal of laughter. "Yes! Yes! Exactly! Oh, my God, that makes me feel so very validated. Thank you."

Evan smiled at her. "Sorry about your mom."

"Sorry about your family."

He shrugged. "It is what it is."

She nodded, and he thought it was rare to meet someone who actually could accept that.

They got out at the eighth floor and unlocked his front door. She stepped inside and he tried not to watch for her reaction. He hadn't had anyone over since… He tried to remember. Probably the last model? The one with the big teeth? God, she had been boring. They had all been boring. When he'd given up going to Fetish, the highly discrete, highly exclusive S & M Club, he'd been worried that he'd miss it. And he did, just not for the reasons he'd thought. He didn't miss the pain or the latex or Leona Meade, or the endless amounts of feeling like a horrible fucking human being, but what he missed was sex that wasn't boring. He didn't understand why there couldn't be a middle ground between white bread and jalapeño.

"Oh, look at your view," she said, her accent pulling out *view* to multiple syllables.

"It's pretty much why I bought the place," he said, tucking the box into the front closet.

"I can see why."

"Will wine do in the alcoholic beverage department?"

"Yes, please," she said, still staring at the view.

He paused halfway to the kitchen. "Should you have alcohol?"

Olivia gave him a sour look. "I have so little left in my system that the doctor accused me of making it up. I think I'm fine."

"Right," said Evan, feeling a sympathetic fury on her behalf. "Wine coming up."

"Thanks."

He went into the kitchen and unstoppered the wine he'd opened the previous night. He'd used the new air sealer system his cousin had bought him last Christmas and the stopper released with a wet pop. He poured two glasses and took one out to her. She was standing on the edge of the step down from the dining area into the living room.

She accepted the glass without tearing her eyes away from the windows and took a healthy drink.

"Oh, that's nice," she said, looking down in surprise at the wine, then she held the glass up to her nose and inhaled. Her appreciation pleased him; most people didn't enjoy wine properly.

"Mm… summer in a glass," she murmured. She took another sip, smaller this time, savoring it in her mouth, and then closed her eyes as she tipped it down her throat.

He blinked. He felt incredibly turned on just from watching her drink wine.

"Summer?" he asked, clearing his throat, and yanking his eyes back to the city view on the other side of the window.

"It's the blackberry notes," she said. Her accent was now like syrup. He smelled his glass. He knew what she meant. The wine was a Syrah and the hint of blackberry was distinct. "I used to visit my grandparent's farm in the summer. My brother and sister and I would go out and pick the blackberries. We'd come back with purple fingers. Purple everywhere really. We'd always end up in a blackberry fight."

He smiled. That sounded nice and *so* far removed from his childhood. His father had been an abusive alcoholic. And when his father, uncle, and aunt had died in a plane crash, Evan and his cousins Aiden and Dominique had gone to live with their grandmother. But Eleanor Deveraux had never allowed them to indulge in messy outdoor adventures—those did not reflect well on the family.

"Evan," Olivia said, sounding nervous and he turned toward her, "can I ask for another favor? Do you have some sweats or something I could borrow until the cops come? I'd like to not be wearing lycra for a while."

He looked down at her costume. One look at Olivia with her cascade of red hair and Dark Phoenix costume of crimson lycra with a splashy yellow sash, thigh-high boots, and phoenix logo on her chest, and he'd let himself be coerced into going into Isabelle Elliott's stupid Halloween party. He hated Isabelle Elliott. She consistently tried to corner him in the parking garage and invite him to dinner. But Olivia looked like every fantasy he'd ever had when he was fourteen and how was he supposed to resist that? If nothing else, he wanted to know if she was padding her bustier for better comic book accuracy. Of course, he hadn't counted on Olivia's date putting a roofie in her drink or having to help her through the morass of the criminal justice system for the rest of the evening.

"Sure, of course."

He took her upstairs to his room and pulled out a pair of sweats and a t-shirt. Then he grabbed a t-shirt for himself and went back downstairs, changing out of his button-up as he went. When she came back down, he was most of the way through fixing them some dinner. He looked up as she walked down the stairs and watched as her breasts bounced under the soft cotton of his shirt—she defi-nitely had not been padding the costume.

"Go ahead and sit down," he said, gesturing at the dining table. "I'll have food in a moment. Sustenance, as you say." He found himself smiling. Her Southernisms were hilarious.

She picked up her glass of wine and sat down, pulling her feet up into the chair. He dumped the vegetables on her plate, tossed some parmesan over them, and took it over to the table. She looked down at the plate as he set it in front of her and then back up at him, her green eyes suddenly enormous in her face. He didn't know what the expression meant.

"Did you cook for me?"

"You said you were hungry," he said, backing away.

"But I could have had a sandwich or something," she said, her eyes still big.

"It's just chicken," he said, sitting down on his side of the table. "That's OK, right?"

"Yes! Yes! It's fine!" She picked up her fork and seemed to try and pull herself together.

"OK," he said picking up his own fork. He felt like he was missing some sort of subtext. She took a bite and he relaxed, preparing to cut into his food.

"No," Olivia said. "No, it's not fine."

He put his fork down and looked at her in exasperation.

"I can't play this off. You don't understand. I have been in this stupid city for six months and no one has cooked me anything. Not a cookie, not a cake, not a casserole." She ticked them off on her fingers like a checklist, as if people just randomly made casseroles. "Every piece of food I have put in my mouth I either made myself or paid someone to make, and that's fine, but it's like paying for a whore."

"What?"

"The sex is good, but it's not real love if you know what I mean."

"I love the way you talk," Evan blurted out. "But it's still just chicken. I didn't even cook it tonight. I reheated it from last night."

"And I really, really appreciate it."

"Then I won't tell you about the vegetables."

"I love the vegetables."

"You haven't even tried them."

"I still love them."

"Eat your food."

"Thank you," she said smiling as if she had won. "I will."

He glared at her as she popped a piece of broccoli in her mouth. He was uncomfortable having someone thank him. He was used to doing things for other people and expecting something in return. That was how things worked and it kept him in control of who owed what. He didn't know what spontaneous thanks meant.

Olivia – New Rules

Olivia sipped her third glass of the Syrah Evan was pouring and looked around his living room. This was by far the best not-a-date she'd been on in…year? No, it was over a year. She'd broken up with Clark last July and this was the first time since then that she'd felt like someone might be worth pursuing.

"So you've been here six months?" asked Evan, flipping on the stereo from his watch. "Where are you from?"

"Georgia. I moved for my job." And to get away from Clark and her family, but that didn't need to be said. "And I love my job so far, but I have to say, making friends here has been difficult."

"Is that why you went out with Glen?" he asked.

"He knows a co-worker of mine. She said he was normal."

"I'd complain to her tomorrow," he said. Olivia made an agreeing noise, still scrutinizing the bookshelves. "What do you do for a living?" he asked.

"I'm in research and development, focusing on the biolumi-nescence of the *Vampyroteuthis infernalis*, commonly known as the vampire squid."

"Oh," he said. Which was what most people said when they learned what she did for a living.

"OK," she said turning back to him. "Where is it?"

"Where's what?"

"This is a very lovely entertaining space. Very comfortable. Welcoming even. With good flow patterns for when you have peo-ple over. But this is not your living room."

"No, it actually is my living room," he said, frowning.

"You laughed at my joke about Wolverine versus Cyclops.

You got my Marie Curie reference. And you never once asked what character I was supposed to be and I think it's because you already know. Where is it? Where's the nerd swag? There's not a single *Star Wars* movie poster in this place."

"I…" His eyes flicked upward to the door at the far end of the upstairs hallway.

"Great," said Olivia, smiling. She carried her wine up the stairs.

"No," he said, trailing after her. "Can't we just assume I'm a nerd and move on with life?"

"How can I judge you if I don't check out your movie collection?" she asked. She walked along the open hallway that looked out over the rest of the loft and down to the closed door at the end of the hallway. "This one?" she asked, hand on the knob.

"This is really embarrassing," he said. "Please don't."

"Why?" she asked, opening the door.

"Because there's a giant poster of you on the wall," he blurted out, hurrying after her, as she swung open the door.

She stared up at the large, framed poster of Dark Phoenix over the couch and burst out laughing. "Yay!" she exclaimed, bouncing into the room, coming perilously close to splashing wine all over his carpet. "I win! I'm the winner!"

"What do you win?" he demanded, leaning against the doorframe.

She wasn't sure, now that he'd asked. When she'd seen the poster, she'd just had the gut reaction that he was already hers and he couldn't take it back.

"I was right," she said. "I like being right." She turned to his movie collection to cover up her sudden embarrassment. "Got it, got it, got it, hated it, got it, got it. Want it," she paused to read the back of the *Adèle Blanc-Sec* Blue Ray.

"So you study vampire squid. What kind of degree do you have to have to do that?"

She glanced up, trying to decide if he was making fun of her or if he was really curious.

"I have two PhDs. One in Chemical Engineering, one in Bio-Chemistry."

"How am I the nerd here?" he demanded.

"You have a poster of me on your wall."

"Who do you have on your wall?"

"No one at the moment," said Olivia, feeling deflated. "I left most of my stuff at home when I moved. I don't even have a cat."

"Do you want a cat?" He looked confused.

"Well, no, but I believe if one is going to be a spinster that it is appropriate at some point to take possession of cats. Or they take possession of you. I'm unclear. But the point is: I have no cats."

He laughed. "Spinster? What are you, like, twenty-four?"

"I'm twenty-seven. How old are you?"

"Thirty-one."

"Well, then you're probably getting it too. Doesn't your family ever pressure you to settle down and get married and not break up with your asshole boyfriend even though he cheated on you and are you sure you couldn't make it work?"

"Literally, no, to all of that."

"Oh," said Olivia, taking another gulp of her wine. She hadn't meant to say that. Talking about an ex was the number one thing not to do with a guy. She had heard it from multiple sources. "That's just so sexist. Why don't men get the same pressure to pair up?"

"I have no idea, but in my case, I think it's because they don't think I should."

"That sounds nice."

"When did you break up with the cheater?"

"One year three months ago."

"Not that you're counting."

"It's hard not to, when—" She stopped herself. "Never mind."

He was watching her with a bemused smile on his face. "Was cheater so great?"

She stared at him, with his penetrating, almost blue, mostly gray eyes and the lips that she could imagine kissing her all over and…oh, fuck it. He'd already seen her puke and he was still talking to her, so why not?

"Cheater was not so great, except in one department. He asked me to marry him, I said yes, we had sex, and the next day I found out that he'd been sleeping with Tara Barnett the naturopathic 'doctor' for six months and I haven't had an orgasm since."

He choked on a sip of wine. "What?" he asked, wiping wine off his chin.

"I think I'm broken."

"No," he said firmly.

"I have had three boyfriends since Clark and I broke up and… nothing. I ended up faking it because I was bored with having someone hop up and down on top of me like a pygmy goat in heat."

He paused with the glass halfway to his lips. "Pygmy goat?"

"There's a surprising amount of bouncing. Anyway, it's hard not to count the time past with that as a marker. Like I said, I think I'm broken."

"No," he said again.

"Oh, really? You know so much?" Olivia was annoyed. He didn't get to argue about her life. It was *her* life. She planted her hands on her hips and stood in front of him.

"About that? Yes." He looked annoyingly confident and he hadn't moved from the doorway. He just leaned there, a glass of wine dangling from one hand a smug smile on his face.

"You just met me."

"I'm still right."

"Fine." She glared at him, assessing how far she was willing to push things. She had promised herself when she moved that she wouldn't get tied up in second-guessing what she wanted. And she was pretty sure that Evan was what she wanted. "Care to put your money where your mouth is?"

"Anytime, anywhere," he said.

There was silence in the room.

"Oh," said Olivia. She blinked up at him. She hadn't expected him to say yes. She actually didn't have any experience with first date sex and she wasn't sure what the rules were. Polite clarification was probably in order. "Um. I was serious. Were you serious?"

His smile broadened to a grin. "Yes."

"Oh." That hadn't helped any. "Um. I don't know what to do next."

He finished his glass in one long swallow and set the glass down on the bookshelf next to the door. "Come on." He grabbed her by the hand and tugged her down the hall to his bedroom, where she'd left her costume on a chair.

"I once met a woman on a layover in Tokyo," he said. "She was a professional, if you know what I mean. And she said that most women have a hard time coming because they can't stop thinking about the next item on their to-do list. They're too busy taking care of other people and they don't take the time to relax."

He reached down and worked his t-shirt off of her. "You're going to relax me into an orgasm?" she asked skeptically as the shirt cleared her head.

"Yes," he said, pushing his sweats off her hips. They dropped to the floor with a soft thump of heavy fleece, leaving her standing in her bra and panties. She thought that probably ought to make her embarrassed, but it was her good bra, and from the way he was eyeing her cleavage, he thought it was pretty good too, so it was probably fine. He stripped out of his shirt and then went back to the door, dimmed the lights, and adjusted the heat upward.

"I'm not sure that's pertinent data," she said. "What would a hooker know about making women happy?"

"Well, that was the interesting part," he said. "She only worked with women."

"That is a more relevant sampling," she agreed.

He grinned and reached around to unsnap her bra. His hands caressed her skin for just a second, but she tingled where he touched her.

"Get naked," he said. "Lay on the bed face down."

She did as he said, but watched him. She was suddenly not so sure this was her best plan ever.

"We are using condoms, right?" she asked, resting her chin on her forearms.

"Yes, when we get there," he said.

She watched as he stripped out of his pants. He seemed to have zero embarrassment about flashing his assets, which, as she snuck another look, seemed entirely warranted. He grabbed a bottle of lotion and set it down next to the bed, then disappeared into the bathroom and returned with condoms that he dropped next to the lotion.

"OK," he said, doling out a handful of lotion and rubbing it over his fingers. "Here are the rules."

"Rules?" Olivia felt more skeptical than ever. What had she gotten herself into?

"Yes, rules. Whatever you don't like, you tell me and I'll change it. If you want me to stop, you have to say stop."

"OK," said Olivia. That seemed reasonable.

"But I'm not psychic, so if you like something you have to tell me."

That also seemed reasonable.

"OK, so let's practice. Do you like this?" He booped her nose, and she laughed.

"No!" she said.

"Really? Are you sure?" He kept booping.

"Stop that," she said, swatting at his hand. He immediately stopped.

"OK, how about this?" He ran his hands up the entire length of her back and she shivered.

"That, I like," she said.

"Good."

He swept his hands back down and then up. Evan moved his hands over her entire body, smoothing out knots in her shoulders, her back, and then surprisingly in her ass. He worked his way down to her feet. And she found that by the time he got to her toes she had stopped being able to make coherent statements about what was nice or not and simply went for happy murmurs. As he put her leg back down, she realized that he'd put it in a wider position, so that now her legs were apart. He moved his way back up her legs, fingers working along her inner thigh. He didn't hurry. His fingers simply smoothed the muscles, back and forth. But she found herself breathing more heavily, wanting him to hurry. He slid one hand over her ass and up to her lower back. He stroked the muscles there and his other hand slid gently upward, one finger caressing and exploring. He found her clit, and gently, with hardly any pressure, circled it.

She heard herself let out a little gasp. Pressure was building inside her and she wriggled a little, trying to get him to push harder. Instead, he continued his light touch and she moaned. She knew she was wet, she knew he could be fucking her right now if he wanted. Why wasn't he?

He continued to circle and then abruptly pulled his finger down and back up. The sudden change in rhythm left her gasping. He pressed harder now, as he went back to circles.

"Oh God, Evan," she moaned.

She was closer now to orgasm than she had been at any point in the previous year. She felt the deep aching need to have him inside her.

"Evan, please."

"Please, what?" he asked.

"God, Evan, please, just fuck me." He was pushing faster now and she felt herself involuntarily flex and arch, trying to make herself more available to him. "Please, Evan, please." She was so close. She moaned again, jerking as another spike of pleasure hit her.

"No," he said, his voice in a husky growl as he leaned forward to nibble her ear lobe. "Not yet."

She let out a panting, breathless moan that was half-whine.

"I need you, Evan, please. Please fuck me, please."

"No," he said again, and this time there was a definite chuckle in his voice. She was trembling, on the brink—his goddamn fingers were better than her fucking vibrator. "Oh, God!" She gave a shriek, burying her face into the pillow as she came.

"Not broken," he whispered, and she could hear the smile in his voice.

She blinked at his gray cotton sheets and trying to remember what to do next.

"I like being wrong," she said.

He chuckled, stretching himself out next to her and she groaned as he pulled his hand away from her. She didn't want him to stop touching her ever. He licked his fingers, which she supposed could have been gross, but instead, she found incredibly sexy, and then he leaned in and nibbled her shoulder. She rolled over and extended one leg to loop over his hip. She was going to need a minute, but she was seriously going to fuck his brains out.

Evan - Goodbye

Evan hadn't thought that he'd missed anything about Fetish, but he hadn't realized up until the moment that the words had come out of Olivia's mouth that he missed having someone beg him to be fucked.

What had those fucktards she'd dated been doing? There was nothing wrong with Olivia. She was perfect. He looked over at her, already picturing what he'd do to her for the rest of the evening.

She smiled at him, a lazy, happy smile, and he found himself smiling back as her leg slithered over his hip.

"Is it always like this when you do that?" she asked, her voice a sultry purr.

"I have no idea," he said. "This was a bit of an experiment."

"Oh. Well, in that case, if you have any more experiments you wish to run, I'd like to volunteer myself as a test subject."

"Same time next Tuesday?" he asked, grinning. "See if we can't replicate the results?"

"Exactly," she said.

He reached out for her, sliding a hand along her hip and waist, reveling in her curves. He realized that he hadn't even kissed her, which was clearly an oversight. "Clear your Tuesday then," he said, brushing a lock of hair out of her face. "But I don't think—" he began, intending to say that there was no reason on earth to wait for Tuesday, but the doorbell rang.

"Fuck," she said, sitting bolt upright. "I forgot about the cops. Shit!"

He laughed. "Fuck the police, as my cousin likes to say."

"No! They already think I'm a total slut. This will put the capper on it!"

She scrambled out of bed and onto the floor looking for her underwear. He hated it, but she was right. Officers James and Sanchez had made their opinions of girls who wore superhero costumes perfectly clear.

"Calm down," he said, getting up and pulling on the sweats and shirt, she'd recently been wearing. "I'll go stall them. You put your costume back and I'll say you're in the bathroom."

"OK, right, right."

He went downstairs and checked the small screen by the door. Officer Sanchez and another officer, a woman this time, were standing there holding Olivia's purse and jacket.

"Hi," he said, opening the door. The two police officers shuffled into his foyer and looked around for Olivia.

"Your timing couldn't be worse. She just went to the bathroom, and it's my understanding that getting in and out of the costume is a ten-minute process." Officer Sanchez smirked and Evan fought the urge to punch him in the face. "You don't have a problem waiting, do you, Officer Sanchez?" he asked, staring at the policeman.

"No, he doesn't," said the female cop, and Officer Sanchez seemed to shrink in on himself a little.

"Did you arrest Glen?" he asked.

"Yes," said the female officer. "You will most likely be contacted by the district attorney's office to provide testimony."

"Not a problem," said Evan, already thinking that it was a problem. His grandmother was a senator and she would hate such a public spectacle. He knew what she would want him to do: decline to testify or call his cousin Jackson. But he didn't want to do either of those things. Jackson Zane, now Deveraux, was Uncle Randall's bastard son and when Eleanor had found Jackson five years ago he'd been in prison. Jackson's arrival in the family had changed everything. For the better. His other cousins, Aiden and Dominique, talked to Evan now anyway and he thought that was mostly because of Jackson. Which made sense, in a way, because Jackson was in charge of solving problems.

The Deveraux family was divided into departments. Evan was finance. Aiden was law. Jackson was security. And Dominique… Eleanor said marketing, but Jackson called her the creative director and Evan thought that was probably right. But none of the departments were going to be happy if Evan had to go testify in a public rape case. Eleanor would feel compelled to take an interest, and what was a small-time asshole could suddenly become a very public investigation into just what had happened tonight. He didn't want to explain the glory of Olivia to anyone. And having to ask Jackson to help him clean up one more of his messes was humiliating. Evan was going to have to come up with another alternative.

Olivia came down the stairs and he felt his cock twitch at the sight of her. Their roll through the sheets had given her hair a wild, untamed look and he couldn't believe that the officers couldn't smell sex on them.

"Officer Sanchez! You got my purse! How nice of you!"

The officer mutely held out the bag and she accepted it, plunking it down on the table, and opening it.

"It does look like everything is here," she said. "I hope you've arrested Glen?"

"Yes, ma'am," he said.

"The district attorney's office will be in touch," said the female cop again.

"Great," said Olivia. "I just hate the idea of him being able to do that to somebody else."

"Yes, ma'am," agreed the female officer. "I'm here to drive you home."

"Um, thank you so much," said Olivia. "I appreciate it." She finally turned and looked up at him. "Well, thank you so much for all your help, Evan."

She held out her hand for a handshake and it was all he could do to not laugh.

"Anytime," he said, shaking her hand.

The two police officers escorted her out the door. He raised his hand in an ineffectual wave as she looked back over her shoulder. It was only after the door closed that he realized that he didn't know her last name or how to find her.

Evan – The Storage Unit

The Deveraux storage unit was crammed to the rafters with things that Eleanor Deveraux couldn't quite bring herself to get rid of. Evan's childhood bedroom furniture was over in one corner, along with those of his uncle and father. The first few times Evan had been in the room everything made him cringe. He could almost understand the furniture—much of it was antique, but he couldn't fathom why she would hang on to any of the boxes of clothes, books, and bits of paperwork. Now, although he barely saw any of it, he had come to believe that his grandmother was a secret hoarder who was fortunate enough to have Theo, the family butler, and staff to compensate for her. The saddest box he'd found was one from his grandmother's childhood. It contained a much-worn ragdoll and a photo album. Someone had gone through and ripped her father's head off many of the pictures. His therapist had nodded as though that were the least surprising thing she'd heard about Eleanor. She said it pointed to a history of family trauma. Evan thought it also pointed to the ability to carry a grudge over multiple decades.

Evan stared at the whiteboard. It felt like picking at a scab. His therapist thought it wasn't healthy. She was right, of course, but like so many things, that didn't stop him from doing it. He consoled himself with the fact that it wasn't drugs. He went back to the wicker couch and sat down, the woven white reeds creaking under his weight. After the third month of coming to the storage room, he'd started organizing. His anxiety couldn't take the disorganized mishmash, and he'd discovered that he found the sorting oddly soothing.

He might be no closer to discovering any answers, but he could at least say that he'd sorted all the hats and now had someplace to sit down.

The whiteboard contained the Deveraux family timeline. It started with the death of his grandfather Henry Deveraux from cancer twenty-five years earlier. Then there was his grandfather's proper funeral, followed the same evening by the riotous wake thrown by Randall and Owen. Then came the second autopsy report commissioned by Randall—the one that had thrown Evan's hard-won sobriety and closeness with his cousins into a tailspin.

UNUSUALLY HIGH LEVELS OF CYANIDE. RESULTS ARE INCONCLUSIVE, BUT INDICATIVE OF A MEDICATION OVERDOSE.

He hadn't been looking for the report. It had tumbled out of a box of records he'd been trying to put back. But having found it, he couldn't un-see it. And he couldn't stop himself from asking the same question that Randall asked: had Eleanor killed her husband?

But that led him to further questions—questions that mattered to him far more. Was there any evidence? And who else had Randall told? Evan had no doubt that Randall had told Owen. The brothers had shared everything, including the parenting of Evan, so whatever Randall knew, he had surely told Owen. But had they told their sister Genevieve? And had they ever confronted Eleanor?

Evan had spent close to a year attempting to discover more about that autopsy report. He'd been through every single box in the storage unit. He'd gone through all of the paperwork he had from his father. He'd found the receipt for the work and he'd eventually tracked down the doctor who had performed the autopsy. Unfortunately, Evan had tracked him to a local cemetery—the pathologist had died two years earlier. Then he'd gone out to DevEntier, the company his grandfather had co-founded and where Randall and Owen had worked.

Reluctantly, Evan opened the dingy box that contained the last items that DevEntier had held onto from Randall and Owen. They hadn't asked why Evan had wanted them. After the mess with the Zhao family and Charlie MacKentier a year earlier, they assumed it had to do with the legal case and handed everything over. He'd already looked over the previous night after Olivia left, and this morning—when Olivia still hadn't called him—he'd decided to take it out to the storage unit.

The fragments of paperwork he'd found indicated what Evan already knew—that Randall had been investigating his mother. Randall had pulled the contracts for Henry's care and there were references to witness statements, although Evan hadn't found any. Eleanor had been in charge of her husband's care. She had seen to the nurses, but she had been the one to administer night medication. She had been the only one Henry had trusted.

Evan wasn't sure why Randall and Owen had cared if Henry had been killed. Henry had been an abusive asshole who had tormented everyone in his life, including Randall and Owen. Owen, while being an abusive father in his own right, had always taken great care to never leave Evan alone with Henry. Evan thought that simple fact spoke volumes on Henry's character, and having had a year to ponder it, he'd decided that if it were true, he had no personal qualms about Eleanor hurrying Henry out of life. It had probably been the best thing she could have possibly done for herself, for the family, and for the rest of humanity who had to exist in proximity to the man. What Evan did care about though was the aftermath.

If there was evidence that could harm Eleanor, then he had to find it and get rid of it.

Evan looked at the board again. There, on the right side, was the final defining moment—the plane crash that had killed Randall, Owen, Genevieve, and her husband. Genevieve had hated her abusive brothers. All of them had questioned, at one time or another, why Jack and Genevieve would get on a plane with Randall and Owen. Now Evan couldn't help wondering if it was because Randall had asked them to, with the intention of telling them about Eleanor and Henry. Particularly after he'd found the printed-out email from Randall to Genevieve dated three days before they all took their fateful vacation.

WE NEED TO TALK.

Were there any more ominous words in the English language? Evan was inclined to think not. He hadn't been able to find a response though—-even after going through every single piece of paper in the storage unit.

If there was something to be learned there, Evan thought it ought to be uncovered. Aiden and Dominique deserved to know. It was entirely possible that Randall and Owen had tried to talk to Jack and Genevieve about Henry's death and that was the reason they were all together. Evan couldn't decide what he wanted to be true, but he'd decided that he couldn't take not knowing anymore and Aiden and Dominique deserved to have an answer. But Eleanor had done a complete sweep after the crash. There were no records to be had. Nothing except newspaper articles that he'd printed out from back issues online. Everything else would require a public records request and he wasn't sure he wanted to go on record as having even asked about the crash.

Evan sighed and looked down at the three metal blocks in the DevEntier box. Three hard drives. Three potential pieces of evidence that he couldn't ignore and he also couldn't access without help. He'd considered asking Jackson for help. Jackson had the resources, but it would mean revealing everything to him and Evan wasn't sure that Jackson wouldn't tell Eleanor.

Evan checked his phone again. Still no message from Olivia.

He squelched a feeling of bitterness and pulled open the email with the address to the computer expert who had agreed to take a look at the hard drives.

With a sudden decision, he got up and pulled all the papers off the board, and shoved them in the box. He would take the hard drives to the computer guy and then he would be done with it—one way or another. He had to be done torturing himself for things that his family had done. He shoved the box onto a shelf and put the hard drives in a bag.

Evan exited the storage unit and got in his car. He knew that he could have them delivered, but he also knew that the more people involved, the higher the chances for exposure became, and he had no intention of airing more of the Deveraux dirty laundry.

He drove out to New Jersey. The guy Evan had found was ex-military and worked out of a dilapidated storefront. Evan was buzzed in and the owner, Isaiah, who was in his mid-fifties, dressed in sweats, and leaning on a cane, looked him over. Evan produced a non-disclosure agreement and Isaiah took it. He propped his cane against the counter and put his weight fully on his prosthetic foot to read the document. Then he signed it without comment.

"They're an older model," Isaiah said, looking the hard drives over. "It might take me a little bit to get the right hardware to access the data. But I can do it."

"With my luck, there will be nothing but eighties porn on there," said Evan with a shrug.

Isaiah didn't laugh. "I don't look at the data. I just transfer it to something you access. I don't want to know what's on there. That's your problem."

"That's perfect," said Evan. "Thanks."

But still letting go of the hard drives was harder than the last time he'd held a pill bottle in his hands.

Olivia – Good Values

Olivia stared out the lunchroom window at the incredibly boring office building across the street.

"Hey!" said Alia, dropping into the seat next to Olivia, startling her. "How was your Halloween?"

Olivia cocked her head, trying to formulate an answer.

"This isn't applied physics or anything," said Alia. "Just pick one, good or bad?"

Olivia hesitated again.

"Come on, was Glen so bland that you can't even pick?"

"Glen tried to rape me," said Olivia.

"Holy shit!" Alia clapped her hand over her mouth, her eyes wide. "Are you OK?"

"Um, well, yes," said Olivia and proceeded to fill Alia in on the rest of her evening. "And then," she said, bringing the story to a conclusion, "one thing led to another and..."

"Oh my God! You had sex with the gorgeous knight in shining armor!"

"Well, I was going to," admitted Olivia, "but he wanted to start with um… manual stimulation of… me."

"And did you..." Alia lowered her voice and glanced around the break room. As one of the only six women at the company, and the only two in the same age bracket, she and Alia had become instant friends. She was one of the few that was aware of Olivia's problem. "Um... Have a good time?"

"I had a very, extremely, excellent good time," said Olivia.

"Oh my," said Alia, grinning. "Well, that is very exciting. Are you going to see him again?"

"Well, I'd like to," said Olivia. "But there's a little problem with that."

"What? It sounds like you two hit it off, and he sounds like a really nice guy."

"We did and he is, but..."

"But what? What's the problem?"

Olivia cleared her throat. "I didn't actually get his last name. Or his phone number. We had just gotten done um..."

"Getting freaky?"

"Right. When the police showed up to take me home. And then I couldn't exactly ask in front of them."

Alia laughed at her. "Slut," she said.

"Shut your pie hole," said Olivia. "He was great, and even if I never saw him again, I will not apologize for having fantastic, not to mention extremely safe and consensual sex."

"Sorry, I was teasing! I'm happy for you! What are you going to do? You know where he lives. Can you write him a note and drop it in his mailbox or something?"

"I thought about it, but what if he doesn't call? I was thinking maybe...well, we kind of made a joke about the same time next Tuesday, so I thought I'd go over next Tuesday."

"Whew." Alia blew out a lungful of air. "Gutsy. Could go horribly if he's with someone else or not home or something. Or it could go great and he could swoop you off to his bed for a fuck fest of epic proportions."

"I'm hoping for option two. If he's not home then I'll leave a note and if someone is over then I will say I dropped by to give him a bottle of wine as a thank you and then I will leave and go home and cry."

Alia paused. "That is actually a good plan."

"It should be," said Olivia. "I spent the entire first half of my day thinking about it instead of working."

"Sounds right," said Alia, who had previously expressed the theory that only thirty-five percent of any workday should be spent working. Olivia laughed and they spent the rest of lunch talking about Alia's aunt and her chronic social media over-sharing.

Olivia returned to her desk and was about to settle down to actual work when her phone rang.

"Hey Sofs," said Olivia, picking up her younger sister's call.

"Hi Liv," said Sofia, her tone drooping and sad. "I don't want to bother you. I'd just thought I'd call and see how you were doing."

Olivia felt the old, gut, clenching anger.

"I'm fine," said Olivia.

"Well, you know, it's OK not to be. This is a rough time of year for all of us and you're so far away from home. You don't have to keep up a front."

"Nope, totally fine," said Olivia. "I'm just out here in the city, sleeping with strangers and researching the evolutionary glory of squid. Keepin' it real. Sinner for life! Peace out!"

"Oh, Liv," sighed her sister in exasperation. "Why do you have to make a joke out of everything?"

"Why do you have to sound like a weepy church lady? Why can't you just call and chat?"

"That's what I'm trying to do," said Sofia.

"Well then, my apologies. How are you doing?"

"Well, I'm fine," said Sofia.

"Did you do anything fun for Halloween?"

"I helped out at the church haunted house."

"That was always fun when we were kids. They still doing the hard-boiled egg eyeballs?"

Sofia laughed. "Yes. But Mrs. Button the butcher's wife

brought in a cow brain. I was not all right with that much amount of realism, but the kids loved it. And mostly, I had a good time except for Jimmy Green."

"What did that dipwad do?" asked Olivia.

"Oh, he keeps pestering me," said Sofia with a sigh, and Olivia frowned. Pestering was code for groping when no one was looking. "I've complained to the pastor, but he just said I shouldn't be so cute."

"That's unacceptable," said Olivia. "It's sexual harassment and it needs to stop."

"You've been up north too long. I'll just have a word with Grams and she'll talk to his wife. It's just annoying is all."

Olivia was silent. She didn't think that Grams would be that effective. Jimmy Green had been married fifteen years and he was always *pestering* someone.

"Well, how about next time he pesters you, you just knee him in the balls and tell him that if he touches you again, you're going to take your sewing scissors to the same spot?"

"Olivia!"

"What? There's no reason he should get to touch you."

"It's fine. I don't know why you're harping on this."

"Neither do I," said Olivia, rubbing her head. "Did you do anything else fun?" she asked, forcing a smile into her voice.

"I went out to dinner with George Hatterson."

"Isn't he the one with the lazy eye?"

"No, you're thinking of his older brother."

"Oh, right. George was the good-looking one."

"Yes. How about you? Did you do anything fun?"

"Yes," said Olivia. "I went to a party and met a guy."

"Oh! That's exciting! What's his name? Was he cute?"

"Evan, and very cute."

"Are you going to see him again?"

"I hope so," said Olivia. "We'll see. How's everyone else? Tyler and Dad, OK? Grams and Pops still in Washington?"

"Yes," said Sofia with a sigh, the creepy sincere church tone returning to her voice. "I talked to Grams already. You know how she always has a hard time."

"Sure. But she pretty much has a hard time all the time. You know that, right?" asked Olivia. "It's called a drinking problem."

"Olivia! Grams does not have a drinking problem!"

"Sure," said Olivia, "and Pops isn't sleeping with his assistant."

"Our grandfather is an upstanding, church-going man," said Sofia icily. "He is not having an affair. I don't know why you insist on saying these hurtful things."

"Pops is a hypocritical blowhard. Which you would know if you listened to anything but Fox News and bothered to read something that wasn't the Bible. Or you know, opened your eyes and ears for once," said Olivia. "I mean, I pretty sure that one girl had an abortion because of him."

"I'm hanging up," said Sofia. "I will not listen to you talk about Pops like that."

"No, but you'll listen to him call me an immoral harlot who couldn't keep a fine man like Clark Stewart."

"Goodbye, Olivia," said Sofia and hung up.

Olivia took a deep breath and set down the phone with a shaking hand. Over a year since breaking up with Clark and she still got mad just thinking about it. Sofia was right. They all did get weird around this time of year. The anniversary of her mother's death loomed over everything, making holidays weepy and tempers flare over imagined slights. But this was no imagined slight. Their grandfather had built his career on solid Christian values. And that was fine as far as it went, but Olivia didn't see what was so Christian about wanting her to stick with a man who couldn't stick with her. Her break up had crystallized many things for her, one of which was that she needed to get the hell out of Georgia.

Jackson – Hipster Vegans

Jackson Deveraux slid into the booth and waited for his cousin Dominique while scrutinizing the restaurant décor. There were crystal chandeliers, but the walls were lined with roughly sawn wood and chalkboards. It looked suspiciously trendy.

"Nika, this is some hipster vegan place, isn't it?" he demanded as she sat down. Tall, blonde, and wearing heels that made a lot of people think dirty thoughts, Dominique caused head swivels around the room as she entered. He decided that she must have the day off. Dominique worked under her father's name—Casella—and usually dressed plainly to keep her Deveraux identity, and money, hidden.

"Hipster, yes. Vegan, no," she said, dropping into the seat opposite him. "Why are we meeting?"

"Why do you think?" he asked.

"Grandma?"

"Of course, but it's not a thing, so don't stress. I just want to strategize. This is going to cost more than my rent used to, isn't it?" he asked, pulling the menu toward him.

"Your rent used to be covered by the state. I don't think that's a fair comparison."

Jackson grinned and picked up the stiff sheet of paper that constituted the menu. Then, keeping an eye on Dominique, he used one hand to cover up the price column. She snorted and perused the menu herself.

Until five years ago, Jackson Deveraux had been Jackson Zane. He'd been an orphan, a thief, and an inmate. And then his grandmother Eleanor had found him, plucked him out of prison, and brought him into the Deveraux fold with the express intention that he should look after his cousins. He didn't mind. He'd always wanted a family, and now he had one. And he'd thought that looking after some spoiled rich kids would probably be easy. He'd been wrong on both points—his cousins were neither spoiled nor easy.

"Pickled... What the fuck, Nika? We can't just go somewhere that makes omelets?"

"They make omelets. It's the third one down."

"It comes with a compote. I don't know what compote is, but it sounds offensive."

Dominique giggled, and Jackson shook his head. When the waiter finally took their order, Jackson took a chance on the compote but thought he might be stopping for a burger later.

When Jackson had first come to live with the Deveraux, the reactions from his cousins had been mixed. Their parents, including Jackson's father, had all died in a plane crash, leaving Evan, Aiden, and Dominique in the care of their grandmother Eleanor. Most people had taken the plane crash as a mixed blessing. Genevieve Deveraux and Jack Casella were sweet, honest people whom everyone loved. But Owen and Randall Deveraux had been described, at best, as cold-hearted, abusive bastards.

Evan, Owen's son and the oldest of the cousins, had accepted Jackson easily. But then Evan had a drug problem and probably would have accepted just about anyone. Aiden, Dominique's brother, had been resistant. Aiden was territorial and protective of his sister and he wasn't particularly interested in having another potentially violent relative around. Dominique, on the other hand, *had* been interested. Interested in what Jackson could do. Interested in what Jackson wanted to do. Simply interested in Jackson. Interested in the intensely focused way that Jackson had come to identify as a Deveraux trait. She had been his first ally in the family. Aiden had taken a bit longer, but now that Jackson knew his secret—illegal MMA fighting—he and Jackson were finally on the same page. It was Evan who had drifted away in the last year, even as his sobriety and stability had increased. Jackson wasn't sure what to make of that.

"So," he said when the waiter left. "The new shitty job. How is it?"

"Slightly less shitty than the last one. You know, I was pissed when those stupid mercenaries attacked me and blew my cover at work, but it has turned out to be a good thing!"

"A good thing?" asked Jackson with a laugh.

"It totally threw off my timeline—so inconvenient. I was not planning on making some of the job switches I have made so fast. But I feel like it forced me to step up. I'm now managing five people and only two of them are idiots. And I've officially got Marketing Director on my business card. So that's nice. Although, of course, fuck Absolex and J.P. Granger, and I hope they all go down in a flaming ball."

"Naturally," said Jackson.

Some people might have characterized being attacked by mercenaries as a bit more than *inconvenient,* but Dominique recovered from shocks easily. She also cherished her string of anonymous shitty jobs and was hell-bent on pulling herself up by her bootstraps. Never mind that she was already up. She wanted to work her way to the top and then probably rule with an iron fist.

"Actually, where *are* we on the Absolex situation?" Dominique asked, frowning.

"We'll have to check in with Evan at Sunday dinner," said Jackson and Dominique accepted that with a half-shrug and a nod.

When Eleanor Deveraux had pushed for a senate investigation and hearing on the subject of why the PTSD drug that Absolex had developed and sold to the VA seemed to cause *more* suicides in veterans, someone at Absolex had hired mercenaries to attack the Deveraux family. An investigation had pointed toward the CEO J.P. Granger, but after being charged, Homeland Security had blocked access to the mercenaries that attacked the Deveraux family, which meant those charges couldn't be pursued. All that was left were some financial indictments, which were ongoing and annoying for Granger, but they weren't the punishment the Deveraux had been hoping for.

"What about you?" she asked. "Anything good this week?"

"More situational awareness seminars," he said.

"What the hell is that?"

"Most of it was stuff I'm already doing. Knowing what's going on in my surroundings, blah, blah, blah. I think the minions, as you call them, got some good stuff out of it though."

"No, seriously," she said, "what is it?"

"Keeping an eye on exits, not burying your head in a phone, and you know, being aware that there's a photographer outside taking our picture," said Jackson.

"Is there really?" asked Dominique without looking around and Jackson smiled at her. She'd once given him a twenty-minute lecture on how to get good paparazzi photos. Apparently, suddenly turning toward an unexpected photographer led to awkward photos and the blogs and mags always seemed to run the worst photos on purpose.

"Yeah, at least since you got here."

"Aren't they over us? Why the sudden interest?"

"Eleanor, I think. That diversity and inclusion speech on Monday set off a little shit storm. The Huffington Post picked up a clip and so did some sort of positive thinking page with like a million followers."

"Ooh! I knew that one had promise. Excellent!" Dominique was beaming, and Jackson shook his head. In many ways, she and Jackson had opposite goals. Dominique had gone into marketing, which meant that Eleanor promptly expected her to assist in the PR for the seemingly never-ending Eleanor Deveraux for Senator campaign. Whenever Dominique excelled, Jackson's job as head of family security got a lot harder.

"I'm going to pretend to go to the bathroom then head out the back and see if I can roust him."

"Is that a good idea?"

"No clue, but it sounds like fun."

"Suit yourself," she said, laughing. "Just don't make Aiden get you out of jail again."

"Wouldn't dream of it."

He ducked out the back of the restaurant and worked his way around the block to get in position behind the photographer, who was leaning with a faux-casual attitude against a car parked across the street from the restaurant. Dominique adjusted to a modelesque pose and flipped her hair, probably attempting to look as photogenic as possible and keep the attention on her.

Jackson walked closer. The photographer was intent on Dominique and didn't notice him. Apparently, situational awareness really was something that needed teaching.

"Hi," said Jackson directly into the man's ear. The photographer, yelped, jumped, and dropped his camera, then fumbled with panicked hands, trying to catch it. Jackson grabbed the camera out of the air and began to look at the photos. The photographer reached for the camera with angry, wild hand gestures. Jackson merely pivoted away.

"Give it back!" the photographer demanded, a note of panic in his voice.

"What? This? You want this?" asked Jackson, swiveling away from his grasping hands. It was so childish, but he couldn't stop himself. The pictures were nothing special. A couple of shots of the restaurant. Jackson arriving. Dominique getting out of the cab. Dominique had selected the place and Jackson had made the reservation. He suspected someone must have tipped off the cameraman. He flipped back further to see who else was on the hitlist and felt a flutter of fear as he saw Aiden going into work, and then, even earlier, Evan, coming off the train.

"Give it back to me or I'm calling the cops!"

Jackson took another look at the photographer. He was a medium height with a slight build. The clothes were non-descript: puffer jacket, jeans, and sneakers, ball cap pulled down low on his face. Jackson reached out and knocked the hat off.

"Hey!" The man dove for his hat, pulling it out of a motor-oil scummed puddle. He had brown hair, brown eyes, nothing particularly remarkable about him. Perfect for his job, in other words.

"Why are you following my family?"

"It's the gig, man," said the photographer, shaking off his hat. "It's not personal. Give me back my camera!"

"What's your name?"

"I'm not telling you that!"

"Who do you work for?"

"I'm not telling you that either!"

"Then I'm keeping the camera."

"Fine," said the man, reaching into his pocket. Jackson tensed, his fingers curling around the camera. "Here. Happy?" He shoved a business card at Jackson. Jackson took it.

INTELLIGENCER MAGAZINE

MONROE HARDING

"Intelligencer? I've never heard of it."

"That's not my fault," said Harding. "Give me back my camera."

"Who sent you?"

"My editor."

"What's his name?"

"*Her* name, and go fuck yourself. Camera!"

"Are you going to go away and leave us alone?"

"I have a right to be here!" Harding's face blazed red in fury.

"And I have a right to punch you in the face."

"That's a threat. I can call the cops!" Harding was angry, but he had yet to even reach for his phone. Not only was that a secondary camera that he could be using to film, but if he were truly serious about the cops, he'd have it in his hand. Either Harding wasn't that scared or he wasn't anxious to call the police.

"Word of advice: don't make threats you're not going to follow through on," said Jackson. "It's a principle I try to live by."

Harding froze and licked his lips. "Yeah, OK, give me back the camera and I'll leave."

"Sure," said Jackson, baring his teeth in what might have passed for a smile. He tossed the camera back to the man, who scrabbled and nearly dropped the camera again, but managed to keep it off the ground.

"Fucking Deverauxes! You're all assholes!" yelled Harding as Jackson walked back toward the restaurant. Jackson didn't turn around but held up one middle finger. On the other side of the glass, Dominique smiled and waved. Harding snapped one last angry photo, before running off.

"Funny," said Dominique as he sat down. "You're going to be lucky if he doesn't sue for assault."

"I did not touch him or damage his equipment. I think I'm good." He pulled out his phone and texted a picture of Harding's business card to Pete. Peter Schalding was Eleanor's private investigator. He'd been instrumental in helping Jackson acclimate to the security role. The reply pinged through moments later.

Who's this douchebag?

Don't know. Find out.

On it.

"Are we focusing on me yet?" asked Dominique.

"Yes," said Jackson, smiling. "We are."

But Dominique frowned. "Was that photographer something I need to worry about?"

"Not at the moment," said Jackson. "Maybe just have Max drive you to work for the next few days."

"He usually does anyway," said Dominique, still frowning. Max was Dominique's six-foot-five, US Marshal boyfriend. Jackson liked Max, but he sometimes wondered how Dominique squared her periodic desires to beat mercenaries with bats with dating a total do-gooder.

The waiter appeared and placed their food down on the table and seemed disgusted when Jackson asked for ketchup. Dominique waited until the ketchup was in place and the waiter had left before speaking again.

"What's going on? You're…" She waved a hand at him open-palmed as if feeling his aura. "Unhappy."

"Eleanor's speech," said Jackson. "It touched a nerve. She's received about fifty letters and quadruple that in emails and tweets all telling her to stop betraying the white race."

"Ugh," said Dominique, sitting back in her chair, disgust on her face.

"Those are the nice ones," said Jackson. "The others range from telling her that she should be raped to death to threatening all of you."

"It's Absolex all over again."

"Pretty much," said Jackson. "And we all know how well that went."

"I can see why you're tense."

"You can see why I… Nika!" said Jackson, laughing. "You're the one that ended up with bullet holes in your wall. Why aren't you tense?"

"Well, I'm sure you'll take care of it. Oh, you can take the Evan look off your face. Honestly, it's no wonder everyone thinks you're brothers. I know that I sound all devil-may-care, but what I mean is that having you and Max around lowers my stress level about threats considerably. I do not mean to imply that I am not aware of your efforts or that they are not appreciated. And of course, I'll take all the precautions you recommend."

"Mm-hmm. Aiden says exactly the same thing."

"Yes, well, I actually mean it."

"Yes, and speaking your brother. He's part of what I want your help strategizing about. I'll be bringing this up at Sunday dinner," said Jackson.

"And you want me to help beat it into his head that he needs to do what you tell him?"

"Him and Evan, yes."

"Evan usually takes your advice."

"Not about this. He likes to ride the train."

"And aren't you looking after that angle?" asked Dominique, raising an eyebrow.

"I don't know what you're talking about," said Jackson. He had no idea how Dominique had caught wind of that particular angle.

"Mm. Well, it's for his own good, so I'm sure we don't need to mention it. But are you really worried about these messages?"

"Yes. No? I don't know. It feels… *pogano*."

"I have no clue what that means."

Jackson rummaged in his brain for a decent translation from Ukrainian. "Bad," he said at last. "It's giving me the heebie-jeebies."

"Well, I think that at dinner, the best we can hope for is to lodge it in Aiden's brain. You know how he hates doing what he's told. We'll just have to work on him a bit until he decides it for himself. Plus, I'll call Ella. She won't mind having the Zhao keeping an extra eye out."

Jackson laughed. "Ella won't mind. But the Zhao security may. I don't think they've ever quite forgiven us for being us."

Ella Zhao was the niece of Bai Zhao head of Zhao Industries, the massive multi-national solar energy firm. Their security forces were not used to being given the end run quite the way Jackson and Aiden had done. Even with the hatchet buried between the Zhao and the Deveraux families, and Ella and Aiden dating, Jackson knew that the Zhaos' security still viewed the Deverauxes as threats.

Dominque shrugged. "They'd better get over it. Bai Zhao has Ella pegged as the heir to the throne. And she and Aiden are firmly glued together at the lips. Seriously, it's disgusting. He floats around the place like he's on cloud nine. It's been a year already. We get it—you love her. Move on!"

Jackson laughed. "Oh, whatever. You're just mad because he's stealing the shmoopsy crown from you and Max."

"When Max and I do it, it's adorable. When my brother does it, it's gross. Meanwhile, do you have any idea what's going on with Evan?"

"Evan…" Jackson sighed. "is going through one of his phases."

"You mean the ones where he doesn't talk to us about anything real? He's been doing so well with his sobriety and he was wonderful at Christmas. Coming out of last year I thought… Well,

I thought things were only going to get better. But I feel like he's retreated again. And I think it's my fault."

"That seems unlikely," said Jackson.

Dominique let out a heavy breath of air. "Grandma talked to me prior to you know… what we're asking Evan about on Sunday."

Jackson nodded. He appreciated Dominique's discretion in the crowded restaurant.

"And I signed up for it. I thought I could gain more of Grandma's trust and I thought it would put to rest any reservations she had about Max moving in with me. But I didn't realize that it would be Evan taking most of the risk. I think he felt pushed into it. And I'm not sure… I don't know how to talk to him about it."

"Mm," said Jackson. He'd had similar thoughts.

"I feel like I made a choice to go with Grandma's plan for the good of the family, but maybe it wasn't a choice that was good for Evan. And that really, really bothers me."

"Mm," said Jackson, nodding.

"I hate it when you *mm* me," said Dominique.

"I *mm* because I'm not sure what else to say. I'm not sure you're wrong. But I'm not sure you're completely right either. The four of us discussed it without Grandma. Evan agreed."

"Yes, but… Evan has never… Going against Grandma… I'm not sure his therapist has got him to that place yet, you know?" Dominique's phone pinged and she pulled it out of her purse and made a face. "As if neo-Nazis weren't enough. I cannot convey how much I hate Ralph Taggert."

"What's he done now?"

"I do not understand how a senator from Georgia can spend this much time in our state or why he feels the need to horn in on everything Grandma does. He is still shooting his mouth off about the Absolex hearings."

"He wanted to glory hog that so bad," agreed Jackson.

"He's still pissed Grandma shut him out," said Dominique. "Ever since she got the Sixty-Minutes interview, he's been gunning for her. He's just mad because he feels like protecting veterans is some sort of Republican birthright."

"Maybe they should stop cutting funding to the VA then," said Jackson, tentatively trying his potatoes. There was a lot of paprika going on.

"Exactly Grandma's point. Anyway, he honestly seems to feel that he should have been in the lead on the Absolex hearings, never mind that Grandma's the committee chair, and he's been whining about it to the press ever since. And now!" She waved her phone angrily. "He's made some sort of statement about how she's grandstanding and drawing out the hearings on purpose when she should be letting the authorities handle the investigation. Which is unfair, because the only reason they weren't closed out two years ago is because she *has* been letting the authorities investigate and now all the reports are finally in. But he's acting as if she did it on purpose and that she's a glory hog who is trying to bring up her greatest hits for the election. Only he used a lot more syllables because he's Southern."

Jackson chuckled. "I'd tell you to let it go, but he's part two of my strategy question."

"What do you mean?"

"She's got that health bill coming out. Taggert's been running his mouth more than usual and I think he's laying the groundwork to attack her and the bill. I want to start digging into him and see what we can find for counter ammunition, but so far Eleanor is taking the high-road. She wants to stick to the merits of the bill."

"You want me to bring up the low road on Sunday?"

"Just float it out there," he said. "See if she shoots it down.

"Yeah, no problem," agreed Dominique. "The potatoes are weird, right?"

"Yes," he agreed. "They fucking are. I don't know why you bring me to these places."

Dominique grinned. "I like to broaden your horizons."

"You like to torture me."

"Well, I didn't grow up with you, so I have to make up for all the torturing I didn't do when we were kids."

Jackson laughed. "Love you too, Nika."

Evan – Sunday Dinner

Evan stared at his dinner and ignored his cousins. He still showed up for Sunday dinners. He liked seeing his cousins. They made him laugh. But after what he'd discovered the previous year, he felt like a liar every time he was in the house. So much of his sobriety had been predicated on being honest and open and he felt he could no longer do that. He wasn't even sure that being honest was the right answer. How was telling his cousins that he thought Eleanor was a murderer going to help at all?

A year ago, he'd been on a tentative path to happiness. He had been sober, he thought his cousins had almost forgiven him. But now that he knew that he wasn't sure who to tell, or if he should tell them at all. And if he did tell them, what was there to do about it, with no evidence? Sunday dinners had become a torture of nodding and keeping his mouth shut. A torture compounded by Eleanor's plan to ruin J.P. Granger. Not that he minded exactly. At least it was a concrete way to prove his loyalty. Something he could point to if the autopsy report ever came out.

And today was even worse than usual since he was fighting off a monumental case of wounded pride. He had not called lots of women the next day, and there had been several evenings where the understanding was that no one would be calling anyone, but he couldn't remember a time when he had wanted someone to call and they hadn't. But here it was, well past the three-day rule of calling, which meant she wasn't going to call. He was a goddamn Deveraux. Everyone wanted a Deveraux. Everyone, except, apparently, Olivia.

And now he had an additional thing to talk to his therapist about. He was trying to eliminate things off that goddamn list—not add to it.

"Evan?"

He realized that Dominique had been talking to him, but he had no idea about what. Dominique was five years younger than he was, blonde, pretty, and smarter than almost anyone gave her credit for. If she wanted to, he suspected that she could give their grandmother a run for her money. It was his estimation that Dominique specifically did not want to.

"Hm?" he said, he said looking into her cornflower blue eyes that always reminded him of her mother Genevieve.

"I asked if you were getting ready to dump the Absolex stock and then you stared at me like I was an alien," said Dominique.

"Sorry, I was thinking of something else."

"Yes, I could tell."

In the past, their entire exchange would have been larded with sarcasm and disdain. But the previous few years had been different. Evan's efforts at self-improvement had resulted in an uneasy truce between himself and his cousins. He got the feeling sometimes that they were waiting for him to revert to being an asshole. His therapist said that was normal. He found it exhausting. But at the moment Dominique merely looked amused by his inattention to the conversation over Sunday dinner.

"Yes, I've stopped purchasing the Absolex on all of my channels—not that they can be traced to me. I'll do the short sale on Friday at the end of the day and dump all of it. By Monday the stock will be next to worthless. Considering the other scandals that have broken recently on their research fraud—"

"Thank you, Jackson," said Aiden.

"I do my part," said Jackson with his usual equanimity. "I do enjoy being an unnamed source on page one."

"And the social media campaign against them," continued Evan.

"Facebook ads," said Nika, shaking her head, "so worth it for the money."

"By my calculations, with the devaluation stock, and the stock dump, Absolex should announce bankruptcy by the end of next week. Since J.P. Granger's net worth is tied up in his company's stock, that should pretty much ruin him. And with any luck, his lawyers will quit when they realize he's not going to pay them, and then he'll go to prison."

"Your father would be so proud," said Eleanor.

He looked down to the head of the table where his grandmother sat. Eleanor Deveraux was over seventy but looked barely sixty with carefully coifed blonde hair and subtle cosmetic work. She was the epitome of speak softly and carry a big stick. There were many people who hadn't seen the stick coming, but Evan hadn't ever been one of them. He had never dared to cross her about anything important and he had always done what she considered most vital: he made the family look good.

Evan tried to decide what she was trying to imply. She rarely mentioned his father. It was his impression that the only child she'd cared for was Genevieve. Like almost everyone else, she'd hated her sons Owen and Randall. And yes, the Absolex situation was something straight out of his father's playbook, but since she had been the one that asked him to do it, he didn't think she had much of a reason to object.

"Well," said Dominique, smiling at him as if to make up for their grandmother's comment, "I think it's great. I personally did not appreciate their attempts at intimidation, kidnapping, or murder, so good job."

"Passing off fake research and bad PTSD medication to veterans pretty much sealed the deal for me," said Aiden. He was blond, like his sister, but a shade darker and two years older. "And trying to squish me with a car didn't improve my opinion any. So, I say, good riddance. Job well done." He lifted a glass to Evan, and Evan found himself smiling awkwardly.

"Wait and see if it works first," he said.

"It'll work," said Jackson confidently, and Evan gave him an actual smile. But from the moment their grandmother had dropped the bomb of his existence on them, Evan had wanted Jackson. He had always envied Aiden and Dominique, and the idea that maybe he could have an even a sort of, maybe sibling-cousin who belonged to him was attractive. He'd been certain that would work. Grandma would bring Jackson home and then Evan would have a brother of his own and that would be that. Of course, at the time he'd been flying high on some sort of drug cocktail so that kind of thing made sense.

The strange thing was that it was almost true. At least Jackson behaved as if it were true. The problem was that now that Evan was sober he had no idea what to do with that. Jackson, from the day he'd arrived, had seemed to like him, and Evan found that deeply suspicious. He kept waiting for the switch to cruelty. It was what he always expected from Owen and Randall, and he had a hard time believing that Jackson would be different. And then there was the fact that Jackson was one of their grandmother's few confidants. He couldn't trust Eleanor. So how could he trust Jackson?

"You seem very confident," said Evan.

"You don't miscalculate," said Jackson and Evan felt as though he should go home and mark the date in his calendar. An evening where all three of his cousins complimented him was unlikely to come again.

"We'll see," said Eleanor, and Evan nodded. Eleanor was always the thumb on the scale to provide balance. These days he was never sure where he stood with Eleanor. As a child, she had been the one person that he believed with any certainty loved him. But now he felt as if he had been pushed into the ranks of people she didn't trust. He wasn't sure why. He had never once breathed a word of what he knew or suspected about her, but it was as if she could smell it on him.

For a moment, Evan thought Jackson's face registered annoyance at Eleanor's comment, but then it smoothed out and he turned to the cousins.

"Hey, reminder, we've been seeing an uptick in Neo-Nazi bullshit. Eleanor's getting some hate mail."

"More than usual?" asked Dominique.

"Yes," said Jackson. "Her anti-discrimination speech last week kind of pushed some buttons. I don't think they'll target any of you, but Evan, you might not want to ride the train to work for a few days and Dominique maybe get Max to give you a lift in the mornings?"

"He usually does," said Dominique.

Evan felt a flutter of discomfort. He had been intending to mention the photographer that had been lurking around the day before, but now he wasn't so sure.

"I like riding the train to work," said Evan, weighing his options. If he mentioned the photographer, how likely was it that Jackson would freak out? Or that Eleanor would demand that he take a car? He didn't want to have that argument.

"It's a pretty big window of opportunity," said Jackson. "I don't like that you do it."

"It's fine," said Evan stubbornly. "No one bothers me."

"Fine," said Jackson. "Just keep your head on a swivel. Don't nose dive into the paper or anything."

"I will keep that in mind," said Evan. Jackson looked like he was entirely unconvinced by Evan's lie, but he shrugged.

"What about you, Aiden?" asked Jackson.

"What about me?" asked Aiden, blinking at Jackson.

"Can you make sure that you're not loitering in conveniently dangerous public spaces?"

"Oh, sure. I mean, it's November. I don't think I'll be doing a lot of standing around outside."

"I was thinking more of your social life," said Jackson drily.

"I don't think I frequent Neo-Nazi bars," said Aiden. "I'm sure I'm fine. Besides Evan's not doing anything extra."

"I will drive or take the car service to anywhere besides work," said Evan.

Jackson looked over in surprise. Aiden looked annoyed. Dominique chuckled.

"Really, Ev?" demanded Aiden. "You can't be a little more stubborn?"

"It's a negotiation," said Evan. "If I give him something, he'll focus on you and leave me alone."

"Throwing me to the wolves," said Aiden, shaking his head. "Fine. I do solemnly swear to avoid dive bars and generally follow all of your *Don't Do This* list."

"Thanks," said Jackson. "Meanwhile," he said, turning back to Eleanor, "what did you want to do about Ralph Taggert?"

Eleanor gave a soft snort of annoyance. "What do I ever want to do about Ralph Taggert?"

"Besides drop him off a cliff, I mean," said Jackson. "You

know after the holiday break he'll come out swinging on your healthcare bill, right?"

"Yes," agreed Eleanor. "I think the only thing I can really do is discredit him on his own record."

Dominique made a disagreeing noise. "Can we dig up some sort of dirt instead?"

"I'll talk to Pete on Monday," agreed Jackson.

"He got re-elected?" asked Aiden, who tracked politics the least of all of them. "How?"

"He wrote some sort of anti-gay legislation, got the Republican-based whipped up, and then drafted up some mental health bill, which he knew would get shot down, and then dredged up his daughter's suicide again. He hit the hate, sympathy doubleheader," said Dominique.

"Asshole," said Aiden.

"We don't swear about our opponents," said Eleanor.

"We're at home, Grandma. Who will know?" said Aiden with an easy smile.

"Someone is always listening," said Eleanor. "Swear about your friends if you like, they'll forgive you. But never say anything about your opponents."

"Regardless," said Dominique, "that's why attacking his record on health care doesn't work. He plays the dead daughter card and anyone who tries it looks like an asshole."

"I think it can be done," said Eleanor. "I think we just need to make him stick his foot in his mouth."

"He'll just Southern his way out of it," said Aiden.

"What do you think, Evan?" asked Dominique.

"I think he's a bully," said Evan. "I think he counts on other people fighting fair and sticking to the rules, while he does not."

Eleanor looked thoughtful and then nodded.

"Well, your team can dig into the opposition research," said Jackson, "and I'll see what Pete and I can come up with. No reason to pursue all options."

"I suppose," agreed Eleanor with a reluctant nod.

Evan looked down at his dinner. He wondered if other families had these kinds of conversations. He suspected not. Evan exited dinner as soon as possible, and for a moment he was alone in the hall and he thought about ducking into Eleanor's office. He was fairly certain, with her hoarding tendencies, that she would have kept files on the plane crash.

"Ah, Mr. Deveraux," said Theo, coming into the hall. "I believe the chauffeur has just pulled up with your car."

"Thanks, Theo," said Evan, straightening his coat. There probably wasn't anything in the files anyway.

But as he went out front to collect his car, he was surprised to see Jackson pull up behind the driver's seat instead of Eleanor's chauffeur.

"Hop in," said Jackson with a grin. "I want to take your car for a spin. I'll drive you home and then get an Uber."

"Can't you just take your own car?" asked Evan, confused.

"No, I know how my car drives. And Aiden will get all peeved if I steal someone else's car."

"So steal Aiden's car," said Evan, climbing into the passenger side.

Jackson laughed. "I would but that thing's a piece of shit. I hate vintage. Give me a modern motor any day of the week."

"And legroom," said Evan, sliding the seat back and stretching out. "I don't know why he's obsessed with owning an old Aston Martin. The new ones are perfectly nice."

"James Bond," said Jackson, peeling out of the drive.

Evan stole a glance at Jackson's profile as he drove. Jackson was fiercely protective of the Deveraux family, something that confused Evan, although he appreciated it. Jackson hadn't liked what Fetish did to or for Evan and he had voiced that opinion strenuously. Evan had been shocked that Jackson knew about Fetish, but he suspected that everyone would be shocked at all the things Jackson knew.

"Pretty sure that traffic cam just flashy thinged you," said Evan as they slid through an intersection.

Jackson chuckled wickedly. "You have no idea how much I allocate monthly for speeding tickets."

"I probably don't want to know," said Evan.

"Hey, speaking of not wanting to know," said Jackson, and then he paused as he was forced to downshift and negotiate around a double-parked cab. The speed picked up again and Evan glanced over at Jackson, now dreading whatever his cousin had clearly wanted to talk to him about. "Maybe you've been avoiding. Or maybe not. I don't know, but I think I should talk to you about Dominique."

"What about Dominique?" asked Evan, a cold lump forming in the pit of the stomach.

"She's freaking out that she screwed you over."

"What?" demanded Evan. There was no way in which he could make that sentence make sense.

"She's really worried that she helped bully you into doing this Absolex thing."

"What? No. I didn't... No one... I wanted to." He shook his head, still confused.

"She's kind of spazzing. She feels like this last couple of years you two have worked hard to be honest with each other and she feels like because Eleanor talked to her first that she went behind your back."

Evan let out a half-laugh in surprise. Dominique was worried that she had damaged their honesty. The irony of that burned with a fine guilt. When had she ever been anything but honest with him? He was the one who was hiding everything.

"It's fine. Grandma is Grandma. There's nothing Nika can do about that."

Jackson glanced over at him before turning back to the road. Evan was relieved to see that they were approaching his building. This conversation was making him sweat. Jackson pulled into the parking garage and punched in the access code as if Evan had already told it to him.

"Seriously," said Evan, "tell Nika not to worry. I'm not worried about the Absolex situation."

"Yeah, OK. It's just…"

"Just what?" asked Evan as Jackson parked.

"You've been kind of AWOL lately," Jackson said, shutting off the engine. "Is everything OK?"

Evan looked at his cousin in frustration.

"Keys," he demanded, holding out his hand. Jackson handed the fob over without protest and Evan got out of the car, surprised to find his hand shaking in suppressed anger.

"Evan," said Jackson, following him.

"You want a pee test?" demanded Evan.

"No, that's not what I'm saying," said Jackson.

"Then what are you saying? Is this why you were all nice to me at dinner?"

"What?" Jackson blinked in a way that Evan thought meant he was genuinely confused. That was nice, but it didn't mean that they all weren't waiting for him to screw up and he had no other way of showing them that he wouldn't. "I show up to family dinners. I answer all the calls. I make all my therapy appointments. What more do you fucking people want?"

"Hey," said Jackson, holding up his hands. "I'm not trying to say anything like that."

"You obviously know how to get in and out of my building," said Evan. "You can let yourself out."

He turned on his heel and left Jackson standing in the parking garage.

Jackson – The Intelligencer

Jackson waited on the rooftop reading a book on his phone. At some point, he switched over to a video that Aiden sent him and then got lost down the rabbit hole of TikTok, but when his phone battery started to tick toward the halfway mark, he switched off and stood up. He did a couple of laps around the roof and some basic calisthenics to get warm. Waiting for the right moment was always the most boring part of breaking and entering, but now that he did it as a hobby rather than as a profession he was finding it a lot easier. Of course, having all the gear and cold-weather apparel his little law-breaking heart desired also made things a bit easier.

At 10:30 he pulled on gloves and strapped on his headlamp and set to work on the elevator shaft. In old buildings, the elevator shafts were rarely alarmed. They relied on the alarm systems on each floor and the basic premise that people interested in theft would either break a lock or attempt it during convenient daytime hours. Once inside the elevator shaft, he climbed down the service ladder to the eighth floor and popped the electrical panel outside the doors. He triggered the right little diode and the doors slid open. He stepped off the ladder and walked into the offices of *The Intelligencer* Magazine.

Jackson knew Pete was working on the photographer Monroe Harding, but the more he thought about the pictures on Harding's camera, the more nervous Jackson had become. It wasn't just Harding's existence; it was the fact that the photographer was tied to a real publication. Jackson wasn't sure what the Intelligencer would want with the Deveraux family and he didn't feel like spending the time to sift through the clues to guess. Not when there was an easy shortcut to be had for the price of a few hours and a quick climb down an elevator shaft.

Jackson was choosing not to admit that part of his impatience was a result of his conversation with Evan. It bugged him that Evan thought Jackson was checking up on his sobriety. Not that Jackson wasn't checking up on it, but Evan wasn't supposed to *know* that. And Evan certainly wasn't supposed to feel like Jackson was putting pressure on him. As far as Jackson could tell, all Evan got from anyone was pressure. Jackson wanted Evan to feel like he was safe with his own family, but the conversation in the car had only shown how little Evan trusted any of them.

The Intelligencer was tucked in a little rabbit warren of grimy offices on the eighth floor and seemed to be composed of cast-off cubicles and whiteboards so old that they no longer erased properly. Jackson started at the front desk. Front desk computers were frequently not password protected because they were considered group property. A quick cruise of the desktop gave him access to the employee calendars. The editor's name was Marnie Perrault. She had a meeting with Monroe Harding booked for later in the week. He opened the event and saw that Marnie had added a note.

I'M GETTING A LOT OF PRESSURE FROM UP TOP. GIVE ME SOMETHING USEFUL ON THE D. STORAGE UNITS AREN'T IT.

Jackson frowned at that and made a note to have Pete look up the Intelligencer parent company. Jackson shut the computer back down and made his way through the cubicles, looking for Monroe Harding's desk. It turned out to be easy to find. The outside was covered in photographs, mostly of celebrities on the streets of New York without makeup on. Someone had been writing 'funny' captions on them. Jackson wasn't sure how calling someone a fatty for eating lunch qualified as funny, but clearly, his tastes and Monroe's didn't align. Inside the cubicle, more pictures papered the walls, but these were more neatly organized under taped-up banners that appeared to denote ongoing projects. He surveyed the wall behind the desk and then turned to the desk itself. Jackson froze. Evan was the entire interior wall in front of the desk.

Jackson's fingers itched to rip down all of the photos and his heart was racing. Instead, he forced himself to take a deep breath and then another. On closer inspection, there were a few pictures of Dominique and Aiden and one or two of himself, but Monroe Harding had spent far too much time focusing on Evan. Jackson felt a surge of rage. Previously, Monroe Harding had been an irritation, but he was about to become the focus of Jackson's attention. Jackson looked at each of the photos, trying to gauge how long Harding had been following Evan. As he looked from photo to photo, Jackson found himself frowning. In at least four pictures, Evan was visiting the Deveraux storage unit. The date stamps on the photos said the visits were only a few days apart and in the most recent photo, Evan was carrying a bag out of the storage unit—one that hadn't been in his hands in the previous photo of him arriving. What the hell was Evan doing?

With no other clues popping out at him, Jackson rummaged through Harding's desk but didn't find anything else interesting. Then he moved on to the editor's office. She had a stack of resumes in her desk drawer and was working on editing her own cover letter, but other than the stench of desperately wanting out of the Intelligencer, Marnie's office didn't yield anything interesting. She kept her computer locked down and her files organized, but she didn't have anything filed under Deveraux.

Jackson shook his head, relocked Marnie's office, and went back out to the elevator. He climbed down to the fifth floor and then crossed the hall and took the service elevator down to the loading dock. He left by the back door and walked quickly down the alley that he already knew didn't have any security cameras. He got into his car and sat for a long moment before starting the engine.

This trip was supposed to have answered questions, not raise more of them.

He dashed off a quick message to Pete to hurry him along on his report on the Intelligencer and Harding and then sent a second one to Theo. Theo had all the keys to Deveraux House and he would know what was required to get into the Deveraux storage unit. When Jackson had visited the storage unit the previous year with Evan, he'd noted the sign-in station and the passcode on the door, but Evan had taken care of it.

Jackson frowned, remembering last year's excavation of boxes of paperwork during the lawsuit with the Zhao. The paperwork had been from Randall and Owen Deveraux and it had been an unpleasant trip down memory lane for Evan. It hadn't bothered Jackson—he never felt particularly interested in the things his father left behind, mostly because the things Randall had left were useless trophies. Jackson was far more concerned with his current living, breathing cousins than his abusive dead relatives. But Evan took Randall and Owen's abusive behavior much more to heart. When Evan had volunteered to take the boxes back to the storage unit, Jackson had meant to go with him but had ended up getting called away by Eleanor. Whatever Evan was doing in the storage unit, Jackson didn't think it could be healthy for him. Jackson drummed his fingers on the wheel. He was tempted to send an email to Evan's therapist, but the woman was obstinately closed-mouthed about Evan's therapy. Which was good. For other people.

His phone chirped an alert and Jackson saw with surprise that it was from Theo. It contained the storage unit address, passcode, and a quick note about front desk sign-in procedures. Jackson checked his watch.

I DIDN'T THINK YOU'D SEE THAT UNTIL MORNING. SORRY IF I WOKE YOU.

I was just on my way to bed. It only took a moment.

Thanks.

You're welcome.

Jackson shook his head again. Nearly six years in and he still wasn't used to Theo. From the first, Theo had been an ally, but Jackson wasn't entirely sure why. The only explanation that Jackson could come up with was that Theo liked the Deveraux family and wanted them to succeed. It seemed like an unlikely motivation, but Jackson had come to rely on the butler as much as the rest of his security team.

Jackson stared again at the text and debated waiting until the morning to go to the storage unit and then decided against it. The whole point of twenty-four-hour access to the storage unit was that they could go whenever they wanted. And the whole point of inheriting millions was so he could sleep in whenever he wanted. Why else would money exist if it wasn't to allow for periodic slothfulness?

Jackson put the car into gear and navigated toward the storage unit. The building was well lit, but he couldn't decide if the plethora of security cameras was a good thing or not. He used the pin number to unlock the door to their unit instead of rolling up the large garage-door-like portion and stepped inside. Jackson paused and blinked in surprise.

The last time he'd been in the storage unit it had been a disaster zone of piled furniture and boxes. Whatever Evan had been doing, it had included organizing. Jackson felt a tremor of unease to see that the wicker furniture that he had previously climbed over had now been set up to face a whiteboard. There were tick marks and numbers on the board, and Jackson stepped closer, trying to assess their meaning. A few newspaper articles were taped to the board with blue painter's tape and he flipped through them. Henry

Deveraux's obituary featured prominently near the left side of the board. Jackson looked it over curiously.

Entrepreneur and innovator, Henry Evan Deveraux passed away in his home on Tuesday from complications relating to cancer. His wife Eleanor Hicks Deveraux was by his side. Born in New York…

Jackson skimmed the obituary. It was a full page and only reiterated what Jackson already knew—his grandfather had a lot of money and connections. Whoo-de-freaking-hoo. The obituary read like a resume—it was a list of accomplishments and not much more. There weren't any quotes from friends and family. No funny stories. Nothing that amounted to a worthwhile human being. Jackson let the sheet of paper fall back onto the board and looked around again.

Why had Evan been here? What did he need with Henry's obituary?

He went to the next tick mark on the board, figuring the numbers above them were dates. But that tick mark was empty. Sticky ghosts of tape marked the board there indicating that something *had* been there, but wasn't any longer. He traveled the board, none of the dates stood out as important to him until he got to the end. The Deveraux plane crash stared out at him from a scanned copy of a newspaper.

All three Deveraux children Randall, Owen, and Genevieve Deveraux, as well as Genevieve's husband Jack Casella, were pronounced dead Thursday after their private plane crashed in the Rockies. The pilot reported turbulence shortly before the plane went down. The pilot is still listed in critical condition.

Jackson sighed. Whatever Evan had been digging into, Jackson was sure it wasn't a good thing. Evan could be obsessive and stubborn. Fixating on their parent's death could not be mentally healthy.

Three years ago, Jackson had convinced Evan to stop going to Fetish. The stupid sex club hadn't been about pleasure for Evan—it had been away to punish himself for being too much like his father. Jackson hadn't had any patience for that and when he'd gotten the call that Evan was in the hospital, he'd finally been unable to respect his cousin's privacy.

Evan was sitting in the hospital room when Jackson walked in. He went directly over and looked at the x-ray on the light-up box in the wall.

"How'd you get in here?" asked Evan.

"I bully people," said Jackson. "And I said you were my brother. Radial fracture."

"Yeah."

"How'd that happen?"

Evan didn't answer and Jackson could see that Evan had no intention of answering. Jackson sighed.

"Did I ever tell you about my mom?"

"No?" Evan looked off-balance.

"She liked S&M. It was one of the reasons we got booted out of her family. They said she was a whore. Which was kind of true, although unrelated. And they thought she… defiled herself. I believe that was the term my grandfather used."

Evan swallowed hard. "Defiled?" he repeated.

"I punched him in the face," said Jackson with a shrug. "Not that it did much good. I was twelve. He just threw me out of the house. It doesn't matter anyway. I told you—they abandoned us. They are not my family. This is my family."

"Evan stared at him mutely and Jackson decided that there wasn't going to be any commentary.

"My point is that I'm not unfamiliar with people or places like Fetish. And I'm telling you that the good part about those places is that they are all about consent. When to use it, when to give it, when to take it away. The bad part, the part I don't like, is that you are consenting to this." Jackson gestured angrily to the x-ray, and Evan looked down, avoiding eye contact. "My question to you, is, are you sure that *you* like it?"

"What?" Evan looked up, startled. He looked down at his arm and then back at the x-ray. "It's a broken arm. Of course, I don't like it. It was an accident. I just didn't… It wasn't supposed to happen. I'm stubborn."

"Yes. I see that," said Jackson. "I see that you don't like being told what to do. I see that you like controlling things. But there's a big difference between control and pain. And if you don't like it, why are you doing it?"

"It's better," whispered Evan, his voice hoarse.

"For who? It's not better for you."

"It's safer."

"Again, for who? Not for you. I can't have people hurting you Evan. It's unacceptable."

"There can't be any more monsters in the family," said Evan, his face deathly pale.

"There aren't any."

"Are you sure?" demanded Evan.

"Yes," said Jackson. "I am. This is my family now, Evan. You know why Eleanor brought me in, right? Instead of leaving me to rot in prison."

"To keep tabs on us," said Evan tiredly.

"To keep all of you safe. This is not safe!" This time, he found himself flapping his hands at Evan's arm. "I cannot have this shit."

Evan seemed to be chewing over Jackson's words. "What about the others?" he asked.

"I won't let anyone hurt them either."

Evan eyed Jackson carefully. "Anyone? You promise?" Jackson knew what he was asking. Evan was asking Jackson to protect Aiden and, more specifically, Dominique from him.

"I promise," said Jackson, looking him in the eye.

It was an easy promise because Jackson knew Evan wasn't the monster that Evan believed himself to be. But Evan had taken years more work to believe that about himself. Evan had always taken too much of the family history as his own burden and now the storage unit had become a testament to that burden. The worst part was that Jackson didn't know what to do about it.

Evan – Tuesday

By the time Evan left work on Tuesday, his head was pounding from too much staring at the computer screen. When he received the phone call from Last Stop Computing, he almost didn't answer. But finally, he gathered up his energy and answered.

"This is Evan Deveraux," he said as he picked up, hoping he sounded calm.

"This is Isaiah, from Last Stop Computing. I wanted to update you on the hard drives you dropped off."

"Great," said Evan, forcing a smile to his face so that it would come through in his voice.

"I picked up the equipment and I've got the hard drives up and running, but I can't copy them over."

"Why not?" asked Evan.

"They're encrypted. It's not the end of the line, but it's going to take me another week or two."

"Oh," said Evan, trying to decide if he felt grateful for the reprieve or not. "Well, thanks for letting me know. Just give me a call when it's done, I guess?"

"Yeah, no problem," said Isaiah.

Evan hung up and walked up the stairs to his unit, only to find Martin, the condo board president knocking on his door.

"Evan! Good to see you! I have gotten four super weird messages from Isabelle Elliot. Something about that Glen guy in C8 being a serial rapist?"

"Yeah," said Evan. "I was going to call you. He tried to roofie someone."

"Are you sure?" asked Martin, looking shocked.

"I was standing right there and watched him do it," said Evan sharply. If the disbelieving response he was getting was anything to judge by, he had no idea how women dealt with these situations. No wonder rape got under-reported. "I was going to call and see if there was anything we could do to get him evicted."

"Well, gosh," said Martin, in possibly the most fifties response to a rapist that Evan had ever heard. "I'm just so shocked. Um… Let me think."

But a prolonged conversation didn't lead to any solutions. Martin was sad to inform him that there was not much they could do… legally. But Martin and his partner were kings of the gossip chain, so at the very least, Evan was certain that the entire community would know about Glen's rapist tendencies by the end of the week. Evan was not entirely happy with that, but it was the best he could do for the moment. He wondered if he could just buy Glen out of the building.

He had barely shut the door and taken off his coat when someone knocked on the door again. Evan rolled his eyes, deciding it was probably Martin with one additional thought. Evan didn't know what his loquacious neighbor could possibly have left to say other than his usual pitches to get Evan *involved*, but Evan didn't want to join the condo board. He didn't want to participate in his community. He didn't like groups and he had no intention of being wrangled into anything where he spent time with Isabelle Elliot. He yanked open the door intending to clarify his position with Martin once and for all.

Olivia stood in the hallway. She was carrying a bottle of wine and her purse and wearing a pair of jeans, boots, and a motorcycle cut jacket that only emphasized how adorably un-tough she looked.

"You said to clear my Tuesday," she said.

One thought managed to elbow its way to the forefront, pushing out thoughts of Eleanor, Glen, and his family. He had won—Olivia was his.

He reached out, grabbed her by the jacket, and pulled her inside. Slamming the door shut behind her, he wrapped his arms around her and kissed her, claiming her, putting his mark on her lips. There was a thump as her purse hit the floor and she wound her arm around his neck. At least, he hoped it was her purse and not the wine. He finally realized that possibly, as a greeting, that his approach might be a tad aggressive and leaned back to get a look at her face.

"Hi," he said.

"Hi," she replied, smiling up at him.

"To clarify, I was joking about Tuesday. You didn't need to wait that long."

"Well, I might have called," she said, letting go of him, and taking a half step back. He was not happy about that. "But I don't have your number. And I might have looked you up online, but I don't know your last name."

"Right," he said, feeling like an idiot. He was so used to people knowing who he was—he had just assumed she would reach out. But she was new in town. Why would she know him?

"And I'm assuming that's also why you didn't call me," she added.

"Right," he said again, "because we kind of skipped that part."

"Right," she agreed, her green eyes sparkling in laughter.

"Olivia?"

"Yes, Evan?"

"What is your last name?"

"West. What's yours?"

"Deveraux," he said evenly, hoping it meant nothing to her.

"Well, Mr. Deveraux, it's very nice to meet you." She held her hand out as if to shake.

"No," he said, batting her hand away and sliding his arms back around her waist. "We're not doing that again."

"But we're doing this again?" she asked, nibbling tiny kisses along his jaw.

"Among other things," he agreed, leaning into her.

She tasted sweet like sugar, and her lips met his with a matching eagerness. He let one hand slide downward, to feel the curve of her ass, pulling her tight to him, while the other went upward, burying itself in her hair. He found himself hampered by the wine bottle between them and he stepped back.

"You brought wine," he said.

"I brought wine," she agreed, blinking at him.

He plucked the bottle out of her hand and glanced at the label. "Oh. I like this one." He was surprised. It was rare that anyone brought him a bottle he actually liked.

"Do you? Good. It's one of my favorites."

He was torn between approval and mentioning that he had three in the cellar.

"I like it," he said. "I just like it better when you're not holding it while I kiss you."

That made her laugh. "So," she leaned forward and let her hand drift up his thigh, "I shouldn't hold…*anything* while you kiss me?" He found his breath suddenly short. "I'm not sure that was mentioned in the rules."

"Oh, there are additional rules," he said. "Did you not get the handbook?"

"Why, no, I did not!" She pulled her hand away and placed it with mock shock on her chest. "I hope I have not violated any Evan Deveraux policies. Do I need to take a class? Is there going to be a test? Do I get a hand-out?"

"Hand-out?" he asked, sliding his hand along the buttons on her shirt and popping them one at a time. "Sure. Hand, out." Her breasts pushed the shirt open as if they had resented being covered. She looked down at herself as he slid his hand inside her shirt and along the smooth skin of her ribs. He pulled her to him again, leaning in to kiss her.

"Stop holding the wine," she said before his lips made contact.

"Right," he agreed. He turned around and walked the few steps into the kitchen and dropped the wine on the counter, then he grabbed her by the hand and tugged her toward the stairs.

He had her mostly undressed by the time they reached the bedroom. He was hampered by the boots.

"Evan," she said, as he unzipped a boot, enjoying the fricative sound of the zipper.

"Yes," he replied, pausing briefly and hoping that she wasn't going to do anything pedantic and normal like talk about relationships or where they were going because at the moment he was more worried about coming than going.

"Do you think…" she bit her lip and he raised an eyebrow. "I'm up for whatever, but I was also kind of hoping for dinner."

He laughed. She never said what he thought she was going to say. "Yes, I'll make you dinner."

"Well, food in general. You don't have to cook. I just haven't had dinner."

He yanked off the other boot and slid the jeans over her hips, kissing along her thigh as he went.

"I," kiss, "will," kiss, "make," kiss, "you," kiss, "dinner."

She made a little moan of happiness at the end of the sentence and he was fairly certain he could make her come based on promises of food alone. One of her bra straps was sliding off her shoulder and her breast was tumbling out of the cup. Her bra and panties were gold and pink lace that matched her nipples perfectly.

"You're still dressed," she complained.

"You should probably do something about that," he said, running his tongue over the escaping breast.

"I, oh…" Her nipple became taut in his mouth, firm, while the rest of her breast was soft. He undid the bra and ran his hand over the other breast. She was pulling, ineffectually, at his shirt. "God, that feels good," she groaned, giving up on his shirt in favor of letting him do what he wanted.

"You'll never get me naked that way," he said, letting his teeth barely touch her breast. She let out a little gasp but reached again for his shirt again. He let the other breast roll through his fingers pinching the nipple right at the end and her gasp this time was more pronounced.

"You're making this very difficult," she said, her voice higher than normal and breathless.

"Am I?" He kissed along her neck. She finally managed to get his shirt untucked and was working on some of the buttons, but he put a stop to that, by moving one hand down between her thighs. He pushed the panties aside and ran his entire palm over her roughly and then gently pushed inside with one finger.

"Evan!" she gasped, arching back for him and he could not stop himself from smiling. "Evan you're being very, oh…"

"Very what?" he asked, circling her clit with his now wet finger. "Nice?"

"Yes! No."

"No? I should stop?"

He stopped and she glared up at him. "Evan Deveraux, you take your clothes off right now."

"I never should have told you my full name," he said, yanking his shirt off over his head. "You're going to use it against me."

She was wriggling out of her underwear and she glanced up at him. "Well, yes," she said, her accent pristine in her agreement, "because I want you to use other things against *me*."

Her red hair tumbled down around her shoulders and her pale skin stood in stark contrast to his dark gray sheets. He found that he was grinning down at her like a fool. "We are going to have so much fun."

"Well," she said, unzipping his fly slowly, and sliding her hand inside, "I hope so."

She kissed along his chest, as her hands ever so slowly worked his pants off his hips. He let her push him off the bed to get him out of his pants. He was standing there while she knelt on the bed, running her thumb up and down his cock, when she bit his chest with a stinging nip. He found himself gasping and his hand came down on her ass with a sharp smack. He looked down at her, petrified.

"Was that not in the rules?" she asked, her eyes wide in mock innocence.

"You tell me," he said, breathing heavily. He hadn't hit anyone during sex in two years. He wasn't sure that counted, but he really didn't want to screw this up.

She looked over her shoulder, to where his hand still rested on her ass. "I don't see a flag on the play."

"Then I should see if I can make it to the goal line," he said and pushed her onto the bed.

She watched him with flushed cheeks as he pulled the condom on, reaching for him eagerly when he was done. But instead of complying he dipped his head and ran his tongue along her thigh and slid two fingers inside her.

"Oh God, Evan, Evan."

She moaned his name as he found her G-spot. He pushed his tongue onto her clit and she bucked against him with a little shriek of pleasure. She was trembling as he circled her clit again and again.

"Evan, God, Evan please, please I'll come if you just fuck me."

"Come and I'll fuck you," he said.

She made a noise that was half angry, half ecstatic.

He switched to using his fingers on her clit and sat up, letting his cock rest at the entrance to her sex. She pulsed against him and he wanted nothing more than to give in to her, but he held off a moment longer.

"Evan, Evan, please," she begged.

"Please what?"

Her eyes closed and her body tensed underneath him, rocking with the pressure of his fingers. Her hands clenched at the sheets and her hair spread out in an arc across the bed.

"Please, fuck me, please!"

He let out his air in a woosh and drove into her, unable to restrain himself any longer. She came immediately, screaming his name and wrapping her legs around him. He gave her a moment and then began to fuck her in earnest. She moaned and pulled his head down to kiss him as their bodies moved in unison. She came again when he did and he collapsed into her, sweaty and happy.

Later, when he could think again, he decided that half the fun of sex with Olivia was not letting her have her way. The other half was giving her exactly what she wanted.

Olivia – Dinner

Olivia tried to get her breath back and maintain enough self-control to keep from blurting out the thought that was uppermost in her mind: this had been even better than last time. Last week had been fantastic, but she had failed to realize that last week had merely been a warm-up for Evan Deveraux. She had never reacted to anyone like she did to him. His lightest touch had set her on fire. She tried to roll over to snuggle against Evan and found that her muscles didn't respond to her commands. He had turned her to jelly. Fortunately, he pulled her to him, settling her against his chest with a satisfied grunt.

"God, I love Tuesdays," she said.

"Again, I was just joking about Tuesdays," he said.

"I am not laughing," said Olivia.

"Neither am I," he said cranking his head down to kiss her. They settled back into comfortable silence and Olivia ran her hand over the sheets.

"Where did you get these?" she asked fingering the material. "They are seriously the nicest sheets ever."

"No clue," he said.

"That's such a guy thing," she said. "I don't generally believe in gender stereotyping, but seriously, men need to learn that sheets matter."

"I believe that they matter," he said sounding amused. "For instance, I hate flannel. It's like being Velcroed to one spot in the bed. And I hate satin. Having satin sheets is just begging for a sex-related injury when someone goes sliding right out of bed."

Olivia laughed.

"No, the only real answer for sheets is cotton with a ridiculously high thread count. Which is what I believe these are. I just have no idea where they came from."

"Well, then I take back my harsh words regarding your gender," said Olivia with a laugh, but privately she wondered just how much Evan had spent on the sheets. She wasn't making bad money, but she was starting to think that Evan made ridiculous money.

"Thanks," he said. "Dinner?"

She groaned. "How do you have energy for that?"

"Stay here," he offered. "I'll bring you dinner in bed."

She stared at him suspiciously. "This is a ploy to keep me naked, isn't it?"

"Entirely," he agreed, and she found herself laughing at his blatant honesty. In Georgia, she had never been naked. After sex, she'd been up and clothed in short order. She had always wished she were brave enough to be more of a nudist but privately thought her boobs were a bit too floppy to be wandering around naked. She looked at Evan and made a decision.

"Well, I don't mind being naked, but I'd rather come down and watch you cook."

"As long as you stay naked, you can do whatever you want," he said with a shrug.

"Oh," she said, suddenly remembering the layout of his condo. "Doesn't that mean that half the city is going to see me in your living room?"

He grinned. "No, there's a coating on the glass. You're safe."

"Oh, all right then."

Ten minutes of making out later, Olivia was nakedly drinking wine while Evan made dinner in his boxers and t-shirt, which he deemed necessary for cooking purposes. She watched him moving around his kitchen with the easy familiarity of someone in their element.

"What do you do for a living?" she asked.

"I'm an investment manager."

She tried to square that with what she knew about him. Every financial guy she'd met since moving to the city had been a complete douchebag. She could see his career working with the condo, but it didn't seem to match the comic books and the way he'd leapt to her rescue.

"That doesn't seem like you."

"It's what I do," he said with a shrug. His face seemed to close off a little.

"But do you love it?" she asked.

He stared at her. "That isn't a priority," he said after a moment.

"For who?" she asked, laughing. "You do realize, that our entire generation is predicated on pursuing our true passions?"

"Um, I'm pretty sure mine was predicated on doing what my grandmother told me to do."

"That also doesn't seem like you," she said.

"You haven't met my grandmother," he said.

She realized that a line of tension head formed in his back and had been there since she asked about his work. She was making him uncomfortable.

"Evan?"

"Yes," he said, smiling at her, but it seemed a little forced.

"Here are the rules: I'm prone to asking completely the wrong thing and not noticing, so if you want me to stop, you have to tell me to stop. I won't mind."

"You can ask," he said, with a real smile. "And I'll even answer. It just doesn't make me happy."

"Then tell me something about yourself that does make you happy."

He stared at her as if she'd asked for the moon. The silence stretched on and she had a nervous thought that he wouldn't have anything.

"I speak halfway decent Japanese, but I've never taken a class."

"Have you been to Japan? Wait, yes you have because you said you were on a layover in Tokyo."

"I go a couple of times a year for work."

Olivia sighed in hopeless jealousy.

"You like Japan?"

"I like anywhere that isn't here. I've always wanted to travel abroad but never had the chance."

"Never?" His eyebrows flew upwards in surprise.

"Well, I could have gone with some friends when I was in college, but my grandparents disapproved and, since they were the ones paying for college, that was that."

"Mm," he nodded his understanding.

"And then Clark said he'd go with me to Mexico."

"Clark?"

"Cheater. I got my passport and everything, but it turned out he lied about that like he lied about everything else."

"I don't like Clark," he said.

"That makes two of us," she said, smiling at him. "I think the thing that pisses me off the worst is that I knew I didn't… I didn't like him. I let myself love him, but I didn't actually like him very much, and then I found out that he cheated on me and I felt so stupid. I should have dumped his ass a year before. I shouldn't have wasted my time on someone that wanted me to…"

"Wanted you to what?"

She floundered, realizing that she'd wandered into a thorny topic.

"He never liked my Dark Phoenix costume and never wanted me to go ComicCon. And he didn't want me to use my title."

Evan was frowning at her. "Why not?"

"He said I wasn't a real doctor, like a medical doctor, so I shouldn't use my title in social situations."

"Clark doesn't live here, does he?" asked Evan.

"No. That was one of the attractive things about moving."

"That's probably good. I probably shouldn't go around punching people I don't know."

Olivia laughed. "I wouldn't mind. Anyway, my point is, that when I moved here, I promised myself that I was going to do as the wise one, Snoop Dogg, once advised: I'm gonna be me at all times."

"Unless you're Dark Phoenix," said Evan with a grin.

"Well, I figure that's like being a unicorn. Always be yourself, unless you can be a unicorn, then you should be a unicorn."

Evan chuckled. "I've never been to a ComicCon," he said. "I've never had the courage. My family is much more on the Clark side. They would not approve if they found out."

"That is why you go in costume," said Olivia. "No one has to know."

Her phone burbled and she went to finally pick up her purse from the floor where she'd dropped it earlier. She put it on the table and pulled out her phone, happily aware that Evan had checked out her ass when she'd bent over.

Automated alert: refrigeration unit 246 has failed.

"Fuck!" She looked up at Evan in panic. "Fuck! The refrigeration unit failed!"

"I don't what that means," he said calmly.

"It means that if I don't get my samples moved in the next hour I'm going to lose six months' worth of research!"

"Go get dressed," he said. "I'll drive you to work."

"Dressed! Right!" She started to run for the stairs, realized she was still carrying a wine glass, and ran back to set it on the table.

Twenty minutes later, Evan wove through traffic, driving through three red lights before pulling up in front of her building with a jerk.

"Thanks!" she said, leaning over the emergency break, and kissing him as hard as she could. "Call you tomorrow!"

It wasn't until she was halfway through moving her samples to the smaller unit that she realized she still didn't have his number.

Evan – Cookie Crumbs

Evan was waiting for the meeting to start. Bob Degrossier was talking to Tall Todd about the impending Absolex collapse.

"It feels like insider trading," said Tall Todd.

"No way," said Bob. "I bought some of those shares. And no one tipped me off. It just looked like a good deal. Do you know the kind of network you'd have to have to start a cascade like that?"

Evan continued to sip his coffee and check his phone. Ignoring Bob's blatant lie about being tipped off. Evan was well aware of the network he'd need. It was his network after all. It was just that most of the network didn't know it belonged to him.

"I'm just saying," said Tall Todd, "it feels…" Todd hesitated and made a hand gesture that expressed some form of oddity. "hinky. The market doesn't usually move that way."

"You've been smoking that market voodoo shit," said Bob. "It feels like just another sloppy decision from their management. Last year it was the utter bomb of the Zanilex product line and those senate hearings all over the news. Someone probably dropped that they were heading for a devaluation in the fourth quarter. Ask Deveraux."

"Ask me what?" asked Evan, looking up.

"Your grandma was doing those senate hearings, right? And weren't there rumors they tried to put a hit on her or something?"

"They made some threats," lied Evan. "Some people showed up to be threatening. It never tracked back to Absolex, of course."

"But you still had some of their shares, right?"

"Business is business," said Evan with a shrug. "With the way things are shaping up, I'll be taking a loss though. I should have sold last week, apparently."

"I did," said Bob smugly.

Evan shrugged. "Can't win them all."

His phone beeped with an incoming message and he looked down and saw an unknown number. He hesitated and then pressed to receive the message.

DELICIOUS. BUT I'M HAVING A PROBLEM WITH CRUMBS.

There was a second delay before an image loaded. Evan managed to not spill his coffee on his phone, but it was a near thing. The picture was of a cookie. Well, partially a cookie, but mostly Olivia's cleavage with a smattering of cookie crumbs. He'd stopped at her work earlier in the morning and dropped off a package at the front desk with cookies and his card taped to the inside of the box. That had definitely been the correct decision.

COME OVER TONIGHT AND I'LL HELP YOU OUT WITH THAT.

YOU'RE GOING TO SPOIL ME.

Evan found himself smiling. The last three women he'd dated had expected very expensive somethings for two dates and half-assed sex. Olivia was spoiled by cookies.

YES, THAT IS MY PLAN. SEVEN?

SEE YOU THEN! XOX

"Lingerie model?" asked Bob, craning to look at Evan's phone.

"None of your business," said Evan, tucking the phone away.

The staff meeting was as boring as always. The Absolex collapse was touched on, but Tall Todd's opinion seemed to be an anomaly. Short Todd even went so far as to say that Tall Todd needed to stop doing so much coke, which made everyone laugh.

Back at his desk, Evan found himself wandering away from his to-do list—both Olivia and the encrypted hard drives. He'd done the usual newspaper archive search on Randall, Owen, and the plane crash, but they hadn't told him much more than what he remembered from when it happened. What he wanted was the FAA's report on the crash. He knew his grandmother had it, but he couldn't ask her for it without her wanting to know why. And he couldn't ask Pete or Jackson to get it without them reporting the request to his grandmother. And maybe what he ought to do was simply forget about it and focus on the fact that he was seeing Olivia tonight. He pulled up the text and photo again and couldn't stop a grin from spreading across his face. Olivia was definitely worth focusing on, but… the question of whether or not their grandmother had killed her husband, which subsequently led to the plane crash, wasn't exactly easy to ignore. Finally, he reluctantly dialed Aiden.

"Ev! What is up?"

Evan found himself smiling involuntarily at his cousin's cheerful tone.

"Nothing. Well, nothing big. I have a question."

"Well, I have lots of answers. Some of them are even accurate."

Evan laughed. "Why are you such a dork?"

"Years of practice," said Aiden. "What's your question?"

"How do you file a public records request, and can people find out if you have?"

"Pretty easy and yes," said Aiden. "Most government agencies are required to make available for inspection and copying nonexempt 'public records' in accordance with published rules. Most of them have online public request portals or official channels through to process such an order, but you can also mail in or fax a request."

"Fax?" repeated Evan in disbelief.

Aiden chuckled. "I know, right? But apparently those are still a thing. But as for the second part of the question, the answer is sort of. Public records requests are also public requests, so they can be asked for, but no one usually does and there is some argument to be made that they should be kept private. Also, it depends on the jurisdiction and agency in question. Why? Are you planning on making a public records request?"

"No," said Evan quickly. "I was more wondering if I could tell if someone had made one on me."

"Difficult," said Aiden. "Most of your work is covered by private business and the SEC. I don't think anyone could come up with much on you. Why? Did you see that creepy photographer dude too?"

"Yes," said Evan, startled. "You too?"

"Yeah, but I'm not telling Jackson. He'll flip a bagel."

"A bagel?" Evan repeated. "I swear I only understand about half the things that come out of your mouth."

"It's something Jacks says. I find it so stupid that it's stuck in my brain I can't stop saying it. But my point is, I'm not telling him. The Nazis can shove it out their ear. Besides if this idiot gets too close, I'll just have Ella beat the shit out of him. Nothing is more hilarious than watching my tiny girlfriend stomp on someone's nards."

Evan snorted. "More like she'd just have her security take care of it."

"That is also funny," agreed Aiden. "Anyway, just ignore him is my advice. Haters gonna hate, but they don't have anything on you."

"Yeah," agreed Evan.

"Although," Aiden hesitated, "I don't know, Ev. Maybe you should listen to Jackson about driving to work instead of taking the train."

"Fuck off," said Evan, as pleasantly as possible.

Aiden sighed. "Just putting it out there."

"Well, take it back in," said Evan.

"Fine. Anything else on the public records front?"

"Nope. But thanks."

Evan hung up the phone with a frown. If Aiden was right, he could try to get the report on the plane crash without anyone knowing about it. But he wasn't convinced it was worthwhile. He found himself flipping open Olivia's text again. His thumb hovered over the keypad. Was another text too much?

THINKING ABOUT WINE FOR TONIGHT. HOW DO YOU FEEL ABOUT A CAYMUS CABERNET?

Her response was almost instantaneous.

OOH! DO YOU HAVE A 2018?

Then another immediately after it.

THAT'S PROBABLY TOO EXPENSIVE FOR DINNER WINE.

He tried to remember how much it was. Probably around seventy-five bucks, but he couldn't remember. It seemed fine.

I HAVE ONE ON HAND. NEEDS TO BE DRUNK. IT'S TAKING UP SPACE IN THE CELLAR.

WELL, THEN, YAY!

This text had kissy-face emojis and some wine glasses. Evan put the phone down feeling smug. Talking to Olivia was so much easier than talking to other people. She seemed so upfront about everything and he loved that. He also loved that she didn't come with any preconceived notions about the Deveraux family. He wondered how long he could keep it that way because he really, really liked it.

Evan successfully avoided another meeting and headed out for lunch. There was a Greek place around the corner that he liked. The shop smelled like roasting lamb and honey, the windows were steamy in the winter, and Stavros always seemed happy to see him. But he'd barely gone a block when he spotted the photographer across the street. He was ninety percent certain it was the same asshole from the previous week. He tacked across the sidewalk until he was on the inside edge of the crowd by the buildings and ducked into the corner Forester Building, which had two entrances. He stretched his legs and hurried to the far exit and came out on the cross street. He loitered behind the bonsai-sculpted boxwood in the pot by the door and saw the photographer come hurrying across the street, camera in hand.

Evan waited until the man approached the door, squinting through the winter glare on the windows, then he stepped out behind a herd of lunchtime walking secretaries in sneakers and skirts. The photographer was still looking in the window, scanning the interior intently. He didn't see Evan approach.

Evan kept his speed neutral until he was an arms-length away. Reaching out, he swatted the camera hard and it bounced out of the photographer's hand, hitting the sidewalk with a hard plastic crunch. The man spun around eyes wide, clearly uncertain of whether to go after the camera or face Evan.

"This is your only warning," said Evan. "Leave me alone." Then with a swift kick, he sent the camera sliding further down the cement. The photographer chased after it and Evan walked quickly in the other direction. He kept an eye on the reflections in the windows he passed. The photographer failed to reappear, but he was still relieved when he reached the restaurant and slipped into the steamy warmth of the interior.

Jackson – Oars in the Water

Jackson approached the building that Aiden referred to as the Deveraux satellite office, with the fading peeling sign that read Cheery Bailbonds. The sign had been part of the appeal of the place and he had never bothered to change it. Between the sign and the building's run-down, gritty appearance, the dozen or so tough-looking individuals who filtered through its doors on a daily basis looked perfectly reasonable. No one in the neighborhood questioned why they were there. The only problem was turning down real customers.

"Yo," said Devonte from one of the desks as Jackson entered. Devonte was in his morning attire of construction worker's clothes. But he was wearing a shoulder holster over his Carhartt shirt.

"Hey D," said Jackson. "How'd the commute go?"

"Same as always," said Devonte. "Got some good stock tips, but I'm about to go get changed. Pete wants me to go case out some photographer's apartment."

"Great," said Jackson. "That means he's made progress."

"Yeah, sounds like. My time sheet's filled out for last week. I don't like this new software."

"Well, I like it because I don't have to try and read the shit you guys call handwriting."

Devonte's umber face flashed in a smile, and he shoved an errant dreadlock behind his ear. "You just hate paperwork."

"Fuck yeah, I do," said Jackson. "And if I make you do more work and the accountant do more work, then I have to do less work. And that's what it's all about. I mean, hell, what kind of lost-heir lifestyle am I living if I have to do paperwork? The point of inheriting millions is *not* to do paperwork."

Devonte laughed. "I'll keep that in mind for when I win the lotto."

"Do you dislike this software more or less than the last one we demoed?"

"That's too many double negatives for me to keep track of. Overall, I like it more than the last pile of crap, but still not as much as the one that had phone integration."

Jackson made a face. "I liked that one too. Just not the price tag. I swear for that amount I could have Kerschel build us a custom app."

"There are worse plans," said Devonte. "OK, I'm going to go change, and then I'm out. Holla if you need shit."

"Will do," said Jackson as Devonte headed for the locker room in the back. He sat down at his desk and began to rummage for some gum.

"Hey," said Pete, coming out of the kitchen with a cup of coffee. Pete was fifty-ish, middle height, and had a comfortably friendly face that made people want to tell him things. He was ex-Army Intelligence and had been working for Eleanor for about a decade before Jackson came along and kicked his operation into high gear. "I ran down your photog. Little shit's a restraining order magnet. I'm sending Devonte over to check out his place."

"He said. What else did we find out about him?"

"Well, he won't be winning any Pulitzers but he really is a photographer and he does work for the Intelligencer. He also freelances for a couple of other places, but his main income is the Intelligencer."

"What about the Intelligencer? What the hell is it? I've never heard of it."

"Some sort of right-wing nut magazine."

"So why the fuck is it sending a photographer after my family?"

"That," said Pete, "is an excellent question."

Jackson stared at Pete and tried to decide how much he wanted to admit to the detective. Pete's eyes narrowed.

"Jackson… you have that look."

"What look?" asked Jackson innocently.

"That shark look. Like, all I'm seeing is the fin, but there are about twelve more feet of shark down there and I need to make a decision about whether I need to get my oars in or out of the water and I need to make it fast."

"I think you should look into who owns the Intelligencer. I don't think the editor, Marnie Perrault, decided to go after Eleanor on her own. She has to know that Eleanor has sued larger organizations over less. Also, they're not targeting Eleanor. They're targeting the family and specifically Evan. It's making me uncomfortable. If I can't dig up something soon I may have to bring in the legal department."

"Are you sure Aiden is going to want to be involved in this? And do I want to know how you have come to these conclusions or know the editor's name without reading my report?"

"Um, no?" offered Jackson. "Probably to both questions."

"Uh-huh. OK. We'll run with that for the moment," said Pete sourly. "Anything else?"

"Um…" said Jackson.

"Oh, God, what now?" demanded Pete, pulling his coffee cup away from his mouth.

"Nothing big," said Jackson. "I just ran across some old paperwork the other day at the house. It seemed a little weird. Do we have any files on the plane crash?"

"The plane crash," repeated Pete, his face carefully blank.

"Yeah, the one that killed all our parents," said Jackson sarcastically. There was no other plane crash in the world of the Deveraux es and Pete's expression said he knew damn well what Jackson was talking about. "I don't have anything on it. I had a little poke around and couldn't find anything."

Pete shifted uncomfortably. "You're not going to either."

"What do you mean?"

"Eleanor took possession of all of the files on the plane crash—digital and paper."

Jackson frowned. "You didn't keep any back-ups?"

Pete shook his head. "I gathered all the reports. I compiled the files and I handed them over. She said the matter was closed and that if I kept any copies I'd be fired. I'd just started working for her at the time, so I was pretty thorough. Pretty sure I got everything."

"That didn't strike you as an odd request?" asked Jackson, and Pete took a breath.

"At the time, not really. There were pictures of the bodies and toxicology reports. Those files were a tabloid's daydream. I thought she was trying to control the information pipeline. In retrospect… yeah. Not that I have any intention of doing anything about that."

"OK," said Jackson with a shrug. That seemed fair enough. "Well, I guess, I can ask her for them."

Pete grimaced. "I don't know, kid. That doesn't sound like the best idea. She's pretty private in general, but the only time I've seen her be more touchy about a subject was when I was looking for you."

"Huh," said Jackson. "Well, OK, don't worry about it. I'll deal with it one way or another. Thanks."

"Uh-huh." Pete nodded, still looking suspicious. Jackson didn't blame him—Pete was a smart guy after all. "Meanwhile, FYI, Granger's going to be in court this morning, probably around eleven."

Jackson grimaced in dislike.

"You want me to send someone?"

Jackson shifted in his seat, trying to decide. "Nah, I'll go myself. I'm tired of reading the reports. I want a look at Granger."

"You've seen him," said Pete.

"Yeah, but not lately. I want to get the vibe in the courtroom."

"Well, word to the wise, keep it low profile."

Jackson gave him a look. "Because I'm so well-known for my publicity stunts?"

Pete grinned. "Just saying."

Jackson slid into the back of the courtroom. Unlike what was shown on every TV show ever, the courtroom was utilitarian and the audience was virtually empty, consisting of three interested-looking college students who were probably there as homework, a homeless man who was sleeping in the corner, and a couple of reporters who looked bored. One of the reporters was a sketch artist and he was waiting for the court to convene by sketching the students and homeless man. Jackson sat in the back row, but behind the artist so that he wouldn't be sketched.

When Granger had first been indicted, the courtroom had been packed and Aiden had forbidden any of the Deveraux from attending. Since Eleanor's senate hearings were also in full swing, there was too much opportunity to look like they were interfering in the case. For almost a week, it had looked like Granger would be indicted for hiring the mercenaries who had attacked them, and the Deveraux children had watched the news with bated breath. And then Eleanor had gotten a call.

Homeland security was not granting access to the mercenaries. They were too valuable to ongoing security efforts. They would not be allowed to testify in open court. And without their testimony, no charges could be brought. Fortunately, the evidence Eleanor had already turned up in the Senate allowed for indictments on governmental fraud. Granger wasn't being charged for the fraudulent research or the deaths of veterans, but defrauding the government… sure, that was a crime.

Aiden's most recent update on the case said that it was not going well for Granger—tax fraud, perjury, and three other legalese phrases that meant nothing to Jackson had been heaped on the initial charge. Granger had been summarily replaced as the Absolex CEO and the company was doing all it could to distance itself. Granger had made a stand, saying that they were trumped-up charges based on the work of people he'd already fired or let go. But it hadn't flown legally. Socially, Dominique and Eleanor had ensured that J.P. Granger could not get a reservation anywhere and was no longer invited to participate in anything. And Evan's most recent efforts to bankrupt Absolex would probably put the nail Granger's coffin financially. The short story was that Granger was in a world of hurt.

The bailiff entered, then the lawyers, then Granger came in with his team, although, his "team" had now been reduced to one lawyer and a woman who Jackson thought was probably a junior clerk. The bailiff called for them to rise and Jackson stood along with the others. He'd always hated this part. It was the height of absurdity that some rich pompous old man in a robe could make a judgment on any part of his life. To knuckle under and stand for some a-hole who had simply managed to blow the right people in college and line the right pockets on the way to ballot box galled Jackson. He was a little surprised to find that being a Deveraux hadn't made that feeling go away, but he was amused to see that it was a feeling that Granger shared. The lawyer had to poke him sharply to get him to barely stand and then he dropped into his seat on the first syllable of "You may be seated."

Jackson eyed Granger. He was broad-shouldered and thick across the middle, hazel eyes and dark brown hair going gray rather abruptly because he must have stopped dying recently. He had probably been good-looking enough in his youth, but currently, his eyes were bloodshot and bagged and his skin was sallow. He looked like he'd been on a three-week bender and was still hungover. He also looked bitterly, venomously angry.

The lawyers stood and took their turns talking. Jackson looked around the empty courtroom. Granger had three ex-wives and a child somewhere, an aunt up-state, and a smattering of cousins, but no one was here. No friends, no relatives, nothing. It was just Granger and the people he paid to be there. Jackson remembered the last time he'd been in court. It had been much the same for him. Only his lawyer had been appointed by the state.

Jackson wondered what would happen now if he were arrested and hauled into court. Aiden would be livid for a start and then start building his defense. Pete would probably say *I told you so*, since the odds of him being arrested for something he hadn't done seemed slim, and then try and dig up evidence to help him. Dominique would be very disappointed and then probably start some sort of vicious smear campaign against the prosecuting attorney and a marketing campaign on what a saint Jackson was. Eleanor would probably publicly distance herself while privately pressuring a good many people to do the "right" thing. And Evan… Jackson wasn't sure what Evan would do.

The argument in front of the court today, as far as Jackson could tell without Aiden to interpret, was about whether or not Granger would await trial as an inmate or a free man. The lawyer was arguing that Granger had made every court date and appearance and not even been out of state, that the Federal government had frozen many of his assets and that his net worth had recently taken a significant hit in the stock market. In essence, Granger was not only trustworthy but broke.

The problem with this argument from Jackson's perspective was that the judge did not like Granger's attitude. The palpable waves of fury coming from Granger made the idea of giving him anything he wanted seem like losing and the house always had to win.

Finally, J.P. Granger stood and shuffled to the microphone to make a personal statement. He had a three-by-five card and read from it word for word through clenched teeth.

"Thank you for your time this afternoon. I am respectfully requesting that I continue to be free on my own recognizance. I have always supported the court system and continue to be invested in this process. I look forward to my day in court."

Granger sat down again and Jackson thought his lawyer looked relieved.

"Any final thoughts from the state?" asked the judge.

"No, your honor," said the prosecutor.

The judge stalled, fiddling with his gavel. Finally, he seemed to come to a decision.

"Very well. Then, Mr. Granger, I will expect to see you at trial. Don't abuse our trust."

He swung the gavel and Granger immediately stood, snatching his coat, preparing to leave. The lawyer barely restrained him until the judge was off the bench. Then Granger swung around and began to move back up the aisle. He stopped halfway, seeing Jackson, and going red in the face.

"Come to gloat?" he snarled. Jackson said nothing. He didn't see the percentage in it. Granger took a few more steps, his stride stiff and short.

"No, no, no, no," said his lawyer catching up to him and

grabbing him by the arm, but Granger continued to move toward Jackson. Jackson stood up and waited.

"Leave it!" barked the law clerk, standing in between Granger and Jackson. She pointed commandingly toward the door as though Granger were a bad dog, and with a snarl, Granger went.

Granger paused at the door and took one last look at Jackson. "I hope you all die," he said and then slammed the courtroom door in the law clerk's face. She took a deep breath and then pushed through the door after him.

"Mr. Deveraux," said the reporter, shoving his phone at Jackson. "Any comment on today's proceedings."

"No comment," said Jackson, and he left quickly, taking the opposite direction in the hall, away from Granger who was heading for the stairs and probably the parking garage. Jackson ducked into the men's room, and then loitered in the lobby, before finally headed outside, intending to take the long way to his parking spot to give Granger plenty of time to clear the building. He had made it barely three steps out of the front door when he realized his error.

In the middle of the stairs, grandstanding in front of a gaggle of reporters beneath the statue of Blind Justice was Ralph Taggert.

Ralph Taggert was round like a Thanksgiving turkey and liked to wear suspenders under a pinstripe blue suit and carry a handkerchief to mop the fat sweats he was prone to.

"Eleanor Deveraux is trying to enforce her grudge against J.P. Granger," said Taggert. "Now, I'm not saying he's an entirely upstanding character—that's for a jury of twelve fine men to decide. But that's just my point. She's using the Senate to do her bidding and we're a democracy. We don't work that way. We don't roll over for anyone but Lady Liberty here."

He jerked his thumb at the statue of Justice carrying her scales, and Jackson bit his tongue to keep from shouting out a correction of the statue's name. Authority figures always brought out his childish side. Instead, he did what he figured Aiden would want him to do and turned around and went back inside. Unfortunately, one of the reporters was quicker than the rest.

"Mr. Deveraux!"

Jackson ducked into the stairwell, slamming the door on the pursuant sounds of "Mr. Deveraux!" He put on a burst of speed and went up two flights instead of down, jogged down the hall and went to the opposing stairwell, and then sped down the stairs, popping out in the parking garage. Only once he was in the car and well away from the courthouse did he breathe a sigh of relief. He had almost made it home when his phone rang.

"Visiting the courthouse today?" asked Aiden.

"Saw the news?" asked Jackson, wincing.

"I got a Google alert," said Aiden. "So that's fun. Ping! Your cousin did something stupid."

"Well, admittedly this was not my best day," agreed Jackson.

"Didn't I say: don't go to court?"

"I wanted to see Granger. And it would have been fine. I just didn't know Taggert was going to be showboating on the courthouse steps."

"That guy pisses me off so much!"

"So much," agreed Jackson.

Aiden made a growly unhappy noise. "How was Granger?"

"Mad as hell," said Jackson. "They let him stay on the outside. All of his assets are frozen. It doesn't seem like he should be a threat, but…"

"But you don't like it?"

"He hates us. I don't mean that in any metaphorical, hyperbolic way. I mean, he actually hates us."

"I tried to talk to Evan today," said Aiden. "He says he saw some weird photographer."

"Mm," said Jackson. "Just Evan?"

"Apparently," Aiden lied blithely. "Anyway, he was concerned that someone was digging into him. I thought you should know."

"I'm looking into it," said Jackson. "It's some sort of low-rent magazine called *The Intelligencer.* I might need your help on it. I'll send you an email. They're taking too close a look into us, and Evan specifically."

Aiden grunted unhappily. "I don't like the sound of that. Anyway, I tried to talk to him about maybe not riding the train and he told me to fuck off."

Jackson let out his breath in a gust. "Yeah. He's stubborn."

"It's probably OK though, right?" asked Aiden hopefully. "It's just one stalker photographer, that's not exactly hitmen or anything. We can deal with that."

"Yeah," said Jackson. "I think so. I just wish I knew why they were focusing on Evan."

Aiden was silent for a moment. "Yeah… Send me the details on this magazine. I'll see about a cease and desist. Might as well get something on record even if it doesn't go anywhere. You're right. I don't want them bothering Evan."

Jackson smiled. It was nice to finally have Aiden as an ally.

Evan – Lunch

The photographer had not been seen since last week, but Evan still took the back way out of work and jogged across the inside of the parking garage to pop out on the far side of the block. He turned up the collar on his overcoat and shivered in the bright, brittle November sunshine. He usually tried to rotate his lunch spots, but Stavros and a warm gyro were calling to him again, so he headed uptown, keeping an eye for any tails in the windows of the buildings as he passed.

He picked up the pace as he caught the wafting scent of roasting meat and was already trying to decide if he would vary from his usual for the special when he heard the tinny beep beep of a vintage horn. He looked up and saw Jackson waving at him from Aiden's sky-blue Aston Martin. The Aston Martin flipped a u-turn, darting through traffic, and wedged itself into an almost legal parking spot just ahead of him.

"Hey!" said Jackson cheerfully, exiting the car like a piece of unfolding origami.

"Jackson, did you steal Aiden's car?" asked Evan, trying not to laugh.

"I did," said Jackson, grinning. "I took it to a guy I know. He thinks he can drop a vintage race car motor into it. I was thinking it might be a good Christmas present."

Evan laughed. "Yeah, but nothing is going to fix the legroom."

"True, but at least it won't feel like I'm in Mario Kart when I'm riding with him. Are you getting lunch? I'm starving, but I need to get the car back before Aiden notices."

"I…" Evan looked at Stavros's restaurant with longing. But it was definitely not a Deveraux style of place. Jackson looked around and spotted the restaurant.

"Oh my God, is that what's making the smell? I could smell it in the car. Can we go there?"

"If you want to," said Evan cautiously.

He swung the door open and Stavros looked up beaming. "Evan!"

"Hey, Stavros."

"And brother!"

"Yes," said Evan. He never bothered to correct anyone about his relationship to his cousins. It was too complicated and, secretly, he liked it. He glanced at Jackson, who was grinning. "Shut up," said Evan.

"And here I always thought you were posh-club, three-scotch-lunch guy," said Jackson.

"I like well-cooked lamb," said Evan.

"Well, if it tastes as good as it smells, then how could you not? Although, I suppose I shouldn't. I have put on so much weight since becoming a Deveraux."

"You were too skinny to start with," said Evan dismissively. "Just start working out with Aiden again and you'll be fine."

Jackson laughed. "I'm going to have to. Is that your diet plan? Aiden workouts?"

"Oh please, I don't hate myself *that* much," said Evan. "I just have a trainer who wakes me up five three times a week and yells at me until I sweat through sheer anxiety."

Jackson let out a startled bark of a laugh.

"Hey, Evan," said Stavros, arriving at the table and depositing two water glasses. "The usual?"

"Yes, please," said Evan. "And the same for my brother, but with extra vegetable skewers. He's trying to be healthy."

"Coming right up!" Stavros bustled away and left the two men staring at each other.

"Extra vegetable skewers," said Jackson. "I feel healthier already."

"They might be fried in butter," said Evan. "But, yeah. Definitely. So, to what do I owe the pleasure of your company?" asked Evan, crunching an ice cube from his water glass and trying to decide if Jackson being here was as a result of anything in particular. So far Jackson appeared to be pretending their argument in his parking garage hadn't happened. "I'm assuming you weren't just driving by."

"Nope. Was heading for your office. Wanted to talk to you before I called Aiden."

Evan tried not to look worried. "What's up?"

"I went to lunch with Nika the other day. Although," Jackson leaned in, "seriously, what is a *compote*?"

"It's like fresh jam. Fruit in syrup. You cook it down, but stop before it's total mush."

Jackson made a face that said he was unhappy with this information. Evan was always surprised by which parts of the Deveraux lifestyle were a shock to Jackson.

"I don't think that's what they served me and now I'm annoyed."

"Stop going to lunch with Nika then. You know she likes to go to all the hipster places. I don't know how Max stands it."

"Pretty sure he puts his foot down and they go places that serve actual food. Last time I went out with them they went to some Italian place that made me want to dunk my face in a plate of noodles."

Evan tried to picture someone putting their foot down with Nika. "I'm having trouble with this whole concept," he said.

"I know. But I've seen him do it! It's weird! Anyway, compote aside—which believe I did shove over because I don't think there was supposed to be curry in it, let alone whatever else was fucking in there—while we were at lunch, I spotted this guy taking our picture."

"Mm," said Evan.

Jackson looked up at him from where he was arranging the silver to a more precise angle. "Oh, Nika's right. That is annoying. I wonder how often I *mm* at her?"

Evan laughed. "I don't know, but I've heard you *mm* Grandma, so I'm assuming often enough."

"OK, but if it was me mm-ing, I'd be thinking: should I mention that I also have seen a photographer stalking me?"

"Yes, I have," said Evan with a sigh.

Jackson grunted and leaned back folding his arms over his chest. "This, I don't like."

"It's one photographer," said Evan. "They show up occasionally. Hardly the second coming of Absolex."

"I already looked into the photographer," said Jackson. "He works for some rag called the *Intelligencer*. I'm about to sic Aiden on them."

"Good," said Evan with a shrug.

"Evan…" said Jackson, sounding frustrated.

"What?"

"When I was talking about being more careful and not taking unnecessary risks, this was the kind of thing I was talking about.

All of you are supposed to tell me when you see shit like some rando photographer."

"I only saw him a couple of times and I haven't been doing anything that would embarrass anyone, so… he can run whatever photo he wants."

"I don't want him to run any photos," objected Jackson, aggressively rubbing his eyebrows and then pushing his hands through his hair. "I just want people to fucking leave my family alone."

Evan nodded sympathetically.

"Also, you walked to lunch," said Jackson, glaring at him. "You said you would drive places."

"It's just lunch," said Evan.

Jackson sighed. "Well, maybe you should stop riding the train for a bit."

"Go fuck yourself," said Evan.

"I wish I could," said Jackson thoughtfully. "Other people say it's fun."

Evan snorted. "You're an idiot."

"As long as I get the laugh," said Jackson.

"I'm careful," said Evan. "And I listen to you more than Aiden ever does."

"Yes, he routinely complains that you're making him look bad."

Evan paused with a water glass halfway to his mouth. "What do you mean?" He had no idea what his cousin was talking about. He was the fucked up druggie cousin. "How can I possibly be making anyone look bad?"

"Oh, come on," said Jackson, in exasperation. "You're always way more put together than the rest of us. But I believe Aiden has general complaints about a childhood's worth of *why can't you be more like Evan?*"

"No one should ever be like Evan," said Evan firmly.

"I could do worse," said Jackson with a shrug.

Evan tried to think of an adequate response to that. Fortunately, Stavros returned with food, saving him from having to say anything. "Oh my God, that smells amazing," Jackson burst out, causing Stavros to grin.

"That is how I get you," said Stavros, tapping his nose. "I lure you in and once you taste it you have to come back."

Jackson shoved half the gyro in his mouth and grinned around the mouthful and gave a thumbs up. Stavros laughed and scuttled off to help the next customer.

"Can I ask you something?" Evan asked, putting down his gyro. He rarely got to talk to Jackson without another family member around and he felt like he should take advantage of it. Jackson nodded, his mouth still full. "Does Grandma ever…" He trailed off, trying to formulate the question he wanted to ask. "Does Grandma ever talk about us?"

"Yeah, of course," said Jackson.

"Maybe I don't mean us. Maybe just the family in general. I mean, I know she cares about us, but other families seem to… reminisce? Maybe we just don't have anything good to reminisce about."

"Mm," said Jackson, nodding, and Evan grinned. Jackson rolled his eyes. "I think, reading between the lines, that she grew up very poor and married Henry pretty young. I don't think she was even eighteen when they tied the knot."

Evan looked around and leaned across the table. "I'm pretty sure her family owed Henry money."

Jackson let out a hiss of dislike.

"I've never had any proof of it," said Evan, sitting back. "Just something Dad said one time. He was quoting Grandpa though and that makes it seem even more likely."

"Well, that fits with some of the things I've heard her say," agreed Jackson. "But my point is that we know what kind of person Henry was, and I think that basically until after the plane crash her life was pretty hard. I think she is extremely hesitant to point out happy times, even in retrospect, in case someone comes along to ruin them."

"Yeah," said Evan, itching the back of his neck. "Yeah, that makes some kind of sense, I guess. My dad… He was truly afraid of Grandpa. I don't remember him very much and that's because Dad would go out of his way to keep me away from him. It was the only thing I remember Dad and Grandma and Randall all being on the same page about."

"She doesn't talk about Henry at all," said Jackson. "Like zippo. Not bad or good. If he comes up then she keeps it factual. No reminiscing."

Evan frowned, trying to dig through his memories for something concrete about Henry.

"I would have thought Owen and Randall would have stopped being scared of him after he got sick," said Jackson. "There wasn't much Henry could do them as adults."

"Not to Randall," said Evan. "But Dad…" Evan petered out and looked up in embarrassment at Jackson. "Things were different back then. I know that sounds dumb because it wasn't that long ago, but Dad, um, he didn't… He wasn't straight."

"Well, all of the Deveraux keep secrets… Right, not what you meant. Sorry. That was dumb." Jackson looked so embarrassed that Evan laughed.

"In the Deveraux context, I see how you got there," said Evan. "But yeah, I meant that Dad was bi, and in retrospect, he was ashamed of it. I think Randall was the only one who ever made him feel accepted. And I think he was afraid of what Henry and Eleanor would do if they found out."

"Do we really think Eleanor didn't know?" asked Jackson.

Evan shrugged. "I don't know. As we've just been discussing, she never talks about the past."

"You know what I love about Nika?" asked Jackson and Evan shook his head. "She is so dang smart, but damn I hate when she's right."

Evan laughed. "What's she right about this time?"

"We need to be more honest with each other. It feels like every time we peel back a layer on this stupid family we find one more, but we can't figure it all out until we start talking to each other." Evan sighed and hung his head. Now he felt guilty.

"You're not going to stop taking the train, are you?" asked Jackson, taking another bite of his gyro.

"No," said Evan, feeling stubborn, but also a little worried about Jackson's reaction.

"You all are going to be the death of me," said Jackson, shaking his head.

"We keep your life interesting," said Evan, feeling relieved.

"I don't want it to be interesting," complained Jackson, but he was smiling and Evan smiled back.

Olivia – Anniversary

"Liv," said Evan from the couch in the nerd den. He was lying on his stomach picking a playlist for the stereo and Olivia was watching from the armchair and admiring his butt. It was Tuesday, so they were naked. In her head, Tuesday was now designated naked day. She hadn't told him that yet, but so far he wasn't arguing. She had never loved Tuesdays so much. Of course, they had been naked pretty much every day for the last three weeks, but there had been attempts to leave the condo on other days. He rubbed the stubble on his chin and she thought he looked uncomfortable.

"Yes?"

"It's November," he said.

"Yes, I had noticed. It comes right after October."

"Mm, and more specific to what I'm about to say, it comes right before December."

"I have noticed, in the past, that it does do that," she agreed.

"Which is the holiday season, or at least holiday party season."

Olivia froze. She could see where this was going. "Well, I hope you enjoy karaoke," she said. "Because I'm pretty sure my boss plans on making all of us sing at the party. Even weird nose hair Jim from accounting."

"I will come and enjoy karaoke," he said. "But um… OK, remember last week when I wanted to go to that restaurant and you freaked out and made me stop at the store because you didn't think your pants were good enough?"

"They had bleach stains on them," said Olivia.

"OK, well, all of the parties I'm currently RSVP'd yes to are going to have people that think that restaurant is casual dining."

"Oh, God," said Olivia, blanching. "I don't have the wardrobe for parties like that."

"Yes, I know," he said.

"I only packed one dress when I moved!"

"You packed a dress?" He looked surprised.

"It's a summer dress."

"Oh. Anyway, my thought is that I would like to take you shopping."

She stared at him.

"To buy you dresses for parties that you would not attend unless I made you go. So really those are clothes you shouldn't have to pay for."

She stared at him some more. She had no experience with this. Her family had money, but Evan's type of money was outside of her experience. She had the feeling it was some sort of taboo that her mother would disapprove of. On the other hand, her mother was dead and had abdicated any sort of right to make beyond-the-grave judgments.

"I don't know what your expression means," he said.

"I don't know either. I've never had a man offer to buy me clothes before. I'm processing."

"Processing what a good idea it is?" he asked hopefully.

"You really want to take me to fancy parties?"

"Um, yes," he said.

"I can't decide if that's weirder than the clothes part or not."

"What is wrong with you?" he demanded. "You're hot. You're brilliant. Aside from your shocking lack of clothes, why wouldn't I take you anywhere?"

"I have clothes."

"I've seen your closet. You have four shirts."

"I purged when I moved, and I hate shirt shopping. My boobs pop out of everything and nothing fits and then I get mad and throw hangers and the clerks don't appreciate that."

"We'll get you dresses that keep your boobs in."

"That's harder than it sounds."

"We'll make it happen. And then we'll come home and I'll make it un-happen."

Olivia laughed. "I feel like I shouldn't, but it does make sense. I'll buy you a Gen-Tech polar fleece to wear to my party."

"Please don't," he said firmly. "And I mean that really, really a lot."

"No, it's only fair," said Olivia. "I'll get you one of the ones in bright green."

"Oh, God."

Olivia laughed. Her phone rang and she saw it was her sister. She bit her lip. Sofia hadn't called since the day she'd hung up on Olivia. Reluctantly, she picked up the phone.

"Hey, Sofs," she said, putting on a false note of cheer.

"Hello, Olivia," said Sofia, sounding stiff and formal.

"What's up?" she asked. "How's your Tuesday going?"

"You know how it's going," said Sofia.

"Nope. I really don't. You could be doing anything."

"I am at our grandparent's house," said Sofia. "And you haven't called."

Olivia was silent, realizing between one breath and the next why Sofia was calling.

"No, I haven't," agreed Olivia.

"Have you forgotten what the date is?"

"I am very aware of the date," said Olivia, trying to ignore the fact that Evan was watching her.

"Then why haven't you called?"

"Why haven't they called me? Why should I comfort them?"

"They lost their daughter!" snapped Sofia.

"And their needs come first? Always? What about Dad? What about us?"

"You're being a bitch," said Sofia, lowering her voice on the B-word.

Olivia thought about that. "Possibly," she said. "Or maybe I'm just tired of being told how to feel. Maybe that is being bitchy. I can't postulate a theory on that right now."

"And you're just going to go off and leave us and be happy out in there in the city by yourself?" demanded Sofia.

"At the moment, yes, I'm very happy, but no, I'm not by myself. So if you don't mind, I have to get back to my date."

"Pops is right," said Sofia. "You are a harlot."

"Fuck you, Sofia," said Olivia and hung up the phone.

She stared at her phone, unsure of what to do next.

"That didn't go well," said Evan.

"I actually did forget the date," she said, a tear dripping down her face. "It's the first time I ever forgot it."

"What's the date?" he asked.

"My mom committed suicide twelve years ago today."

He got up and came over to her chair, scooping her up so she was sitting in his lap, wrapping his arms around her. Olivia pressed her face into his shoulder, trying to not give in to the terrible pressure of tears in her chest.

"My dad died when I was fifteen," he said. "I hated him," said Evan. "He used to hit me. So it's not the same. But I know how the date sort of… clouds things. I used to get high every year on the anniversary. I kind of miss that. Damn you therapy for pointing out my unhealthy coping mechanisms."

Olivia laughed a little hysterically. "I hated her after she died," she said the laughter dying out of her voice. "I was so angry at her. I'm still angry. But mostly now I'm mad at my grandparents. They pick at it. Every year. Pulling out her photos, her clothes. There's a vigil of sorts. They make a thing of it. They can't just let her be buried. She wanted to escape this life and it's like they won't leave her alone, even in death. And the truth is that it's not about her, it's about them and I hate that."

"Yeah," he said, tucking his face into the curve of her neck, his breath was warm and his stubble tickled. "My grandmother… it's always going to be her first, the rest of us second. I know that. I accept that. But sometimes, it's like she sucks the air out of the room. I wish I had space to breathe my own air once and awhile."

"That's why I moved," said Olivia.

"Glad you did," he said, smiling at her.

"I want you to buy me dresses and go to your fancy parties," she said. "And I want to be happy and naked on Tuesdays."

"We don't have to stick to Tuesdays."

"I'm fine with other days, but specifically, I want Naked Tuesdays."

He grinned. "My Tuesdays are all yours."

Jackson – Marnie

Aiden looked around the grubby lobby of The Intelligencer and sneered at it. He straightened his face before turning back to the secretary.

"We are not waiting for an appointment," said Aiden, sounding so authoritative that even Jackson felt like this was going on his permanent record.

"I think she's on a call," the secretary squeaked. The Intelligencer secretary had been painting her nails when they arrived and Jackson was pretty sure she was going to have to re-do at least one.

"I don't care if she's on a weeble-wobble," Aiden said. "I want to see her now."

"Um… one moment," said the secretary, hitting the numbers on the phone again.

"It's down here at the end of the row on the right," said Jackson.

"Great," said Aiden, detouring around the front desk. "Do I want to know how you know that?" murmured Aiden as they ventured into the back area.

"No," Jackson muttered back.

Aiden nodded and proceeded along the row of cubicles as Jackson tried not to grin like an idiot. Having been told about the situation with the Intelligencer, Aiden had gone from his usual athletic wear to his full lawyer costume. He was dressed to an Evan-like level of perfection, and his every step managed to imply that he was a golden god striding through an imperfect universe of some lesser being's creation.

"Um," said a reporter stepping in front of them. He looked like he was in his sixties and had a mustard stain on his shirt. Aiden looked the man over, focusing on the stain, and then raised an eyebrow. "OK," said the reporter and slunk away. "The power of a good tie cannot be underestimated," said Aiden, before proceeding. "I learned that from Evan." Jackson nodded and tried not to laugh. He just hoped that he wasn't letting the Deveraux team down with his peacoat and jeans.

Aiden walked into Marnie Perrault's office without knocking and stood staring down at the editor who turned out to be a thirty-something woman with dark hair and fringe bangs.

"Is there something you would like to ask us?" asked Aiden.

"Wha?" she asked around a mouthful of sandwich.

"You're having your photographer follow my family around. I can only assume that there's something you would like to know."

"I'm…" She set her sandwich down and looked from Aiden to Jackson and back again. "Oh."

"Yes," said Jackson. "Oh." He went over to her window and adjusted the blinds so no one could see in. People generally found this intimidating. He leaned against the window frame and waited for Aiden to do his thing.

"It's not illegal," began the editor, who looked like she was sweating.

Aiden threw down an envelope on her desk. "Cease and desist," he said. "Or I'll sue. And not just the Intelligencer. You personally, Marnie."

"I… This is not… I didn't…"

"Didn't what?" demanded Aiden. "Direct Mr. Harding to stalk myself and my family?"

Marnie's mouth pinched in an uncomfortable straight line. "I apologize," she said. "I will tell Mr. Harding to stop."

"What I'm more interested in," said Jackson quietly, "is why you sent him in the first place."

Marnie shifted uncomfortably.

"We've taken a look through the Intelligencer back issues, we've taken a look at you."

Marnie looked up at him, shocked.

"You write a reasonable editorial in every issue. And you make, at least, an attempt at fact-checking. You've also got student loans and a mounting rejection pile from job applications. You want out of this place, so why are you targeting us?"

"I'm not," she muttered.

"Someone is," said Aiden, sitting down in the seat across from her desk. "And I want to know who." Marnie didn't say anything but looked uncomfortable. "I have a friend at the American Bureau of the Guardian. He could use someone who can translate right-wing bluster into coherent news. That person could be you." Marnie's eyes widened. "Or I can go ahead and file my lawsuits."

"I roll over and you pay up."

"That is the general gist," agreed Aiden, leaning back in the chair, looking relaxed. Marnie looked tense enough that Jackson was a little worried about her crying or something equally awkward. Suddenly, she straightened her spine.

"And what's he along for?" she asked, jerking her head at Jackson.

"The ride," said Jackson.

"Really? Because I have to say that it feels very intimidating for you two to barge into my office and threaten me."

"And I have to say it feels very intimidating to have Monroe Harding following my relatives around," said Aiden.

Marnie rolled her eyes. "Your family is already costing us an arm and a leg in damages and hospital fees. I wouldn't worry about her if I were you."

"I beg your pardon?" Aiden glanced at Jackson in surprise. Jackson shrugged.

"Evan threw Monroe's camera on the ground and Dominique stomped on his foot with one of those five hundred dollar stilettos of hers yesterday and broke his third metatarsal or something."

Aiden burst out laughing. "Well, to be perfectly honest, he's lucky that she didn't take a baseball bat to his head."

"Or that Evan didn't do more than break his camera," said Jackson. "Not to mention what would happen if Max got a hold of him."

"Also true," agreed Aiden. "That is the lovely part about her being shacked up with law enforcement. But it doesn't change anything—I'm still going to sue you. And then I'll probably sue Harding and demand that he be arrested for assault."

"Him?" gasped Marnie, flushing in outrage.

"I have a lot of money," said Aiden, in his sweetest tone. "And I like to put places like this out of business. Don't tell me you're actually attached to it? Do you really want to defend this…" he waved around the office, "place?"

For a moment Marnie looked like she was going to argue. "No," she said, deflating. "I don't. It's a bullshit hell-hole for people that have no soul and have lost their minds to a fear of a changing racial landscape."

"Tsk," said Aiden. "Come to the good side. We like universal health care and we bury our hypocrisy under layers of political correctness."

Marnie snorted. "Do you really have a contact at the Guardian?"

"I do. And I have even taken the liberty of setting up an appointment for you with Sam tomorrow at three."

Marnie hesitated a moment longer. "It's not us," said Marnie. "No one here gives a shit about any of the Deveraux except Eleanor and even then I can't sell copy on her as long as she insists on protecting veterans."

"I know," said Aiden sympathetically. "It's a terrible habit of hers. But if it's not you, who is it?"

"Last year, the paper was bought about by an outfit called Interferon. Their goal is to put together a network to combat the mainstream fake news. But since we're already in line with their agenda, they pretty much leave us alone. I meet with an owner's rep every couple of months and that's about it. Then a few weeks ago I got a call from the owner's rep. She sounds freaked. She says she just talked to the CEO and he's requested a personal favor for a friend. She's going to send me contact information. I'm going to do what the person asks or I'm going to be fired."

"Who was the friend and what did he want?" asked Jackson.

"I don't know," said Marnie. "Not really. It was an email address for a John Patches. It's bullshit. It doesn't go anywhere. But the requester asked for information on all of you and specifically Evan and Aiden Deveraux. He said not to worry too much about Dominique and Jackson, but he wanted to know about you and Evan and what you were doing. So I sent Harding. He's good at that sort of shit. I thought it was probably for some sort of hit piece on Eleanor. I thought there would be more coke and hookers and less going to work and the gym. At least Evan dates. You don't even cheat on your girlfriend. You're boring."

"Thanks," said Aiden. "I try."

"I sent Patches the report and a couple of days ago he emailed back and said to switch focus to Evan. I don't know why Harding decided to follow up on Dominique except that he was pissed about some sort of run-in he had with her and you." She pointed at Jackson.

"So of course he decided to go after her?" asked Jackson, annoyed.

"Dumb move," agreed Aiden. "I think the last guy that tried to intimidate her is still in physical therapy."

"No, they canceled that program in his prison," said Jackson. "I'm pretty sure he's just stuck with a limp now."

"Oh good," said Aiden. "I'd hate to think that he didn't learn his lesson."

Marnie watched the two of them with an unsettled expression. "You can't just go around beating up people."

"We didn't. The man broke into her house and tried to kill us," said Aiden. "But if you come after us, there are consequences. Now tell me all about this Patches person. There wasn't any clue about who he is?"

Marnie hesitated, then sighed. "I thought it sounded bullshit and I thought the entire mess sounded guaranteed to expose us to liability, so I did a little digging. The email address isn't connected to anyone. No social media, no websites. That means it's a bogus account. Probably created just for communicating with us. I had one of our tech reporters do his thing." She dug into her desk drawer and pulled out a manila file. "You can't have the digital files, but you can have my paper back up. With the request coming from Interferon, I figure it was someone who knows the CEO. That limits the suspect list right there. It could be political, but since we're not focusing on Eleanor, that makes me think it's personal. I put together a shortlist based on who's been linked with your names and is a prominent shareholder."

Jackson took the folder and flipped it open. There were five names. He recognized all of them, but only one stood out. He held out the paper to Aiden.

"Granger," hissed Aiden.

"Yeah," said Marnie, "that's where my money is at. I think Granger invested in Interferon, but currently, the stock is down, so there's no point in selling, and even if he did, the Feds would just seize it. I think the court cases against him are not going well. I think he's desperate and I think he called in a favor. Not that I can prove any of that. And more to the point, I have no intention of even trying to prove it."

Jackson took the folder. "Thanks," he said, tucking it under one arm.

"Excellent," said Aiden standing up. "Here is Sam's business card. The appointment is tomorrow at that address at three. Don't be late. Bring your clip book, but be prepared to talk about how you hate this place and how you never want to work someplace like it again. Also, probably play up how you want to live up to reporting's moral standards or something."

"Thanks," she said, picking up the card with a skeptical expression.

Jackson and Aiden were out on the street before Aiden spoke again.

"He's focusing on Evan?" he asked, folding himself into the Aston Martin. Jackson jammed himself into the passenger seat and slid it as far back as it would go.

"Well, the stock pretty much did just blow up. And if Granger has even the thought that we're responsible then he would have to guess that Evan pulled the trigger."

"I don't like this, Jackson," said Aiden, starting the car. "We've barely got Evan back in the land of the fully functional. We can't have Granger going after him."

"You think we shouldn't tell Evan about it?" asked Jackson, and Aiden made a grumpy noise.

"I'm not sure. He's been really… He's been happy lately, right?"

"Yeah," agreed Jackson. "The last couple of weeks he's been happy to see everyone. He and Nika were getting along great. He even loaned her that stupid suitcase for her conference."

"That's what I'm saying. He never loans out anything. But she starts talking about luggage and he just volunteers it. And he emailed me the name of that wine I wanted. Like he remembered and went out of his way to do it. I have lived too long with abusive drugged-up Evan and I finally get decent Evan back and I'm damn well not having J.P. Granger fucking this shit up for me."

Jackson eyed his happy-go-lucky cousin thoughtfully. "I'll look into it," he said. "Granger's under indictment for six different felony charges. You'd think he'd be too busy to take swings at us."

"You would think," agreed Aiden, angrily pulling out into traffic.

"But if it is him… Well, I'll figure out something."

"Good," said Aiden vehemently. "Meanwhile, can you also do something about Grandma? She's working my last nerve."

"What do you mean?"

"She keeps being mean to Evan! He is really fucking trying, and she just keeps poking at him like he's a bear in a cage."

"I think that's the point," said Jackson. "She wants him to snap."

"What the actual fuck?"

"Your grandfather—"

"Yours too," Aiden reminded him, sharply.

"Our grandfather was, well, he was a twisted son of a bitch."

"I have gathered that," said Aiden. "From Randall and Owen if nothing else. They used to raise hell in his honor on the anniversary of his death. I always thought we were lucky that all Evan does is disappear and refuse to go to the cemetery on plane crash day."

"Yes, well, I believe that she sees too much of Henry in Evan," said Jackson. "I don't think she believes he can change."

Aiden was silent for a moment. "This isn't the change," he said finally. "This is the change back. This is how Evan was when we were kids. This is the Evan I remember."

Jackson felt a stab of jealousy for all the memories that his cousins shared. "I'll keep working on it," he said.

Evan – Klan Rally

Evan settled his bag onto the second seat in the handicap area of the train and spread out as far as possible to discourage anyone from asking about the seat. He knew the looks he was getting. He didn't let it bother him.

He flipped open the paper and tried to concentrate. It didn't go very well. Olivia kept getting in the way. There had been a lot of that lately. The weekend's shopping trip had been a success. Claude, the Deveraux personal shopper with the discretion of a priest, had made sure that Olivia saw none of the price tags. Which meant that he'd been able to get her dresses, lingerie, shoes, and, miracle of miracles, three more shirts. Which also meant that she'd come home happy, picked out her favorite shoes, and fucked him stupid in her new heels. And that was well worth the twenty grand he'd just spent. He knew he probably ought to tell her that his net worth was somewhere around sixty million on a bad day, but he thought it would make her freak out. She already freaked out enough that he worked in "finance" and made "lots" of money.

At the second stop, someone walked on his toe on purpose, but Evan refused to pull his feet back.

The problem with Olivia was that while she was incredibly smart, she had the nerd myopia that left her unaware of significant chunks of life. Specifically, the chunk of society life that he occupied. Which was adorable. She liked him because he was Evan who made her food and Evan who made her come and Evan who had a better movie collection than she did. But sooner or later, someone was going to point out to her that he was Evan Deveraux, the possessor of a lot of fucking money, who only worked because his grandmother insisted that jobs were important to staying humble. And also, Evan was fairly certain, because his grandmother didn't want strangers handling her money.

At the third stop, someone muttered "asshole" and jostled him as they exited. He flipped to the sports section.

He wasn't sure if he should tell Olivia himself or wait for someone else to do it. If he told her, it felt like bragging. If he waited, then it felt like he'd been lying. Which he hadn't. He hadn't come into his full inheritance until he was twenty-five and by then he'd become used to living where he lived and doing what he did. Probably that was also because, at twenty-five, he'd been monumentally depressed and partially suicidal, but that didn't change the fact that he still didn't want to move, even though his grandmother had been hinting about it.

At the fourth stop, he waited until the doors were almost closing. Timing was everything.

"Hold the door, please," gasped Tired Mom.

Evan got up, gathered his things, and went to stand at the back of the train. Tired Mom, was a young Latina woman who always had two kids and a stroller in tow, and Monday morning was grocery shopping day. Most Mondays she never even knew he'd been in the seat.

He settled against the pole and flipped his paper open.

"Must be Monday," said a deep voice and he found himself looking up into the beefy face of Black Guy with Dreads. Black Guy with Dreads did day-trading from his phone while working construction. With a sigh, Evan handed over the financial section of the paper that he'd already marked. BGD had a habit of pointing out Evan's maneuvers with big booming false cheer if he didn't.

"We have to do this every Monday?" asked Evan and BGD grinned. Evan wondered if he was Skinny White Guy in Suit to BGD.

"Up to you," said BGD, still smiling.

Evan decided not to return comment, but instead shook his head and went back to his paper. After a while, he became aware of shouting further up the train and the clanging of an annoying drum.

"What the fuck?" he said, looking up. A full party of skinheads was making their way down the train. One of them stopped in the middle and began to make a speech. Evan looked around the train and realized that he was the only white male in the car that wasn't part of the skin-head rally. The atmosphere in the train was tense and most people were trying to condense themselves down into their seats.

There was a pause in the speech and the backup band sniggered and whooped.

Evan didn't know what he was supposed to do. Train etiquette generally indicated silence and waiting out the crazies. But this seemed outside the norm. On the other hand, he had no idea how to make them stop. Evan tucked his newspaper into his bag and prepared to get off should things go sideways.

The speaker, a buzz-cut mouth breather in camouflage pants, made a few more comments and then saw Evan and focused on him.

"Are you with me, brother?" he bellowed.

Evan stared at him in disbelief.

"I said, are you with me, brother," yelled the Nazi, screaming it into Evan's face, and then he threw the Nazi salute.

There was silence on the train, everyone was waiting for him to reply. Evan made a choice. Pain was not much of a problem for him. So he'd be late for work. What the hell? Why not?

"This country was built by slaves and immigrants," he said. "And also, fuck Nazis." He dropped his bag and flipped up the middle finger up on both hands.

The Nazi punched him. Which is what he'd expected. He hadn't expected it to be such a weak hit though. So he punched back and then he punched the next white guy he saw, and the next one after that. And then someone picked him up and threw him off the train.

He turned around, preparing to punch that person, and saw BGD.

"That way," said the Black Guy with Dreads, pointing behind Evan.

Evan turned back around again, preparing for more Nazis, but then there was a lot of yelling from cops. Evan put his hands up.

"I want my lawyer," he said, as the cops put him in cuffs. He looked over at BGD; the cops were being a lot meaner to him. "And so does he."

An hour later, Evan sat on the bench with the other four people who had decided that punching Nazis was morally OK and felt embarrassed. Now they were all going to get arrested and while he had the resources to make that not matter, he wasn't sure any of the rest of them did. He had no idea what to say to any of these men. He couldn't figure out why they hadn't just let him get beat up. He had a wad of toilet paper shoved up his nose to stop the bleeding and he wasn't sure where he was in the arrest cycle. At ten in the morning, there was only the five of them and two drunk guys in the cell they were in. Cell? Maybe it wasn't a cell? He wasn't sure what to call it. He saw Aiden come in. Aiden looked pissed.

"So," said Aiden, as the barred door slid open, "how's your morning going, Evan?"

"Could be worse," said Evan. "I could be having your morning."

"Fighting on a train? What the hell, Evan! Like we need this kind of press!"

Evan shrugged. "It seemed like the thing to do at the time."

"Come on," said Aiden, gesturing imperiously, "let's get you out of here."

"What about everyone else?" he asked, standing up.

"I'm not related to everyone else," snapped Aiden.

Evan sat back down again.

"Oh, for fuck's sake!" said Aiden. "Now? Now you want to be a good guy?"

"No," said Evan. "I'm always an asshole. I'm just currently only being an asshole to you."

"Fuck you!" said Aiden, and he stomped out of the room.

"He seems upset," said Black Guy with Dreads, who was apparently named Devonte Miller.

"He doesn't do well with surprises," said Evan.

An hour later, Jackson came in and laughed at him through the bars and then took a picture.

"You're putting that in the Christmas card, aren't you?" asked Evan.

"*Brat moya*," it was Ukrainian for *my brother*. "I wish I could. Meanwhile, you already have five thousand hits on YouTube," Evan groaned, "and you'll probably be on the local news tonight. *Fuck Nazis* always plays well. Way to keep it classy."

"Grandma is going to be so pissed."

"Oh, yes," agreed Jackson. "But don't worry, Aiden's on it.

He has discovered that your arresting officer is a racist asshole who didn't cuff half the skinheads and already let some of them go."

"Seriously?" demanded Devonte, sitting up straighter on the bench.

"Yup," said Jackson, leaning comfortably on the bars.

"Fucking cops," said one of the guys at the end of the line, and he spit on the floor.

"Don't sweat it," said Jackson. "Once Aiden found that out, and saw on the video, he got fucking pissed. Seriously, I haven't seen him that mad since he planted Charlie MacKentier's face into the conference table. Anyway, now it's all holy war up in there. I expect you guys will be released in the next hour or two. No charges."

There was a sigh of relief from down the line.

"Oh," said Evan, repressing the desire to go hug Jackson. "That's good. Hey, Jacks?"

"Yeah?"

"Where am I? I mean, what do they call this?" He gestured around the room and Jackson laughed at him again.

"It's holding. You could also call it the drunk tank."

"Oh, OK. My criminal vocabulary is lacking."

"Yeah, you need to work on that if you're planning on taking my title as the family jailbird."

"Well, this wasn't what I was planning when I woke up this morning," said Evan.

"Which is what I said almost every time I landed in holding," said Jackson. "I'll be back around in a bit. Don't go anywhere."

"Ha. Ha," said Evan.

"Your brother was in jail?" asked one of the other men.

"Jackson did a couple of years for armed robbery," said Evan.

"And you were raised by your Grandma?" asked Devonte.

"Yes."

One of the other men chuckled.

"Why is that funny?"

"I was just thinking the rich people *are* exactly like poor people. That is exactly the family story of about half my neighbors."

"Not really," said Evan. "Rich people have a lot more money."

"Thank you, Captain Obvious," said Devonte.

Evan sat quietly and tried not to do anything else stupid. He was not sure how he was going to explain this to Olivia. She might think it was funny. He wasn't sure.

"OK," said Aiden, striding into the room an hour later, "here's the deal, the ADA is going to come in and ask you all a couple of questions in a minute. Evan, you were acting in self-defense. The rest of you were afraid for Evan's safety and helped defend him."

"Not really," said one of the other guys. "Evan's kind of a dick. I just thought I'd punch some Nazis."

"He's not a dick," said Devonte.

"He takes up both of the damn handicap seats every fucking Monday," argued the first guy.

"He's saving them for Lucinda and her kids," said Devonte. "Or hadn't you noticed how he magically manages to move every single time right before she gets on?"

Aiden was staring at him. Evan felt himself blushing.

"Let's all agree that everyone's right," said Evan. "What Aiden is saying is that the *Get Out of Jail Free* answer is that you were helping me."

"I guess I can roll with that," said the guy who thought he was a dick.

"You're up to thirty-five thousand views," said Jackson, coming in staring at his phone. "Of course, about twenty thousand of them are me. Seriously, I could watch you punch that guy all day. I already sent it to Dominique—she's going to make a gif out of it for me. It does not stop being funny."

"Jackson," snapped Aiden, "that is not helping."

"Punching Nazis *is* always funny," said Devonte.

"Mr. Miller, maybe we could not say that in front of police personnel?" Aiden was somehow managing to look as disapproving as Eleanor.

"OK, OK," said Devonte, "Don't get your panties in a bunch."

"He's right, though," said Evan. He might have to put up with Deveraux disapproval, but he didn't see why Devonte should. "What? Don't give me that look. It *is* always funny." Aiden glared at him but said nothing.

The *Get Out of Jail Free* answers were stated, the formalities were completed and soon they were being handed their possessions.

"Same time tomorrow?" asked Devonte.

"Sure," said Evan. "Why not?"

"No," said Jackson, looking up from his phone. "Evan will be getting a ride for the next few days."

Evan sighed but gave up. He was going to be lucky to get out of this with only having his train privileges revoked. "Next week," he said, and Devonte shrugged.

Aiden walked them by the press with a sharp, "no comment," and got them into a limo.

"Well," said Jackson, settling back into the seat, "could be worse. At least we'll be getting the anti-Nazi vote."

Evan sighed and checked his phone. There were three messages and ten missed calls – all from Olivia.

Sofia called. Dad's in the hospital. He had a heart attack.

Tried to call. Where are you? I'm flying out in an hour.

Call me when you get this. I'll be on the plane for the next little bit and then at the hospital.

He looked up, Jackson was watching him.

"Fucking Nazis," Evan said.

"Damn straight," agreed Jackson.

Olivia – Hospital Stay

Olivia sat in the waiting room and said nothing. No one was speaking to her, so obviously there would be no reason for her to speak. Sofia was sitting facing away from her. Her grandfather was reading work stuff from a mountain of papers. Grams was knitting, because… sure, why not.

Sofia's red curls were shoved into a ponytail that was slowly working its way loose. Olivia thought she looked tired but seemed determined not to admit it. Pops was wearing his customary suit and suspenders. His jacket was set aside on the chair next to him, and he piled ever more papers there from his briefcase—forcing a space between him and Grams. Grams, prim and proper in a sweater set and skirt, was pretending not to notice. Maybe that was why she was knitting. Olivia found the atmosphere depressing.

"I'm going to get some coffee from the cafeteria," said Olivia, standing up.

"That sounds nice, dear," said Grams. "Why don't you bring some for the rest of us?"

"Yes, ma'am," said Olivia.

She decided to take the long way to the cafeteria, going around the outside of the building. She hadn't gone two steps out into the nipping cold when her phone lit up in a cascade of messages. She felt a surge of relief when she saw they were all from Evan and dialed without bothering to read them. He picked up almost immediately.

"Yes! Yes, I'm here."

"Hi," she said leaning against the brick wall.

"Hi," he said, his voice settling down. "How's your dad? Is he OK?"

"They think he will be," she said. "They took him into surgery. He's got some sort of artery blockage. They're doing some sort of rotor-rooter operation and clear it out. We're all just waiting now. What happened to you? I tried to call like fifteen times."

"Um. I punched a Nazi on the train to work and got arrested."

She burst out laughing, but he didn't laugh. "Seriously?"

"There's a video of it on YouTube if you want to search *Wall Street Bro Punches Nazi.*"

She laughed again, sagging against the brick wall, shoulders shaking. "Evan, sugar, what happened?"

"I don't know, this skin-head asked if I was with him and I said *fuck Nazis,* and then he punched me, so I punched back, and then I got arrested."

"Then *you* got arrested? That doesn't sound right." Olivia was indignant.

"My cousin didn't think so either, so he got me unarrested. But yeah, I spent a large chunk of my day in jail while he did his lawyer thing."

"Oh, Evan, that's terrible!"

"But that's why I didn't answer. Sorry."

"Well, at least you have a good excuse. I think I'm just going to start saying that for everything. I'm sorry, I couldn't make it to your baby shower—I was punching Nazis."

Evan chuckled.

"But it's good that your cousin could come and help you out," she continued.

"Yeah, well, nothing looks worse in the family Christmas letter than, *Evan got arrested,* so you know, it's in his best interest."

"That's very cynical. Are you sure he maybe wasn't just a little bit worried about you?"

There was a moment of silence on the other end of the line.

"Maybe," he agreed. "He did get really angry when he found out they let some of the skinheads go."

"I would be too!"

"Jackson thought it was funny. I'm pretty sure he now has a gif of me punching someone as the screen saver on his phone."

Olivia giggled. "Well, punching Nazis *is* always funny."

"That is exactly what I said! When are you coming home? We're going to miss Naked Tuesday."

"I know! I'm very upset about it. I'm also eating into the vacation days I was planning on using to visit during Christmas. Which sounds stupid, but this is throwing all of my plans out of whack and my OCD anxiety is kicking in. Also, Sofia isn't talking to me and, I may be crazy, but I think my grandma is knitting at me."

"How can she be knitting *at* you?"

"I don't know, but it seems like she's purling aggressively in my direction." He laughed and she sighed. She turned to look toward the bright lights of the cafeteria and rubbed the itchy spot on her shoulder against the brick. "Oh, Evan, I don't know what I'm going to do. I don't want my family to hate me, but I just can't be what they want me to be."

"If they loved you, they wouldn't make you try," he said.

"Mm," she said, "I don't think it works that way."

"Never has for me either," he agreed, sounding tired.

"I think I'll wait until Dad's out of surgery, make sure he's OK and come home tomorrow night or Wednesday morning. Tyler is supposed to fly in tonight. I'd like to see him. But then, I think I'd better get back. I didn't prep anyone on the labs I'm running. I already had to spend an hour on the phone today getting Alia up to speed."

"Let me know when you book your flight," he said. "I'll pick you up at the airport."

"Really? Gosh, this boyfriend thing is paying off. I should have got one of you ages ago."

"Who said you could have a boyfriend?" boomed a voice, and Olivia shrieked in surprise as fingers goosed her side.

"Ty! You rat fink. I will smack you!"

Her brother grinned at her, unrepentant.

"Evan, I have to go, my brother has arrived."

"OK," he said. "Call me later."

"OK. Bye!" Olivia stared at her younger brother and shook her head. Tyler's hair was auburn, but he was now sporting a beard that was as red as her hair. He looked indefinably happier than the last time she'd seen him. Moving across the country had been good for him too.

She hugged him tightly and he picked her up in a big squeeze.

"Got yourself a Yankee boyfriend?" he asked, putting her back down.

"Yes, I do," said Olivia primly, and then flipped open YouTube on her phone and typed in *Wall Street Bro Punches Nazi* in the search field. "And apparently he got himself into a little bit of trouble today and punched a Nazi." Tyler laughed as she hit play on the phone and then came around to look over her shoulder.

"Holy shit," said Tyler as the video played. "That's your boyfriend?"

"Oh dear," said Olivia, gaping at the video. "He made it sound like it was just a little scuffle."

"That's a riot on a train where your boyfriend tries to take on a Klan rally."

"Well, no one likes Nazis," said Olivia.

"Yeah, no one likes them, but that's the kind of shit that gets you killed. Is he always like this?"

"No! He's never like this!"

"Well, at least you know he'll back you up in a bar fight," said Tyler with a shrug.

"Because I get in those so often." She watched the video again, shaking her head. "That man just punched him!"

"And he walked through it like it was paper," said Tyler.

"My poor Evan," she said, patting the screen, and Tyler laughed at her.

"It's not funny, Ty! What if he'd really been hurt?"

"He said he was fine, right? Then I'm sure he's fine."

Olivia frowned at the screen again. It was her impression that Evan did not do well with speaking up when he was not fine. "Well, I guess I can check him over when I go home," she said.

"Going to give him a thorough check-up? Play a little doctor?" he asked, waggling his eyebrows.

"Don't start with me," she said, smacking at his arm and he chuckled. Over his shoulder she saw Sofia round the corner, her lips pinched tight in anger.

"Well, at least I know why we don't have any coffee," said Sofia, her tone was one of quiet martyrdom. "You can't be bothered to look after your family in their time of need because you're too busy talking about sex with Tyler."

Tyler eyed their younger sister. "Take it down a notch there, Sofs. If you get any higher on that cross you'll be going head to head with Grams on who's suffering more."

"That is blasphemous," snapped Sofia.

"So's acting like Saint Sofia," said Tyler. "We all know who's been up in your jim-jams."

"Well, at least I don't go around talking about it where everyone can hear!" hissed Sofia, her red curls bouncing in anger.

"I have sex," said Olivia loudly. "With Evan. A lot. Pretty much all the time. We have Naked Tuesdays."

Tyler spluttered out a laugh of surprise, and Sofia made a squeak of horror.

"I'm done pretending that things are other than they are. And I'm done being ashamed of who I am or what I want to do with my life. I'm sorry that you're upset by that, but you're going to have to get over it because I'm not going back."

"It's behavior like this that gave our father a heart attack," said Sofia, and she ran back into the building.

"That's not true," said Tyler.

Olivia blinked back tears. "I'm going to get everyone coffee," she said, turning on her heel and heading for the cafeteria.

"It was bacon for breakfast for fifty-five years," Tyler called after her. Olivia waved but kept walking.

TUESDAY, DECEMBER 5

Evan – Car Trips

Jackson picked him up in the morning.

"You don't have to come get me," Evan said as they settled into Jackson's car.

"Amazingly, I don't think you'd actually get in if I just sent a car," said Jackson.

"I could drive myself."

"Another amazing thought—I don't think you'd actually do that either."

Evan stared out the window, annoyed.

"It's just for a few days," said Jackson.

"I'm perfectly safe on the train."

"Really? How's your nose?"

"Fine," grunted Evan in irritation.

They stopped at a stoplight and Jackson reached over and pulled one of Olivia's long red hairs off of Evan's jacket. "Nice to know you're dating," said Jackson, disposing of the hair out the window. Evan didn't know how to reply to that, so he didn't. Instead, he turned his shoulders slightly and looked out the window. A few minutes later, his phone pinged. It was a message from Olivia with her flight time. She'd get in late tonight, but they might get a tiny sliver of Naked Tuesday.

"Good news?" asked Jackson.

"Yes," said Evan, and put the phone in his pocket without saying anything further.

Jackson exhaled in exasperation and shook his head. "At least I never have to worry about you blabbing family secrets."

"No, you don't," said Evan, wondering if there was a secret meaning in Jackson's comment. Jackson shook his head again, clearly exasperated.

Evan supposed he could tell Jackson about Olivia, but he was fairly certain that Jackson would then immediately run a background check and want to set up a time for her to come to dinner with the family at Deveraux House. The very thought of any of that filled his stomach with knots.

He recognized the feeling. He and his therapist had long chats about that feeling about what to do about it. He took a deep breath and worked through his checklist. Was this fear based on any current actions or were they based on his own projections?

Would dinner with Jackson be that bad? He glanced over at Jackson and felt himself relax. It wasn't Jackson. It was Grandma. Dinner with Jackson probably would be fine. Olivia might even like him. He hoped Olivia would like him. Everyone liked Aiden, and Dominique would be liked if she wanted to be likable, but he thought Olivia might enjoy meeting Jackson. They shared a lack of pretense that they might find refreshing in each other. The problem was that Jackson worked for Grandma, literally and figuratively.

He missed feeling close to Jackson. It was like the stupid autopsy report had robbed him of the ability to connect. Being sober hadn't helped either. Everything that had been easy was now hard. Admittedly, a lot of the things that had been hard were now a hell of a lot easier, but he sometimes missed the social lubricant that drugs had provided. And somehow it had been easier to be blatantly honest when he'd been high. He could always mask it as being rude. Jackson hadn't ever seemed bothered by the rudeness though. Evan sighed. He needed to talk to someone. He wanted to talk to Jackson. But he didn't think he could launch into the autopsy report.

"You thinking deep thoughts or did I miss a spot shaving?" Evan almost smiled.

"I…" he started to speak and Jackson looked over, inquiringly. "I feel like I don't get to run my own life." Evan blurted out to stop himself from talking about anything else. "I like riding the train. It's mine."

Jackson's shoulders dropped a few inches. "I know. I'm sorry. But on the other hand, I cannot, as Dominique puts it, have anyone squashing Deveraux's."

"It sets a very bad precedent?" asked Evan.

"Exactly," said Jackson. "She's been quite firm about it." As if Jackson hadn't been equally firm about it.

"She probably wouldn't mind if I got squashed a little," said Evan, shifting to look out the window.

"No, she's been very clear on the subject," said Jackson.

"You asked specifically if I was included?" demanded Evan skeptically.

"Yes, I did," said Jackson. "Once, when you were being an asshole."

"I'm always an asshole," said Evan with a shrug.

"Yes, but you were being an asshole to *me*. Dominque said *no* though."

Evan tried to process that. He did not doubt that Jackson could beat the shit out of him if he cared to. As yet, Jackson showed no inclination to do so. He also couldn't figure out why Dominique would forbid it. "So I remain unsquashed?"

"Yes," said Jackson, laughing.

"I don't know why," said Evan, looking out the window again.

"Third amazing thought," said Jackson, "maybe we like you."

Evan eyed him and fought the smile that was tugging at the corners of his mouth.

"You people are insane."

"Well, yes, but that's why you like *us*," said Jackson.

"No, I don't. Aiden never talks about anything real. Dominique won't tell anyone what she's up to, and you're hard to get along with."

"I really am," agreed Jackson. "But uh, speaking of people who don't tell anyone what they're up to…" He glanced over at Evan.

"I'm not up to anything," Evan said guiltily.

"*Brat moya*," said Jackson, laughing. "Your face is trying to disagree with you."

"Jackson," said Evan tiredly. "Can't I just have something that's mine?"

Jackson seemed about to speak but stopped as they pulled up a stoplight. The car idled and they both stared at the light. "Of course you can," said Jackson, at last. "But we worry about you. *I* worry about you."

Evan ran his hand through his hair. "I know you do and I'm sorry. This last year hasn't been… I have not been present like I wanted to be. That's my fault. That's not on you."

Jackson looked surprised. "I thought maybe we pissed you off," he said hesitantly.

"No," said Evan firmly. "No, all of you are great. You've been more than patient. I know it's hard to feel like there's a ticking time bomb in the room."

"That is not—"

"I know Dominique feels it. I know she tries not to and I am trying to build trust, but sometimes it's just fucking hard."

"It's hard on you too," said Jackson cautiously.

Evan thought about that and eventually gave up. "Whatever,"

he said. "Look, we have a fucked up family, and sometimes shit just is what it is."

"We're getting better," said Jackson firmly.

Evan eyed him in disbelief and then shook his head. "You are such a fucking optimist that sometimes I want to shove you out a window."

Jackson laughed so hard that he snorted, which made Evan grin in turn. "You're not supposed to laugh about threats of violence."

"Whatever," said Jackson, still chuckling. "I just don't think I've ever been accused of being an optimist before. It's funny. I'm pretty sure the Ukrainian DNA just overrides all potential optimism at birth."

"Is that where we get it?" asked Evan. "I'll have to tell my therapist. I'm sure she'll accept my tendency towards negative thinking as my foreordained genetic heritage."

"Totally," agreed Jackson.

"See? There you go with that optimistic thinking again," said Evan, trying not to laugh, which set Jackson off again.

Jackson stopped at the next light and looked over at Evan again, scrutinizing him.

"You're really OK?"

"I'm really OK," Evan said. "I mean, my nose feels about three feet thick, but Nazis aside, I'm OK. Which feels weird as fuck, but it's still true."

Jackson stared at him appraisingly. "Then why aren't you showing up? You said you wanted to be more present. Why aren't you?"

Evan sighed. "You pry too much."

"Yeah," said Jackson. "But I'm in charge of security, so that's my job."

"You may be taking your job too seriously," said Evan dryly.

"I've been accused of that," said Jackson. "Mostly by Aiden, but still."

Evan chuckled. "Aiden thinks everyone takes their jobs too seriously."

"That is true. Meanwhile, you ever notice how he secretly works on his phone? He puts in more hours than people think."

"And two a day workouts," said Evan. "He thinks I don't know, but my trainer knows his trainer. But if you ask him about his workout he'll shove a donut in his mouth and claim he's lazy."

"Yeah, Mr. Takes-Nothing-Seriously is full of shit," agreed Jackson.

"Well, there's Ella," said Evan. "At least he admits to taking her seriously. I'm glad he found someone smart. He needs that or he gets bored. When we were kids, Aiden could do my homework by the time he was in the fifth grade. He's sweet and he gets hurt easily by people who use that against him, so he acts like an idiot, but he is brilliant. He needs someone who will not just keep up with him but can beat him. His previous girlfriends were nice, but they couldn't keep up."

Jackson gave a half-laugh that sounded somewhat wistful. "I wish we could have grown up together," he said, running his hand through his hair. Evan watched the gesture in bemusement. He remembered Randall doing the same thing and he knew he was prone to making the same gesture when stressed.

"You do?" Evan was uncertain about the abrupt change in the conversation.

"I get so jealous of the three of you," said Jackson. "All of you know each other. You may not get along all the time, but you know each other. I never had that. Do you know how long it took me to figure that out about Aiden? I feel like I'm running like a hamster on a goddamn wheel to barely keep up with any of you."

"No," protested Evan. "You're doing great."

"I'm faking it."

"No. You're doing a good job. Grandma is more relaxed since you got here. And I don't know why Dominique wants her stupid shitty jobs that you helped her get, but she's really happy about it. You got Aiden to stop partying. And Klan rallies aside, I'm usually injury-free these days, so yeah... You're doing great."

"Mm," said Jackson. "I'm not sure I'm solving anything. I think I'm just standing around while you guys do all the work."

"Jackson, I go to therapy once a week," said Evan. "*You can't solve other people* is practically the first thing I learned. The best you can do is make it easier for us to do the work, which you do."

Jackson looked surprised and a little embarrassed.

"Besides," continued Evan, "you do have an entire job doing security stuff for Grandma. Which I'm pretty sure is what you should be doing instead of driving me to work."

"Well," said Jackson, "that is why I have staff—so I can do both. Besides Grandma thinks looking after you guys is part of my job."

"Sure, she probably wants weekly reports," said Evan sourly. There was the root of his problem with Jackson. Aiden had said Jackson kept secrets, but did he really? Eleanor was paranoid about everything up to and including her family. No matter what he wished were true, how was he supposed to believe that Jackson was on his side and not hers?

"She does. But I'm usually pretty careful about what I tell her," said Jackson as he pulled into the parking garage of Evan's work. Evan's skepticism must have shown on his face. "Ask Aiden and Dominique if you don't believe me."

Evan got out of the car with a feeling of unease. This last year had been eye-opening in showing Evan how to function as a somewhat stable human being, but it had exposed the lack of trust that existed between Evan and his family. He wanted to trust Jackson, but he just wasn't sure he could.

Evan went upstairs and headed for his office, but he'd barely stepped off the elevator when he was greeted by a round of applause from the guys at the trade desk.

Evan flipped them off, which made them laugh and ducked straight into his office.

He got settled at his desk and logged into his computer, but was almost immediately interrupted by Saul Rubenstein.

"Fuck Nazis," crowed Saul, flipping him the bird, then plunked a bottle of scotch down on his desk.

"What's this?" asked Evan, picking up the bottle. It was a ridiculously good vintage.

"That is from my father. I was playing poker with him and some of his friends when someone sent me the link to your video. I haven't seen him laugh so hard in years. He said you'd earned it."

"Thanks," said Evan, trying not to sound as annoyed as he felt.

Saul laughed. "Hey, word to the wise, Bob's looking for someone to do the Tokyo trip over Christmas."

"You don't celebrate Christmas," said Evan. "Why don't you go?"

"Can't. I'm celebrating the birth of skiing and models. And besides, it's Eizo," said Saul with a shrug. "He doesn't give a shit about Christmas. Anyway, your name is on the shortlist."

"You mean my name *is* the list," said Evan. Saul shrugged again.

Eizo Matusda was wealthy, possibly a little more so than Evan, and perfectly aware of Evan's financial status. He knew Evan didn't have to work for a living and it amused him to make Evan take the trip to Tokyo. Their firms partnered on numerous ventures in Asia and hammering out partnership agreements had been assigned to Evan for no other reason than it pleased Eizo.

"Avoid him for the rest of the day and maybe you can skate out of it?" suggested Saul.

"This day keeps getting better and better," said Evan.

He had his head buried in a client's portfolio when his cell rang. He picked it up without thinking about it and then saw the number even as he lifted the phone to his ear. He cursed himself but realized it was too late to hang up now.

"Hello," he said through clenched teeth.

"Evan, darling," purred Leona Meade. "I didn't think you'd pick up."

"Well, I thought I'd try telling you not to call directly," said Evan. "You haven't seemed to be taking a hint."

"Evan," cooed Leona. He remembered the way her lips pouted. They'd always looked fucking great wrapped around his dick, but it was never worth it. She made everyone pay one way or another. "I miss you. Everyone at Fetish misses you. I don't understand why we can't put the incident past us."

"You broke my arm, Leona."

"It was an equipment malfunction that wouldn't have happened if you'd done what you were told," snapped Leona.

"Funny how you always want to be the dom, but you never want to take responsibility," said Evan. "Get it through your head: I don't want to talk to you anymore, so fuck off."

He hung up the phone and took a deep breath. Then he texted his therapist to report the conversation. He got back a congratulatory text and an inquiry into how he was feeling about it. He sat back in the chair, considering. Truth be told, he felt pretty damn good about it. The rest of the day might suck, but for once he'd expressed his feelings at the appropriate time. He wished he'd been able to have a little of the same honesty with Jackson. He considered that and wondered just how much of his mistrust of Jackson was warranted. Jackson had been there for him and the others a lot these last few years. Was he clinging to old non-functional and abusive patterns? And if so, why?

Evan avoided leaving the office for the rest of the morning and ordered lunch in. He was halfway through a disappointing chicken salad when Olivia called.

"Hey," he said, picking up with a smile.

"Hey," she said with a sniff.

"Are you crying?"

"I've mostly stopped," she said, and he felt a wave of gut-churning anger.

"What's wrong?" he asked, taking a deep breath.

"I got in a fight with my grandpa and my sister. Um, I think I won't be coming back for Christmas. So, at least that will save on my Christmas budget."

"I don't like your family."

"You haven't met them."

"I don't have to. I hate everyone who makes you cry."

She half-laughed and sniffed again. "Anyway, I just called to say I got my flight bumped up to an earlier time and I'll be in around seven. I'll text you when I have an exact time. I'm still arguing with the ticket girl."

"No problem."

She sighed. "Christmas is going to suck this year."

"Want to go to Tokyo?"

"What?"

"I might have to go for work. I can bring someone. I'd have to work, and there'd be some after-work stuff you'd have to dress up for, but at least you wouldn't be at home moping."

"I was going to stay in bed and eat ice cream."

"We can do that too. We could also do that in Tokyo."

She giggled. "But won't you miss your family?" she asked, switching back to serious.

He thought about the Deveraux Christmas party with half the city packed into the ballroom. He would *not* miss that. He might miss actual Christmas morning with Aiden and Dominique and Jackson. They usually just gave each other dopey gifts and lolled around in their pajamas like they were still twelve. On the other hand, Dominique might be celebrating with Max this year and that would make it less fun.

"Not really," he said. "I think they'll be OK without me for one year."

"Well, OK, then. Let's go to Tokyo."

Jackson – Riley

Jackson handed over a wad of cash to the CNA, who instantly made it disappear inside his baggie scrubs.

"OK," he said holding out a stack of print-outs, "this is everything. But it's nothing too cray. Couple of broken noses and chipped teeth. Scrapes, bruises, etc. Main dude got his jaw broke."

Jackson looked up, surprised. "Broken jaw?"

"They're the 'Wall Street Bro Punches Nazis' crew, right?" The nurse's assistant grinned, flashing gold fronts.

"Yeah," said Jackson cautiously.

"That redhead and the brother with dreads did some damage. Southern boys should know better than to fuck with people on the train. I watched that video like fifty times though, so I'm pretty sure the carrot top is responsible for the jaw."

"He doesn't like Nazis," said Jackson, and the CNA laughed, the beads on the end of his braids clacking together.

"Fuck Nazis," he quoted. "Let me know if you need anything else."

Jackson took the hospital records back to the car. Ten minutes later he had them uploaded to Pete. Pete called back almost instantly.

"They're all over the Neo-Nazi boards and Klan groups," he said without preamble when Jackson picked up. "I barely even typed in this one guy's name and it was like fucking Nazi popcorn there were so many hits."

"Hm," said Jackson.

"What?"

"It feels too coincidental that they showed up on Evan's train."

"There's been a lot of anti-Deveraux chatter in these groups since her speech."

"Yeah, but if you're targeting Evan, then you fucking show up and shank him while he's getting on or off the train. You don't make a whole production of it. Half these guys are from out of state. They made a special trip for this. You don't make a special trip to accidentally protest on the one train a Deveraux is on."

"I see your point," said Pete thoughtfully. "It'll take us a little time to start digging into them, and we're going to have to be careful if the DA is prosecuting."

"Yeah, that's my next stop," said Jackson, checking his watch. Pete snorted.

"I'll see where they're at on charging this bunch."

"I'm sure Eleanor and Aiden are putting the polite hammer down on them."

"Completely," said Jackson. "Aiden's pissed as hell. Eleanor's actually reining him back. He wants heads on a platter for the way the arresting officers acted. She's telling the DA to get it right or she won't be responsible for what kind of legal action Aiden takes."

Pete laughed. "Good for Aiden. All right, I'll start poking at this hornet's nest and see what flies out. Call me later and fill me in on the blow by blow."

"Shut up, Pete," said Jackson, hanging up while Pete laughed.

His phone rang moments later and he saw that it was Dominique.

"Hey!" he said, picking up.

"Oh good, you're you and not the machine. Have you talked to Evan today?"

"Yeah, I drove him to work."

"Oh. Good. I was worried he'd go into hiding. You know how

much he hates being the center of attention. Aiden said he seemed a bit mortified over the fuss yesterday."

"He shouldn't be," said Jackson. "Turns out he broke that guy's jaw."

"No! Well, good for him. I heartily approve."

"So do I. Seriously, that video is the best."

"So he's OK?"

"I think so," said Jackson. "He went to his usual therapy appointment last night and then this morning he seemed… good. Kind of bummed out about the train and the whole situation, but we did actually talk for once. I think I'm going to keep driving him to work."

"Find out anything good?"

"He thinks Aiden is smart and that he's glad Aiden is dating Ella because she'll keep Aiden on his toes."

"Ha! I agree. Plus, their names would look pretty on a wedding invitation."

Jackson chuckled. "You do realize that good design is not a reason to maintain a relationship?"

"Nonsense. Good graphic design is everything."

Jackson snorted.

"Well, I'm glad to hear that he's doing well," continued Dominique, "but I think I might pop in on him tonight and return his suitcase."

"Can't hurt," said Jackson.

"Max wants to know—unofficially, you understand—if you're following up on the *persons*," Dominique's voice was the vocal equivalent of holding a dirty sock at arms-length, "from the train. Because he thought it was weird and it should not be left alone."

Jackson felt his face stretch in a smile. Dominique's boyfriend was very careful to keep the lines between the Deverauxes and his job as US Marshall painstakingly clear. But Jackson knew better than to mistake his professionalism for a lack of interest. Max was a very good addition to the family. He wasn't sure of the design aesthetic on Maxwell and Dominique, but he hoped Dominique planned on making him permanent.

"Yeah, I'm working on it right now."

"Oh, good," said Dominique. "He was starting to get the twitchy, *I-need-to-investigate* look in his eye. But I know he'll relax if you're on it."

"Tell him not to worry."

"Oh, he'll still worry, and he's insisting on me taking zero public transportation until further notice. But he'll at least take it down from DEFCON three."

"I'll have more info tomorrow," said Jackson. "I'll call a meeting if it's crucial. Probably just send a text though and catch up at Sunday dinner."

"Whatever you think best. OK, now I have to go, my intern—I have an intern now," she sounded incredibly smug, "is hopping up and down and waving papers at me."

"A sure sign of distress. Good luck."

"Bye!"

Dominique hung up, and Jackson tossed the phone in the passenger seat while he drove. Once on the eastside he parked down the street from a nice apartment building, ignored the front door and doorman, and slid through the service entrance while a laundry service crew was negotiating the loading dock.

He jogged up the interior stair of the apartment building and knocked on twelve-ohhhh-three. Riley O'Keir had added a series of cute cut-out H's to her number because even ADAs like to craft. His last knock had barely sounded when the door sprang open.

"Hurry up," she said, grabbing him by the lapel and yanking

him inside. She planted her mouth on his and began to push his jacket off. He kicked the door shut and unzipped her dress.

Riley was a Marilyn Monroe type, and while that wasn't exactly his usual taste, he had to admit that only an idiot would turn down a shot at her voluptuous curves. He also didn't generally care for the bleach blonde look, but it covered a first-rate, and creatively dirty, mind. They'd been periodically on fucking terms for the last year depending on her man status at any given time.

She slithered out of her dress and pulled him toward the bedroom, unbuttoning his shirt. "I do need to talk to you about your cousin," she said, giving up on the shirt and going straight for the pants.

"Which one?" he asked, kicking out of his shoes and leaving them in the hall, before pulling his shirt off over his head.

"Aiden," she said, as he unsnapped her bra and kissed her neck.

"Fine," he said pushing her up against the wall. "Wanted to ask you about Evan."

"Yeah, him too," she agreed, giving a wiggle to help in removing her panties. She had pushed his pants off his hips and was working on his underwear. Mostly. Sort of. She was also just working his cock. He groaned as she nibbled his ear and stroked him into hardness. He turned his head and captured her mouth and helped himself to her breasts.

"But you know," she said, pulling away, "afterwards."

"Right," he agreed.

"Right."

She pulled him into the bedroom and he swung her onto the bed where she landed with a giggle and legs flying upward. He pushed inside her and she moaned. He thrust harder and she dug her fingernails into his shoulder.

"God fucking yes!" she exclaimed and he grinned. He loved her enthusiasm.

Sometime later when they were both out of breath and happy, he realized he was still wearing his socks.

"What about Aiden?" he asked, staring at her ceiling.

"Motherfucker is on the warpath," she said rolling over and sounding outraged but amused.

"Yes," agreed Jackson. "He is supremely unhappy with the behavior of the police."

"You need to get him to calm the fuck down. I'm getting race questions from the media and the police union is threatening to go Hiroshima if Aiden gets the Feds or the ACLU involved."

"Well, maybe you should hurry up and charge the fucking Nazis then," said Jackson.

Riley wrinkled her nose, her face scrunching unhappily. "I can't. At least not all of them."

"What the fuck do you mean?" growled Jackson, sitting up.

"Calm down, calm down," she said, retreating from him and sitting up on her knees.

Jackson recognized the posture for what it was—defensive. He took a deep breath and forced himself to lay back down on the pillows. "What do you mean, you can't charge them?" asked Jackson, trying to force a smile onto his face.

"Jesus, I don't like it when you do that," she said rubbing her arm with one hand. It was a self-soothing gesture, and protective, as it put an arm between the two of them.

"Sorry," said Jackson, smiling apologetically. He reached out a hand and she took it.

"I don't like it when you get that aggro," she said snuggling back against him.

"I get upset when people attack my family. I'm not mad at you."

"At me or around me feels the same. It makes you seem dangerous."

Jackson hugged her a little tighter. "Sorry," he said again. "Why can't you charge them?"

"The lead one, Redneck Drew—"

"I'm sure he has a real name," said Jackson drily.

"Yeah, but his official alias is Redneck Drew. It's his social media handle and it's tattooed on his arm. Anyway, Drew's lawyer came in today. He's offering information and testimony in exchange for dropping the charges."

"Testimony on what?" scoffed Jackson.

"Don't get mad," said Riley.

"I'm not going to get mad," he said.

"You're going to get mad," she said.

Jackson didn't want to point out that he was getting mad the longer she delayed, but didn't. "I promise that if I get mad I'll go stand in the bathroom and yell at the wall until my ass gets cold."

That had the desired effect of making her laugh. "Well," she said, "I'm not supposed to discuss it, but I'm worried that if I don't tell you then Aiden will go off on a legal rampage."

"So you have to tell me," said Jackson. "Otherwise it's an atom bomb of police brutality and racism."

"Right." She sat up, chewing her bottom lip unhappily. "He's volunteering to testify about who hired him."

"Mm," said Jackson, nodding. Riley shot him an annoyed glare.

"That's it? That's a bombshell and all you're going to say is *mm*?"

"No," said Jackson. "You're a bombshell. *That* is information that explains what the hell a Southern Neo-Nazi group was doing on Evan's train."

She looked pleased with his compliment.

"Has he said who hired him?"

"I really shouldn't discuss it," she said, getting up and pulling open her lingerie drawer.

"Aren't you just going to put your underwear back on?" he asked as she pulled out a new set of panties.

"Of course not! Those are now floor panties. I know how often I scrub my floor. I'm not putting those back on."

"I'm now feeling less than confident about my boxers. Thanks for that. Meanwhile, seriously, just tell me. You know I'm going to find out anyway."

"J.P. Granger," she said as she strapped into a new industrial-strength brassiere. Big breasts, as far as Jackson could tell, required engineering and structural support.

"Mm," said Jackson again.

"God, we really can never date," said Riley.

"Mm," said Jackson for a third time. He'd formed that opinion a year ago, but he didn't want his fucking pass rescinded.

"I'd end up arrested for your murder after you said *mm* at me for the fiftieth time."

"Sounds like that's my cue to vacate," said Jackson, getting up.

"Thanks for coming," she called after him as he went down the hall, collecting his clothes. Jackson didn't respond that the pleasure was all his, but he thought about it.

"Thanks for calling!" he said, zipping up his pants. "I'll talk to Aiden."

"Great! Can you toss me my dress?"

He chucked her dress into the bedroom and then left, dialing Pete as he went down the stairs.

"Already?" asked Pete.

"She has to get back to work," said Jackson. "Meanwhile, you can start targeting your digging. The lead asshole, Redneck Drew, is flipping and claiming they were hired by J.P. Granger."

"Damn," said Pete. "All right. What do you want to do now?"

"I want to find Granger and punch him in the fucking face until he gets the message that messing with my family is a bad idea."

"Not your best plan," said Pete.

"Just find out where he is," said Jackson. "I'll work on a better plan."

Olivia — Meet Nika

Olivia poured herself the last of the bottle of wine and dutifully stirred the stir fry thing Evan was making. She was standing well back, because it was still Tuesday night, damn it, and she was naked. Evan had disappeared into the pantry to get something and once he came back out she was going to abdicate all of her responsibilities and lounge about and watch her boyfriend cook in his underwear. Because: Tuesday, damn it.

"Hey, Ev," called a female voice from the foyer. "You home? I brought that suitcase—"

A tall, slender blonde came around the corner, and Olivia shrieked and grabbed for the first things that came to hand, which were oven mitts. She slapped them over herself and stared in horror at the girl on the other side of the breakfast bar.

"I'm naked!" gasped Olivia.

"Sorry!" squeaked the girl, turning around.

Olivia rushed upstairs, still clutching the oven mitts, and slammed the door on Evan's bedroom.

The girl downstairs was yelling for Evan. She was yelling? How did she get to yell? Shouldn't Olivia be the one yelling? There was a murmur of voices and then she heard Evan yelling for her.

"Liv?"

Olivia tried to pull on her underwear but found herself tangling in the elastic straps of her bra. Evan walked into the bedroom.

"Liv?"

"I was naked!" she said.

"That is the problem with Naked Tuesdays," he agreed.

The timer went off on the stove downstairs.

"Nika! Can you grab the bread out of the oven?"

"No, Liv took the oven mitts!"

Olivia picked up the oven mitts and hurled them out of the bedroom and over the balcony onto the floor below.

"Thanks!" yelled the girl.

Olivia stood in the middle of the bedroom, her bra still not fastened, and stared at Evan.

"Who did I just throw oven mitts at?"

"That's my cousin, Dominique," said Evan. He walked over, straightened her bra, and fastened it for her. "She brought back a suitcase she borrowed because I need it for Tokyo. You want to put on some clothes, try it again?"

Olivia thought about that. "No?" She thought about it again. "Maybe?"

"Up to you," he said.

"Fine."

He held up one of his shirts and she pulled it on and then the tights she'd been wearing on the plane. Evan pulled on a pair of jeans and a t-shirt and then he held out a hand. She took it, holding tight in nervousness.

Dominique, when Olivia wasn't simply being horrified by her presence, did look related to Evan. She also looked like she was barely keeping in her laughter as she shook Olivia's hand.

"Nika, this is my girlfriend, Dr. Olivia West."

Olivia realized that it was the first time that he had publically stated that she was his girlfriend.

"Not like an actual doctor," she said nervously. "A science doctor."

"She has two Ph.D.'s," said Evan, and she glanced up at him. He was looking very stern.

"Well, that's two more than I have," said Dominique. "How

accomplished of you. It's very nice to meet you. I'm very sorry about walking in on you. I was just planning on dropping off the suitcase. I didn't think anyone was home."

"That's all right," said Olivia, knowing that she was still bright red.

"I didn't know it was Naked Tuesday," said Dominique, and once again the laughter seemed to be bubbling near the surface.

"Nika," growled Evan.

"What? I'm sorry, but Naked Tuesday is an awesome invention. You can't expect me to not laugh!"

"I can actually," said Evan, and Olivia frowned. Evan wasn't usually so grim.

"It was my idea," said Olivia, still feeling nervous. "And he makes me dinner."

"I love the idea," said Dominique, smiling. "And I love that he makes you dinner. Max distinctly does not cook. Which means that if it weren't for take-out, we would both starve."

Olivia felt herself relax. Dominique was being nice? She was pretty sure it was nice. She was smiling and making eye contact and that usually meant nice.

"And does he pour you delicious wine?" continued Dominque. "Evan always finds the best bottles of things."

"Yes, he—oh. I forgot. I brought some home," said Olivia, looking up at Evan. "Tyler sent some back with me. He's working at a winery in Washington now."

"There's a winery in DC?" asked Evan frowning.

"No, Washington, the state."

"That does make more sense," said Dominique.

"My brother makes wine," said Olivia, realizing she'd taken an abrupt turn in the conversation without applying a turn signal. "He's an enologist."

"I've never met an enologist before," said Dominique. "Does he bring great wine to every party?"

"Yes, he does," said Olivia. "But I usually put out crap and then hoard whatever he brings for later."

Evan barked out a laugh. "I do the same thing," he said when they looked at him.

Dominique chuckled. "There's obviously a reason you two get along. It's so unfortunate that my brother is a lawyer. To think he could have been supplying me with wine all this time."

"Well, yes, but we need him to keep Evan out of jail," said Olivia, and then almost immediately regretted it when Dominique burst out laughing and Evan groaned.

"Did you see the video?" asked Dominique.

"Yes! That man punched Evan! I do not understand how the police could arrest Evan when he was the one who got punched!"

"Yes, well Evan won, you see. He broke the man's jaw."

"I did?"

"Yes. Jackson followed up. Aiden wanted to make sure he got charged with assault. But Aiden says that, in general, the police think whoever won was probably in the wrong."

"Well, I don't care if Evan broke every bone in his face. That person started it and he should be arrested."

"Yes," agreed Dominique, smiling. Olivia thought she looked pleased. "We all agree. But not to worry, Aiden will take care of it. Anyway, Olivia, it was lovely to meet you. Sorry for ruining Naked Tuesday. Evan, you saw Jackson's text about meeting tomorrow at the house?"

"Yes, I'll be there," agreed Evan.

"Oh, good. Then I'll talk to you tomorrow." She added a smile and this time Olivia couldn't tell what the smile meant.

"Sounds good," Evan replied, but there was a cautious note to his voice.

The door closed behind Dominique and Olivia sighed in relief. "She seemed nice."

"Yes, Nika is… very gracious," he said. "Should we see if we can salvage dinner? Or just move straight to drinking your brother's wine?"

"You look at dinner. I'll go get a bottle out of my bag."

Evan – Christmas Surprise

Evan climbed the stairs to Deveraux House. Theo, Eleanor's butler, opened the door before he had to knock.

"Miss Dominique is in the study," said Theo.

"Is anyone else here, yet?" asked Evan, shrugging out of his coat and handing it to Theo.

"No, not yet, Mr. Deveraux," said Theo.

Evan had known Theo his entire life. The fact that Theo had decided to call Evan Mr. Deveraux somewhere around the time Evan turned twenty-five was still a mystery.

"Thanks," said Evan, and he headed for the study.

"Hey!" said Dominique from her prone position on the couch where she was tossing M & M's up in the air and into her mouth.

"Hey!" He quickly shut the door and went over to the couch. She pulled her feet up to make room for him. "You haven't told anyone about Olivia, have you?"

"No, but I'm totally about to. This is hot gossip."

"Please don't," he said, feeling desperate.

"Why not?" asked Dominique, sitting up.

"Because as soon as Jackson or Grandma find out about her they're going to do a background check and give her the third degree."

"They didn't with Max," objected Dominique.

"Yes, they did. Jackson was just more discrete because Max is law enforcement."

Dominique wrinkled her nose but didn't argue.

"But, so what if they do," said Dominique. "I googled her last night. There's nothing wrong with her. Double Ph.D.'s, recently published, well-respected in her field, plus, you know, tits for days."

"Seriously?"

"I'm just saying there was not enough oven mitt to cover that action."

Evan grinned. "I wish I could have seen that."

"It was worth seeing. But I mean, come on, Ev, if she's dating you then she has to know that sooner or later she's going to have to meet all of us and generally pass inspection."

Evan was silent.

"I mean, she knows…" Dominique scrutinized his face. "Evan, she doesn't know anything, does she?"

"No, not a damn thing. She moved to the city six months ago from Georgia. She has no idea who our state's senators are. She isn't in the society scene in any way. She doesn't read the gossip columns and, basically, I'm just the guy she met at a party."

Dominique burst out laughing.

"Nika! This isn't funny."

"Oh my God, it's hilarious!" laughed Dominique.

"It is not. If Grandma or Jackson find out about her, then they'll haul her over the coals, and then chances are she's going to freak out and go running for the hills."

"OK, OK, but Evan, you've got to tell her at some point."

"I was thinking maybe after we got back from Tokyo. Or maybe in Tokyo. I don't know…" He trailed off seeing Dominique's expression.

"You're taking her to Tokyo with you?"

Evan realized his error. "Did I not mention that?" He cleared his throat and tried to break eye contact.

"Evan, you're serious about her?"

"We haven't been dating that long, but, I mean..."

"I don't know Evan, a serious girlfriend—maybe I ought to talk to Grandma about this. We can't have you risking the family name and fortune on someone from Georgia of all places."

He stared at her open-mouthed, then caught the evil glint in her eye.

"Oh my God, you almost gave me a heart attack."

She broke down in a peel of laughter, collapsing onto the couch. He pulled the throw pillow out from behind him, put it to its named purpose, and chucked it at her. She seized it and, still laughing, rose to her knees to pummel him about the head with it. He stiff-armed her, laughing at her attempts at pillow-i-cide.

"Evan!" bellowed his grandmother and both he and Dominique stopped. "What are you doing?"

The tone of her voice cut straight through to the child part of him that felt eternally guilty, and Evan straightened up on the couch and tried to correct whatever Dominique had done to his hair. Eleanor glared at both of them, and behind her, Jackson looked like he was laughing.

"Answer the question!" barked Eleanor, and Evan blinked at her. Behind her, Jackson's expression changed to annoyance.

"We were just..." He looked at Dominique, at a loss for what to say. "Goofing around," he finished lamely.

"You are both too old for horseplay. Go fix your hair. Dominique, for God's sake, take your feet off the furniture!"

Eleanor was breathing heavily and she was glaring at both of them, but as he rose she pinned him with an angry stare. He edged from the room, feeling as though he'd somehow done something wrong.

"I'm allowed to smother Evan," said Dominique in her most

petulant tone as he left. "It would be a lot easier if he would stop resisting, but it's allowed."

"Stop being childish," snapped Eleanor.

In the bathroom, Evan stared in the mirror, repetitively smoothing his hair and trying to figure out what he'd done wrong. This wasn't like when they were kids. He hadn't been mad. He hadn't lost his temper. Dominique hadn't been mad either, had she? She had been laughing. Right? He hated this feeling. He felt ashamed, and he didn't know why.

He stared at himself in the mirror. He was lying. He could see it in the set of his mouth.

He knew why he felt guilty.

When they had been children—no, when Dominique had been a child—he had treated her the same way his father had treated her mother. Owen Deveraux had been an abusive, raging, alcoholic who had been twelve years older than his younger sister. Genevieve, like Dominique, had fought back and both had been protected by Eleanor, but Evan knew that there had been times when those protections had failed. They had failed to protect Genevieve from Owen and there had been at least one occasion when they had failed to protect Dominique from him. Evan still remembered the expression on Dominique's face after he'd slapped her. He remembered her, gangly at seventeen, her expression both shocked and scared, as the thin line of blood trickled down from her nose and over her lip. The sick feeling in the pit of his stomach he'd felt afterward had never really gone away. Even now he still felt the acid sense of disgust. The fact that Dominique was willing to be in the same room with him was something that he continued to be grateful for. The fact, that in the last year, she had started to be willing to be *alone* in the same room was some sort of miracle.

He knew why he felt guilty—it was because he should feel

guilty. Eleanor had every reason to keep him on a short leash. Just because he hadn't done anything wrong this time, didn't negate their entire history.

He straightened his tie, squared his shoulders, and put on the Deveraux face. He had to go out and be in the same room with them. There was no reason to make everyone uncomfortable with excess emotion.

They were all waiting for him in the study. Dominique looked up with a smile and patted the couch seat next to her, but he went to get a drink from the bar and then leaned against the windowsill.

"You're not sitting on the couch, Ev?" asked Aiden, getting up from his spot in the wing chair across from Eleanor. Evan shook his head. "Good. I hate having to look at Grandpa. He gives me gas."

Evan glanced at the portrait of their grandfather hanging on the wall across from Aiden's chair. Henry Evan Deveraux glared at all of them with a dismissive smile and gray eyes that most closely matched Evan's own. There was a matching portrait in the dining room as well. It felt like even in death Henry managed to loom over them. Eleanor rarely spoke of him. But Owen, after he hit Evan, would laugh at Evan's tears, then scream at him. *Stop being a pussy. You thank your lucky stars you never had to live with Grandpa. Is that how you want me to treat you? Like Dad?* Evan had learned to stop crying.

"So what horrible thing has happened now?" asked Aiden, dropping onto the couch, dangling his feet off the end to avoid their grandmother's wrath, and putting his head in Dominique's lap.

Jackson took Aiden's chair. He had no remembrances of Henry Deveraux. It never bothered him to look at the man Evan was named after. Eleanor sat with her back firmly to the portrait. Her ankles crossed.

"Aiden and I have been following up on Evan's Nazi situation," Jackson said.

"Yes," said Dominique, twisting Aiden's hair into spikes. "You said Evan broke his jaw."

"He did," said Aiden approvingly. "Did I tell you that?" he asked, twisting his head to look at Evan. Evan shook his head. "I meant to tell you that. He's going to do time and have dental work. It makes me laugh."

"Yes, well," said Jackson, looking apologetic, "I had a word with my source inside the DA's office yesterday. He may plea out."

"What? No. How?" demanded Aiden, almost sitting up. "I will fucking—"

Jackson waved off his impending tirade. "His lawyers have approached the DA. They want to make a deal in exchange for testimony."

"Against who?" demanded Aiden, still looking irate but dropping back into Dominique's lap.

"The person who hired them," said Jackson.

"Fuck a duck," said Aiden, looking annoyed, but uncharacteristically saying nothing further.

"Any thoughts on that, Evan?" asked Eleanor turning to him.

"Absolex," said Evan tiredly. "They've tried it before. They had the most success with me last time. And Granger would know that I'm the one that would have done the dirty work to sink his company."

"Yes," said Jackson, nodding.

"I said last time that we should have gone for a horsehead in his bed," said Dominique.

"Dominique!" snapped Eleanor.

"What? This is ridiculous. He needs to be put in his place."

"I'll make sure he knows what his place is," said Jackson.

"Behind bars," said Aiden sternly, looking from his sister to Jackson.

"Of course," said Dominique, patting his hair.

Aiden looked like he might discuss the point further, but Jackson interrupted. "There is a secondary problem with that though."

"Let me guess," said Evan. "He's claiming he's not responsible. It was the people who worked for him."

"No," said Jackson, shifting slightly in his seat. "No, he's not claiming anything. The DA hasn't approached him yet. I was told in the strictest confidentiality."

"Well, when are they going to move?" asked Aiden with a frown. "New charges should be enough to get his bail revoked."

"I hope so. I think they're trying to get the case buttoned up so they don't have the same problems as last time when Homeland Security yanked the rug out from under them."

Aiden snorted in irritation and sat up, but maintained a slouch that made Eleanor frown at him. "Well, maybe if they didn't let half the Nazis go, they wouldn't have to work so hard now.

"Yeah," said Jackson, "but maybe they can rebound if they don't have you threatening to make this a national-level media circus. Maybe take it down a notch or two until we see how this shakes out."

Aiden grunted. "Maybe. I'll give them a week. I'd better see some movement. But meanwhile, does this take the pressure off? Can we stop worrying for a bit?"

"Not really," said Dominique, and Aiden frowned at her.

"He doesn't do his own dirty work," said Evan. "We don't know that these people are the only ones he hired."

"Oh." Aiden didn't look happy with that, but he also didn't argue about it.

"It's my guess that Evan is the primary target," said Jackson, "but that doesn't mean the rest of you are off the hook. I'm going to be assigning security personnel and you will not walk or take public transportation."

"Nooooo!" Dominique groaned. "Come on. It totally messes with my persona at work to be arriving with a chauffeur and a bodyguard. I don't want to be a Deveraux at work."

"I know, I'm sorry," said Jackson. "You can have Max drive you and pick you up if you want. It's not like Evan likes having me drive him around."

"I don't mind," said Aiden cheerfully. "It gives me time to read the briefs I was supposed to read the day before."

"You suck," said Dominique.

"No, I'm just lazy," said Aiden cheerfully.

Evan glanced at Jackson, who met his look with an equally skeptical one of his own.

"I'll use the car service," said Evan, wishing he could go home and take a nap. "I don't want to bother you. I'm heading to Tokyo over Christmas anyway. At least there won't be any Nazis there."

"You're not going to be home for Christmas?" demanded Aiden, sitting up, looking outraged. Nazis, horseheads, and vengeful CEOs couldn't rouse him, but a threat to the sanctity of Christmas brought him upright.

"Work," said Evan, smiling apologetically.

"But I bought us all marshmallow guns."

"You bought us what?" asked Jackson.

"Marshmallow guns." Aiden mimed shooting a rifle at Jackson, who looked befuddled. Jackson's maternal family had been from a deeply religious Ukrainian sect who didn't celebrate Christmas in the pagan tradition of the west, and his mother had been agnostic at best. He'd never even had a Christmas tree growing up.

Apparently, marshmallow guns had also not been included in his childhood.

"A gun that shoots mini-marshmallows. I need Evan to team up with me against you and Dominique. You're both better shots than me."

"It's fine," declared Dominique. "We'll just have a Christmas repeat day when Evan gets back. We'll save the marshmallows until then."

Aiden looked neither pleased nor convinced. "I don't know…"

"It will be fine," said Dominique firmly. "Evan has to go to Tokyo and that's that."

Aiden looked from Dominique to Evan, still frowning, clearly uncertain why his sister had taken Evan's side.

"I'll bring you back pocky and Sailor Moon," promised Evan, pulling two obsessions from Aiden's childhood out of his memory and Aiden grinned.

"OK, then," he said flopping back into the couch.

"Mochi balls," said Dominique, with a smile. He recognized blackmail when he saw it. This was her price for smoothing over Tokyo and keeping her mouth shut.

"I can't pack ice cream back," objected Evan, mostly on the principle that he should always negotiate. "Besides you can get mochi balls here." He was already thinking he could get a transport freezer for the trip back.

"It's not the same. And Aiden can get pocky and Sailor Moon here too," she pouted. "I want mochi balls."

"Fine," said Evan, rolling his eyes. "I'll ship a cooler home or something."

"Would all of you stop behaving like children!" Eleanor glared at all of them. "We are dealing with serious issues and I would appreciate it if you would stop chattering on about Christmas."

"Well, Christmas is serious, Grandma. Can't believe you're skipping, Ev," complained Aiden.

"We don't need Evan to be home for Christmas," snapped Eleanor.

There was silence in the room.

"See, Aiden," said Evan, setting down his untouched glass. "It's fine if I'm not here. Anyway, Jacks, thanks for the heads up. Let me know what else you need me to do."

Then he headed for the door.

Jackson – Deveraux House

Jackson looked through the window into the yard and wondered what was going on. Theo appeared to be involved in some sort of garden rearrangement. Pavers had been uprooted and were being stacked as if they were going to be re-used. Plants were being bundled and there was a bench wrapped in plastic that was loitering near the drive. He wanted to know what the plan was but he suspected that inquiring into Theo's business would not go well.

Eleanor shut the door to her office with a firm thud. It was as close to slamming a door as she ever got. "This is most upsetting," she said.

Jackson turned away from the view of the back garden. The interior view was not nearly as pleasant. Eleanor's primly feminine office, with the black and white chintz and toile patterns, and yellow trim, was designed to disarm visitors and leave them unprepared for whatever attack Eleanor chose to launch at them. But today there was no disguising the anger in Eleanor's face.

"I'm not happy about it either," said Jackson. "I was looking forward to Christmas."

"Stop talking about Christmas! Who cares if Evan is at Christmas?"

"Well, I do for one," said Jackson. "And Aiden seemed pretty peeved."

"Dominique was obviously not concerned," said Eleanor, her voice venomous.

"Yeah," agreed Jackson, thinking that was suspicious. "I'll have to ask her about that."

"Dominique has a right to feel how she wants," snapped Eleanor.

"I didn't say she didn't. I said I was going to ask her about it."

"Leave her alone," hissed Eleanor. "You should be focusing on doing your damn job. Granger continues to target us and there is only so much that I can do. I was relying on you to take care of this matter."

Jackson eyed Eleanor thoughtfully. She was on edge and angry. Not a good combination.

"I'm working on it."

"Working on it? He should never have been able to get within ten feet of Evan. He is the face of this family and I will not tolerate having him harmed."

"Evan likes to ride the train," said Jackson. "And he's stubborn."

"And it's your job to bring him to heel. You have been too gentle with him. Don't let all this sober living nonsense fool you. Evan is still Evan."

"Which is it?" asked Jackson.

"What?"

"Is he the Deveraux of Deverauxs or is he the bad seed?"

"Don't start with me," said Eleanor. "This is not the day."

"What's going on?" asked Jackson, leaning his elbows on the back of the wingback chair.

"I'm halting the Absolex hearings tomorrow. We're not officially shuttering them, but we'll be sending recommendations to the Justice Department."

"I don't see the problem," said Jackson. "You've got enough evidence of wrongdoing from Absolex that the DOJ shouldn't have a problem making cases."

"That's not the point. There needed to be heads on the wall. If we can't convict Granger then the whole thing fizzles."

"It's still a win," said Jackson. "They'll get him, for the attack on the train if nothing else. It's just taking a little longer than we had hoped."

"It looks weak, right when I need to look strong. Taggert is hounding me on the healthcare bill and things are… tense in the Senate right now. I cannot afford to have things like Nazis and trains happening right now. I need Granger to get prison time. Things need to go according to the damn plan. I need people to stop thinking about Evan, and I need Evan to stop poking into things that are better left forgotten."

"What does that mean?" asked Jackson. "What's Evan been poking into?"

Eleanor glared at him, seeming to bite down on words to keep them from escaping.

"Nothing. Evan's violence just reminds everyone of his father and makes them dig up the past. It is not helpful. This situation needs to go away as soon as possible."

"I can't make the DA move any faster than they are, and while the train situation was unfortunate, you're actually polling up off of that. It looked populist, progressive, and dynamic all in one video clip."

"That is not the kind of help I want," snapped Eleanor. "The kind of help I want is the kind where you do what you're supposed to do."

Jackson held onto his temper with an effort. "I'm working on it."

"Maybe you should go do that then."

"Yeah," agreed Jackson. "Maybe I should."

He left the room and also didn't slam the door. Slamming

doors showed too much emotion. Dominique and Aiden were loitering in the hall and Jackson made an angry face and a Homer Simpson choking motion. Both smothered laughs in response.

He got his coat from Theo and the siblings followed him outside and toward the garage.

"Nika," said Aiden when they were out of earshot. "I am blaming this on you."

"What are you talking about?"

"Evan going away for Christmas. Christmas is the best time for Evan. How could you let him go?"

"He had to go for work," said Dominique serenely. "I have nothing to do with it."

"And if you'd told him not to go he would have weaseled out of it," said Jackson. "What gives? You also didn't look surprised when he said it."

"Yes, he told me before you all arrived. Why do you think I was pummeling him?"

"You can't pummel Evan," said Aiden, looking concerned. "He was just pummeled on the train."

"I wasn't hurting him," protested Dominique. "Just general pillow-i-cide. Which was hilarious until Grandma came in and made everything horrible."

Aiden growled in anger. "She is being a total bitch. I'm going to say something. Seriously, next time she starts in on him I'm not going to be able to hold it in."

"She's got some issues at work," said Jackson.

"Taggert," said Dominique sourly.

"And others," said Jackson. "She's stressed and this Granger situation is not helping."

"Do you think that he'll take another shot at Evan?" asked Aiden, looking worried.

"I don't know," said Jackson.

"From that perspective," said Aiden, "I'm glad he's going to Tokyo. The odds of Granger being able to get to him there seem slim. It might be good to tuck him away in Japan for a bit until you deal with Granger."

"Agreed," said Dominique.

"I am working on it!" Jackson could feel the pressure of their expectations like a physical weight.

"Hey," said Dominique, "we know that. We know you wouldn't let anything happen to us."

"And Devonte Miller won't be letting anything happen to Evan," said Aiden smirking.

"You cannot tell Evan about that," said Jackson, firmly. He'd been hoping that Aiden hadn't recognized Devonte. A hope that was misplaced, apparently.

"Cross my heart," said Aiden, making the appropriate hand gesture but still grinning. Jackson shook his head.

Olivia – Stress Baking

"Olivia Rose," said the voice on the other end of the phone, and Olivia found herself hitching up the neckline of her shirt with one nervous hand.

"Hey, Pops," said Olivia.

"I've been talking with your sister," he said, his voice deep and resonant, reminding her of church mornings and pot luck afternoons. "You've made her very unhappy. And it makes me unhappy that there's so much strife between you two."

As if he hadn't been included in the strife at the hospital. As if it weren't his words coming out of Sofia's mouth.

"I don't like it either, Pops," said Olivia honestly. She found herself walking into her kitchen. She opened the cupboard and got out the mixing bowl.

"Well, it's hard being away from home like you are," he said. "It puts stress on a relationship."

"Yes," agreed Olivia.

"And I know that job you moved for is pretty good, but I just can't believe there weren't equally good jobs here in Georgia."

Olivia got out the flour and went to the fridge for the eggs and butter. "Well, Georgia isn't really supporting science-based jobs right now," she said. She wanted to add that this was partially because of the enormous amount of science skepticism and disbelief engendered by people like him, but didn't.

Ralph Taggert got elected by playing into the fears and willful ignorance of his constituents. The worst was when someone would call him on it, he would say, "I support science education! Why, my granddaughter has a Ph.D. in Chemistry." He couldn't even get her degree right.

"Well, yes, but I'm sure there's something. I think you should look for some jobs a little closer to home."

"I like my job here," said Olivia.

"You like your job or you like your Yankee boyfriend?" asked Ralph. Olivia froze. "Your sister said you had a boyfriend that you seemed pretty stuck on."

She would kill Sofia. She would chop Sofia up into tiny pieces and put her in a blender and feed her to sharks.

"I have a boyfriend, and if I didn't like him, I wouldn't be dating him," said Olivia.

"Well, sure, sure, but you have to see that staying up north for a man is a bad decision. You're a bright girl, but you've always needed guidance and help when it comes to the big decisions in life. You always have your head in the clouds. You need someone to make sure the cows get fed, as the saying goes."

Olivia found herself blinking back tears. He was right. She knew it. She was a stereotype of nerdom. She didn't get half the subtext of what people said. She started thinking about equations and wandered off, leaving the water on in the sink. She fixated on the fake people in comic books because they were quantifiable and controllable. And she often needed someone to remind her that it was Tuesday.

She blinked and straightened up. She always knew when it was Tuesday these days.

"I don't think that's a saying."

"Well, now," laughed Ralph, "you know what I mean. I'm just saying that I worry about you, all alone up there in the big city with some Yankee who doesn't know how to treat a lady. Sofia was saying, and I don't like to be indelicate, that this boy has convinced you to take things maybe further than you should."

Olivia slammed the sugar down onto the counter.

"I took things to exactly where I wanted to go," said Olivia. "I'm an adult and fortunately my work insurance covers birth control because they believe responsible adults should be able to prevent unwanted pregnancies."

"Now, now, Olivia Rose," he chuckled, "don't get testy. It's just that I know you. You're a good girl and I know how those big city fellas can turn a girl's head. And what with you being not the most social girl in the world, I worry about you getting taken advantage of."

"Thank you for your concern," said Olivia tightly. "But, really, I'm fine."

"You know," he said, "Sofia and I aren't the only ones who are worried about you. I saw Clark yesterday. Bumped into him at the club. He said he surely did miss you."

Olivia took a deep breath and thought about hurling the phone across the room.

"Did he miss me? Or do you miss locking down his family's donation to your campaign?"

"Olivia Rose!" he snapped. "You listen to me, you need to stop your whoring ways and get your ass back home. We've put up with this nonsense long enough. Your father is ill and your sister can't manage everything on her own."

"Did you call Tyler?"

"What?"

"Did you call Tyler and ask him to move home?" she asked.

"No, I didn't. He's setting up his career. It's important for him to be out on his own right now."

"You mean that he's of no use to you, and he's not a woman."

"Olivia Rose, you've been allowed to run wild too long. You need to come home."

"I am home," she said. "I'm not moving back to Georgia." Then she hung up the phone. She wanted to cry. She wanted to throw a fit. She wanted to punch something. Instead, she made cookies.

She was putting the second batch in the oven when there was a knock on the door. She looked through the peephole and saw Evan. With relief, she flung open the door and slammed into him, hugging him hard enough that he staggered a little. He recovered his balance and hugged her back just as hard.

She realized that Mrs. Roberson from two doors down was staring at them.

"I like my boyfriend," she snapped. "You OK with that?"

Mrs. Roberson shrugged, tightened her bathrobe belt, and went back into her apartment.

She pulled Evan inside and shut the door.

"Hi," she said, smiling up at him, "did I know you were coming over?"

"No," he said. "I just came. Is that OK?" He smiled, but it seemed like his jaw was clenched and his shoulders seemed tight.

"Of course it's OK!"

He looked around the apartment. "Your wall is smaller," he said pointing to the empty wall above the couch where she kept her brilliant ideas and notes for work taped to the wall. Frequently, notes that were taped up in the middle of the night turned out to be not as brilliant in the daytime. But they were useful at least often enough that she kept to the system.

"I took some of them to work," she said.

He nodded, but it seemed perfunctory, like his mind was a million miles away.

"Why does it smell like cookies?" he asked, frowning.

"Because I talked to my grandfather. I'm a stress baker. The year my mom died my dad and brother both gained twenty pounds each."

"What about you?"

"Once I bake them, they kind of make me nauseous. Like I'd be eating my own stress again."

She stared at him. He looked a little pale. Like maybe he hadn't had the best day either.

"Do you want a cookie?"

"I don't want your stress," he said, then smiled like he wasn't sure that was funny.

"No, it doesn't apply to anyone else."

"All right then."

She handed him a cookie and watched as he bit into it.

"Oh my God," he said around the mouthful of cookie. "How do I stress you into baking at my place?"

"I don't know," she said. "Probably call me a stupid whore, I guess."

His face rippled into an expression of absolute fury. Then, like a magic trick, his face became calm again. "He said that to you?" he asked, and the tightness of his voice and the tenseness of his jaw proclaimed that he was not in the least bit calm.

"More or less," she said with a shrug.

"What did he want?" he asked.

"What do you mean?"

"It's a negotiation tactic. You make someone think that their *product*, if you will, is not valuable so that they will give in to your less-than-optimal offer."

"He wanted me to move back to Georgia and marry Clark."

"I fucking hate Clark."

Olivia scratched her cheek, itching away a dusting of flour. She realized that there was a cheek-shaped flour print on Evan's coat as well.

"I never thought about it like that. Like a negotiation."

"You have all the power," he said. "You have what he wants and he has no leverage to make you do it. Just tell him to go fuck himself. Or whatever Southern people say."

"We generally also say that, but not to our grandparents."

"I'll say it if you want," he volunteered.

"He also said you were the Yankee boy who had turned my head and was taking advantage of me," she said smiling widely.

"Repeatedly and as often as I can," he said, which made her laugh.

"I think I floured your coat," she said, pointing. "Take it off and I'll clean it in a minute. I want to get this next set of cookies on the sheet."

He nodded and did as she instructed before going into the living room. She watched from the kitchen as he kicked off his shoes and collapsed into her second-hand couch.

"You OK, sugar?" she asked.

"Yeah," he said. "Just tired."

She watched with misgiving as he stretched out and crooked his arm over his eyes to block out the light. There was something familiar in the way he simply shut down, which frightened her. It felt like he was retreating into himself. She remembered the terrible feeling of helplessness as she watched her mother crawl back into bed. *No baby, no pancakes today.*

"I bought a shirt today," she blurted out, and he pulled his arm away to look at her. "For Tokyo. And I ordered a new laptop bag and I think I may need some sort of trendier walking shoes than sneakers. Is it super lame that I'm already starting to pack? I'm just really looking forward to going with you."

He grinned at her. "No, I'm looking forward to it too," he said, rolling onto his side to face her. "I've started a list of all the places I want to take you."

She clapped her hands, forgetting she had a spoonful of cookie dough and Evan laughed a deep rolling laugh as the cookie dough flew out of the spoon and across the kitchen.

The next week flew by and Olivia packed and unpacked her suitcase at least three times, trying to find the optimal configuration and perfect list of items. Evan did not help at all. He seemed to delight in suggesting new items that meant that she had to rebuild her list from scratch. She finally gave up staying at her apartment so that she would stop staring into her closet. Evan didn't care about that either. She had a drawer and closet space at his condo, and if she didn't remember to bring clothes, he simply texted someone, and then clothes appeared themselves. She knew she probably ought to object, but it was frankly the most convenient and marvelous thing a boyfriend had ever done for her. It made her want to lick things off of him.

Although, currently, he was licking her in the most delightful, if ticklish, way. Olivia giggled hysterically and her knees clamped around Evan's ears again.

"OK," he said, sitting up. "That's enough of that."

"No, no," said Olivia, "I'm sorry! But you tickled me and now I'm extra sensitive. I can stop."

"Hmm," he said, climbing off the bed.

"No, come back!"

He ignored her and disappeared into the closet.

"Evan!" He came back out of the closet, something in his hand. "I can stop," she promised.

"No, I don't really think you can," he said. "But I'm going to take care of this problem." He reached out and grabbed her ankle. She let out a squeak of surprise as he pulled her down the bed. With a quick movement, he looped one of his ties around her ankle and then lashed it to the bedpost.

"The rules are still in place," he said. "If you want me to stop you just have to say stop."

Olivia didn't say anything. She'd never tried being tied up before. Clark had suggested it once and she'd shot him down before the entire sentence was out of his mouth. The idea of Clark being in control of her body had made her squirm. On the other hand, the idea of Evan being in charge filled her with a delicious fluttery sense of anticipation. His eyes were still on her as he tied her other ankle. Her legs were now spread wide before him. It made her feel vulnerable and sent a thrill of adrenaline coursing through her veins.

Logically, it shouldn't matter. Her hands were free. His knots looked firm, but had she wanted out, she thought she could get out in short order. Not to mention that it was Evan and Evan would never hurt her, and there were rules besides. But she found herself holding her breath in eagerness as he began to kiss his way up her leg.

"Olivia," he murmured, "is there someplace you would like me to kiss?"

"You know where," she said.

"Here?" He dipped his head, gently kissing and nibbling along the soft skin of her inner thigh.

She exhaled a long ragged breath. "That's not where," she said.

"No? Here?"

He was closer. His tongue caressed the hood of her clit, but didn't descend further. She moaned and tried to wriggle into his mouth, but he blocked her. She moaned again as he continued to tease her, his tongue caressing her most intimate places, but not where she wanted him to.

"Evan," she gasped. "Evan, please."

"Am I not getting this right," he asked, laughter cracking through his innocent tone. "Maybe you should show me where you want it?"

Hesitantly, she put her hand down. She'd never touched herself in front of him before. Her clit was swollen and slick and she closed her eyes as she ran her fingers over it.

"Faster," he whispered. She did as he commanded and found herself straining against the ties in her ankles. "Evan," she moaned. "I need you."

He pushed a finger just barely inside her and she gasped. She was writhing now, pulling against her bindings. He pushed her hand out of the way, going down on her. His tongue pushed roughly against her clit and then he pulled it into his mouth. She was trembling on the brink.

"Evan, in me. I need you in me! Fuck me and I'll come."

"Come and I'll fuck you," he said, lifting his head, and she growled in frustration. They'd had this argument before and she usually won. But she usually managed to loop a leg around him and pull him to her. She hadn't realized that this would be a result of being tied up. She panted as his tongue continued to push her closer and closer. The pressure was unbearable. She wanted both to get away from the torturous pleasure and to never have him stop. The inability to close her legs around him tipped the balance, leaving her no ability to retreat, she could only go forward. She finally came with an orgasm that jerked her whole body and left her clutching

Evan's hair. He sat up and cupped his hand gently over her, while he reached for a condom.

When he pushed inside her, she groaned in relief.

"God, you feel good, Liv," he murmured, kissing her neck as he fucked her. Her legs trembled as she strained against the ties.

"Harder, Evan, harder," she begged and he did as she asked. Each thrust tugged against the bedposts, creaking the wood. She was a little bit worried about breaking the bed, but she was past the point of caring. He was fucking her exactly like she wanted.

She shouted his name as she came again, and he came a minute later, collapsing against her sweaty and exhausted.

"Evan," she murmured. "Evan kiss me."

He raised his head and gave her what she wanted, then he rolled away from her and flopped onto the bed. She watched him in amusement. He looked completely happy.

"Evan, can you untie me now? I want to snuggle."

He jerked upright and immediately untied her, then dropped back down the ties still in his hand to kiss her.

"Not too kinky?" he asked, looking down at her.

"Mmmm," she said finally able to put her legs around him. "It was perfect." And he laughed as she squeezed him tightly.

Evan – Burned

"Nice tie," said Jackson as Evan got in the car. Jackson had ignored Evan's promise to use the car service and turned up dutifully every day to drive him to work. Evan was starting to get used to it. He kind of liked talking to Jackson in the morning. Plus, Jackson frequently brought coffee.

Evan glanced down at himself. Last night he'd selected ties he hardly ever wore—a cherry red and a blue fleck that never quite matched anything. This morning Olivia had picked up the red one, carefully ironed it, and handed it to him.

"There weren't any other Property of Olivia West signs in your closet," she had said, her eyes twinkling. In another woman, that would have led to him burning the tie and kicking her out of the condo. Leona Meade had tried on multiple occasions to bring him to heel, but it had never worked. But with Olivia, he found that it was kind of a turn-on. Besides, she'd been screaming his name while she wore it. Who really belonged to who here?

"Thanks," said Evan, fingering the red silk. Olivia had nearly made him late. He'd come into the bedroom and found her retrieving her shoes from under the bed. Her ass-in-the-air system of retrieval had almost caused him to rip the tie and everything else back off. Olivia had not been as convinced, however. He'd seen her to the front door of the building before ducking down into the parking garage to meet Jackson.

Jackson's phone burbled, and Jackson grabbed for it in his coat pocket, but couldn't quite work it out around the seat belt.

"Want some help?" Evan offered, although it felt weird.

Jackson hesitated, but the phone dinged again and he rolled his eyes.

"Yes."

Evan reached over and yanked the phone out.

"Texts from Kerschel," said Evan. He was vaguely aware of the name as one of the people that Jackson had on payroll.

"What do they say?"

Evan tapped the phone, but it went immediately to the lock screen. Without taking his eyes off the road, Jackson reached out and used his thumbprint to unlock it.

"Cryptocurrency workshop a total bust, but double-data encryption is hot," read Evan. "What the hell does that mean?"

Jackson sighed. "OK, so basically I employ a bunch of juvenile delinquents."

"I assumed so," said Evan, eyeing the text about encryption.

"But when I send them to conferences without adult supervision, do you know what they do?"

"Get wasted and fraternize?" guessed Evan.

"Uh, yeah. So I make them text me reports on their sessions. It's not foolproof, but it does mean that they have to work harder to day drink. Kerschel is currently at a tech conference. I understand none of her texts, but that's basically why I pay her."

"She's really good?" asked Evan with a sinking feeling.

Jackson snorted. "The only reason I've been able to keep her from being poached by like six Silicon Valley start-ups is that I provide benefits and periodically she gets to do something illegal and play with guns. Don't tell Grandma any of that though." He added the last part as an afterthought.

Evan looked down at Jackson's phone in his hand. The background picture was the four of them from their first Christmas together in the stupid hats that Aiden had made them wear. Usually, Evan didn't like looking at old pictures of himself—it was too obvious that no one was home. But in this one, he actually looked happy.

"Jackson," he said, swallowing hard. "Jackson, if I tell you something, are you going to tell Grandma?"

"No," said Jackson.

Evan gathered up his courage. He could do this. He should have done it months ago, but he'd been avoiding it like he avoided anything scary and then blaming it on Jackson being untrustworthy. That was bullshit and he knew it.

"I found something in the storage unit last year. When I went to put those boxes back."

Jackson pulled up at a stoplight and turned to look at him more fully. "Like what kind of something?"

"An autopsy report. Uncle Randall had Grandpa exhumed and autopsied. Without Grandma knowing. He was the executor of the will. He could do that. Light's green."

Jackson jerked slightly in his seat and then put the car in motion, but at the next empty spot on the curb, he pulled over. Evan handed him his phone back and Jackson looked like he couldn't remember why he had it.

"OK, I get that Randall *could* do that," said Jackson, tucking his phone away. "The question is: *why* would he do that?"

"Because he thought Grandma killed Grandpa."

"Well, fuck," said Jackson. "Uh… Do you think she did?"

Evan shrugged. "Maybe. The autopsy said it was consistent with a medication overdose. I think at a minimum, that Randall *thought* Grandma did it."

"Well, fuck," said Jackson again. "I'm not sure what I think about that."

"I think I'm fine with it," said Evan. "I've had a year to sit with it and basically… I don't give a shit. I know some of the stuff Henry did to Dad and Randall and he can't have treated Grandma any better. I think he deserved it. But I think I'm fucking scared that someone else could find out about it though."

"Fuuuuuck," said Jackson for a third time. "What'd you do with the autopsy report?"

"I put it in my safe at home. I haven't found any other copies. But, Jackson…"

"Shit, Evan, please don't tell me there's more."

"Randall and Dad never did anything about it. They had ten years and they didn't do anything. And then one day Genevieve and Jack get on a plane with Randall and Owen. I found an email in that box of Dad's stuff we went through. It was dated from three days before their vacations. Randall told Genevieve they needed to talk. What else was there to talk about?"

Jackson made a dissatisfied grunt. "Did Genevieve reply?"

"Not that I found," said Evan. "I went through everything and didn't turn up anything. But then I went out to DevEntier. They pulled two hard drives out of storage. I've got them with a guy I found. But they're encrypted and he hasn't had any luck with opening them."

"I'll call Kerschel and get her on the next plane home. We'll go to your guy tonight after work and get the hard drives. Kerschel is already familiar with some of the DevEntier stuff. Even if your guy is good, she's going to have an edge."

"Jackson, what do we do if…" Evan tried to get the words out. "What if this is the reason they all died?"

"What do you want to do?" asked Jackson.

"Jesus, please don't put this on me," said Evan, feeling a sense of panic in his chest.

"I'm not trying to. I'll have more opinions in a bit, but I need the minute. You've had longer. What do you think?"

"I don't know," said Evan. "I thought maybe if there was something unusual about the crash I might be able to learn more, but there isn't. I requested the file on the crash from the FAA, but there's nothing useful in it."

"Request the… Well, shit. Sure, just ask the FAA."

"What?"

Jackson rolled his eyes. "Sometimes I forget I can go in the front door. There are no files on the crash anywhere. Pete pulled them all years ago and now Grandma's got the only set under lock and key. And me, being me, I have wanted to see them. It never occurred to me to just ask the fucking FAA for them."

"Yeah, you're a next of kin and you can also just put in a public records request. Which is what I did. Aiden said that no one could tell if I made a public records request. Not that I told him why I wanted to know. You can have my copy if you want. It's not very useful. It was just faulty wiring and a storm. There wasn't anything shocking."

Jackson seemed to puzzle over the matter, and Evan watched him, feeling an immense sense of relief at having someone else thinking about it besides him.

"OK, well, even if that is why they got on the plane, it's not why they died. It's like you said, faulty wiring and a storm. It was just an accident."

"Do you think Grandma's going to see it that way?"

Jackson sighed heavily. "No. I think she'll feel guilty as fuck. Even if she didn't kill Henry, she'll still feel guilty if she thinks that's why they all got on the plane."

"So we can't tell her?"

Jackson seemed to consider. "I think we don't tell her. We look at the hard drives. If we find something out then, great, then you and I will know and we can personally feel better about it. If we don't, then, well, as you said a few weeks ago, we have a fucked up family, and sometimes shit just is what it is and I guess we'll have to live with that. Either way, I think we need to destroy the hard drives and move the autopsy report and whatever else you've got to my safe."

"Your safe?" asked Evan.

"I have a very expensive safe in the basement at home," said Jackson. "I could put a body in it and no one would know."

"I don't think that's what safes are usually used for," said Evan.

"No, but I like knowing that I could do it. They said even bugs couldn't get in. A corpse would mummify in there."

"Who sold you this safe?" demanded Evan. "I don't think that's something they're supposed to be advertising."

"I think they're supposed to use whatever makes the sale, and that totally worked on me," said Jackson with a grin as he put the car into gear. Evan looked out the windshield and felt a strange sense of calm as the building passed by, flashing bands of sunlight between them. He'd pictured trying to tell Jackson about the autopsy report. There had been a lot more yelling and disapproving in his head. But in reality, he hadn't even broken a sweat.

"Thanks for not being mad," said Evan.

"Why would I be mad?" asked Jackson.

"I don't know. I just feel like… Every time I go home lately everything is tense, and I feel like it's my fault."

"That's Eleanor," said Jackson sourly. "She's pissed about the Granger situation and work and just… pissed."

"I wish Granger would go away already," said Evan. "I get it. He's mad at us. We screwed up his life and he wants revenge. But

I would think that his time would be better spent focusing on his defense."

"We did not screw up his life," said Jackson. "We didn't make him sell shit drugs to people with PTSD knowing that it would cause suicides. That's what screwed his life up. Had he not been a greedy cold-hearted bastard then he wouldn't be having any of these problems right now. And if he'd just left us the fuck alone then he would have probably skated with minimum jail time and a bunch of fines. But no, he had to hire people to threaten and intimidate us."

"There were guns," said Evan. "Aiden says that makes it attempted murder."

"Yes, it was. So, regardless of whatever he feels about us, my point is…" Jackson seemed to be searching for his point.

"Fuck him?" suggested Evan.

"Yes," said Jackson. "I want to burn his life to the ground."

"We could just let it go," said Evan.

"I keep trying!" snapped Jackson. "He's the one that keeps coming after us for another swing. Considering that you're the one he's swinging at, I'd think you'd be a little more up in arms."

Evan considered that. "I'm trying," he said at last. "But he doesn't really affect my life any, so I'm having a hard time caring."

Jackson laughed. "He sent people to attack you. How does that not affect you?"

"Well, that was very upsetting," admitted Evan. "But it's not like they were very good at it."

Jackson laughed again.

"And I don't know, I just don't think about him, ever. I mean, plane crashes and murder pretty much put me full up on worrying about shit."

"Oh my God, you and Dominique are exactly the same. You're killing me," said Jackson, a smile stretching over his face.

"I'm serious," said Evan, wondering if he and Dominique were as similar as Jackson thought.

"I know," said Jackson. "It's fine. I'll worry about Granger. We'll make Kerschel worry about the plane crash shit. And then we'll move on."

Evan felt his shoulders relax for what felt like the first time in months. Jackson was right. They were going to move on. This wasn't permanent. He took a deep breath and nodded.

"Hey," said Evan, remembering what he'd actually intended to talk to Jackson about, "not to segue from life or death matters to the trivial, but I still have a life."

"Segue away," said Jackson.

"You don't have to drive tomorrow. I'm going to the Wiseman"—he pulled out his phone and checked his calendar—"yes, the Wiseman Christmas party. Castleman's is next week. And my office party is Friday."

Jackson laughed. "How many parties are you going to?"

"Like eight? Twelve? I don't know. December is one long party marathon. It's the social grease that makes our world turn. Anyway, I'm going to drive myself, so I can leave directly from work."

"Sounds good. They'll have a valet, though right? I'd prefer you didn't park on the street."

"Yeah, don't worry about it." With Olivia along he had no intention of taking unnecessary risks. "At least I won't have to go to Grandma's Christmas party this year."

"I thought you liked those," said Jackson, looking surprised.

"Just because I'm good at them doesn't mean I like them," said Evan, deciding that having already discussed murder on this car ride that they could probably also discuss Christmas. He was feeling practically giddy with all the honesty. "By the time her party rolls around, I'm at the end of the holiday season and I'm exhausted. And that party, in particular, is a full house. It gives me low-grade claustrophobia and a desire to knock over the Christmas tree."

Jackson burst out laughing. "What did the Christmas tree ever do to you?"

"Not our Christmas tree down in the study. The big one in the ballroom. I want to plow into it and watch all the ornaments smash."

Jackson laughed harder. "Why?" he demanded.

"I don't know. You ever see one of those videos where the cat just loses it and starts zooming around the room. I think it's like that."

"Caffeine high," said Jackson, nodding. "When you're all jiggly, but your brain is tired."

"Sounds right," said Evan with a shrug. "I wouldn't ever do it though."

"Grandma would be pissed, for one thing."

Evan shrugged again. "It's Theo, really. He'd be heartbroken. That tree is his masterpiece."

"It is kind of his art form," agreed Jackson, glancing at him.

Evan started to feel nervous. He probably shouldn't have said anything.

"I always avoid the tree," said Jackson. "It's so fancy that I have a fear that I am going to knock it over on accident. Like it will be the one Deveraux party that goes down in infamy because Jackson tripped over the model train set, went headfirst into boughs of holly, and took down the entire tree on top of the mayor."

Evan laughed at the unexpected revelation. "Couldn't be any more infamous than the time Uncle Randall peed on it."

"Oh, Jesus! Why is it always my dad that did the horrible shit?"

"Because he didn't give a shit about anyone. Plus, Dad liked to egg him on."

"I don't understand how Grandma produced two such suck-tastic kids and then one nice one."

"It was Grandpa," said Evan. "By the time Genevieve came along he'd had his first run-in with cancer, so he'd slowed down a bit. And then Grandma was able to take Aunt Gen to live at the country house. Meanwhile, Owen and Randall stayed in town with Grandpa. I mean, they were in boarding school, but they still saw him a lot more. Then he got sick again and then he died. So, Genevieve never got the full Grandpa upbringing."

"And Owen and Randall got extra helpings?"

"Something like that," said Evan, staring out the window.

"Makes sense," said Jackson. "Still sucks."

"Dad always said that Genevieve was the only one in the family Grandma cared about."

"That's not true," said Jackson.

"Sometimes I think he had a point," said Evan.

"Sometimes, you save what you can when the house is burning down," said Jackson.

"That's great if you're the one that gets saved," said Evan. "Not so great if you're the one burning."

Jackson didn't reply.

FRIDAY, DECEMBER 15

Evan – Leona Meade

"I think this one was the best one yet," said Olivia, sitting on his desk in his office. "I think I'm finally getting the hang of these parties." He grinned up at her. She looked so sexy perched on his desk in her little black dress. "It's like you said if I just assume everyone is lying, all their behavior makes so much more sense!"

"I liked the Gen-Tech party the best," said Evan, which was the truth. She scooted back a little and her dress rode up. It was giving him some very inappropriate-to-the-office thoughts regarding how to best utilize his desk.

"You're just saying that because of the karaoke."

"I have not laughed that much at a party in years," he agreed. Although, that hadn't been why he liked it. The only person in the room that was aware of the Deverauxes had been Olivia's friend Alia, and Alia had made it clear with a subtly lifted eyebrow and a smile that she had no intention of telling Olivia anything about the Deverauxes. After that, he had just been Evan, Olivia's boyfriend, and that had been fun. Because Olivia's boyfriend could sing karaoke or talk about comic books or make dumb puns that made her coworkers laugh.

He stood up and leaned across the desk to nibble her ear lobe. "You look amazing tonight," he murmured. Jewelry. He was going to have to figure out how to talk her into accepting jewelry next. It was Christmas. He was going to just buy her some and put it in a box. Problem solved.

"I do," she agreed, sounding pleased. "Are you almost done? I want you to take me home and ravish me."

"Almost," he said. "The problem with having our office party, at the actual office is that I end up remembering six things I should email about and the computer is right here…"

"I'm going to go get my coat," she said with a laugh. "And when I come back you'd better be done."

"Yes, ma'am," he said, stealing one of her Southernisms. The last few days had felt like sunshine coming out on a sunny day. With Jackson working on the hard drives and Olivia bouncing around in pre-travel happiness, Evan felt like he was on top of the world.

He was typing his last sentence when the door opened again.

"Just finishing up now," he said, hitting send.

"I don't think so," said a soft voice. "You're done when I say you're done."

He felt a chill run down his spine.

"What are you doing here, Leona?" he asked, logging off his computer.

"I was invited," she said. Leona Meade was a tall woman with dark hair, dark eyes, and absolutely nothing in her soul. She was the lead Dominatrix at Fetish and she had spent a lot of time trying to tell Evan how to fuck her. Not that he had ever done what she told him—submission had never been his thing. A fact that had infuriated her. "You know, Evan," she said, slinking around the desk. Her dress was dark green and skin tight. "I'm starting to think you don't love me anymore."

"I never loved you," said Evan. "I think I was fairly clear on the subject."

"Where are you getting your kicks these days, Evan? Who are you playing with? Not that adorable little angel with the tits to die for? She looks too sweet for you." She leaned down and stroked the side of his face. He twisted his face to try and avoid her and saw that Olivia was standing in the doorway. He froze. Leona saw her too, but instead of stepping away she planted a knee on the seat between Evan's thighs, leaned in, and kissed him. Evan jerked back and raised his hands to shove her away from him, but stopped. A shove was as good as a hit for Leona—he didn't want her to win.

"What the hell do you think you're doing?" demanded Olivia. "Take your hands off of him!"

"No," said Leona. She was leaning on his chest with both hands, pushing her weight down into him.

"OK, fine," said Olivia, sounding befuddled. "Evan, take her hands off of you."

Leona laughed, brittle and bright. "Too bad for you that Evan would rather break his own arm than do what he's told."

Olivia looked at him and back at Leona.

"Evan," she said, her eyes not leaving Leona, and this time her voice was firm and commanding, "take her damn hands off of you."

Leona looked down at him, smug. He grinned at her, then reached down and locked his hands around her wrists and stood up, pushing her away from him. Leona stared up at him in horrified anger.

"Evan," said Olivia, "come."

He did as he was told and went to stand next to Olivia.

"Evan," said Olivia, looking up at him, "kiss me."

He followed her commands, tilting his head to match her angle and letting his lips brush gently across hers.

Olivia looked back at Leona. "Any questions?"

Leona made a snarl of fury.

"See you around, Leona," said Evan and he held the door open for her. She stomped through the door and then turned around to glare at him.

"I hate you, Evan Deveraux!" she screamed and picked up a stapler from the secretary's desk, hurling it at them. Then she ran back toward the party.

"Well," said Olivia, as he swung the door shut, "your ex seems… fun."

"Not my ex. We were never dating or anything."

"Just had a lot of kinky sex?" asked Olivia.

Evan found that he was sweating. "Yes."

She looked like she was pondering that. "Did you really break your arm?"

"It was a radial fracture."

"You hit people, didn't you? And you let other people hit you?"

He swallowed hard. He found that he couldn't take his eyes off her face. "There is a club."

"Fetish?"

"Yes. How did you…"

"One of my shoes escaped under your bed on Tuesday. There was a card under there—I googled. Also under the bed was a Chapstick, those socks you were looking for, and that earring I lost."

He nodded. "I was missing those socks."

"Was the club…" she trailed off. "You tied me up and I thought that was fun."

"It was fun!"

"Are we not…" She gave a helpless sort of gesture. "Am I not enough?" She had a pinched look to her face that said she was holding back tears, and he found his heart was jack-hammering.

"No! Yes! I'm not saying this right." His chest felt like it was being compressed by an anvil. He took a deep breath and then another. Clear communication. Say what he felt. He could do this. He'd done it with Jackson and it had turned out fine. He just had to breathe.

"You are more than enough. I love what we do." Her face relaxed somewhat, and he took another breath. "That place… I quit three years ago. I don't miss it. I don't want to go back."

"Why did you quit?"

He licked his lips. "Aside from breaking my arm, I spent the better part of my twenties being miserable. I thought the club was helping, then I realized it wasn't. So I quit."

"Helping how?"

He licked his lips again. "I thought… I didn't want to end up like my dad. I didn't want to be someone who hurt people. I thought I was being constructive. I thought that was where I belonged."

She made a gesture he didn't know how to interpret. Then suddenly she was hugging him. Then she stepped back and stared up into his face as if looking for something specific.

"We should go home now," she said.

"OK," he agreed. She walked out to the elevators and pressed the button. He followed her because he didn't know what else to do. The elevator doors opened and she walked inside. She leaned against the far wall and pulled on her gloves. Evan stood in front of her, wondering what he was supposed to say or do next.

"She thinks my tits are to die for."

"They are," he agreed. He'd pictured telling Olivia about Fetish and in his head, it had always ended in disaster. It had never once ended in discussing Olivia's breasts.

"They are pretty good tits," she said looking down her own dress. "When we get home you should do something with them."

"Such as?" he asked. He stepped closer to her and ran his hand up her waist and over her breast.

"I would like—" she began.

The elevator jerked to a stop and the doors slid open. Evan dropped his hand and tried to pretend he hadn't just been feeling up his girlfriend in the elevator. Olivia looked like she was trying not to laugh.

They got off in the parking garage and Olivia finally giggled.

"Get in the car," he said. "Seriously, just get in the car."

He glanced over at her as he drove. He couldn't tell if he was in the dog house or not. She was staring out the window.

"Are we OK?" he asked.

She turned and smiled at him. "Yes."

"Are you sure?"

"There are rules in place," she said. "If I don't like something I say stop and you stop. I haven't said stop."

Evan wanted to say right then that he loved her, but he didn't know how to get the words out.

"There was a question of what to do with your breasts," he said. "I was very interested in hearing your thoughts."

They pulled up to a stoplight. "Well," said Olivia, "I would like you to kiss them." She reached down and pulled her skirt up a few inches. The light turned green and he drove as the skirt was inched up by micro-millimeters. "Sometimes you do this thing with your teeth, and Lord knows I do not know what it is, but I love it. It kind of makes me go *zing* all the way down to my toes."

"I believe I know what thing you're talking about."

At the next stoplight, she grasped the hemline and pulled it up another few inches. It was now at mid-thigh. As he drove, she put her hands on her thighs, pushing her legs apart.

"And then, I suppose this sounds weird, but you could rub your cock on them. Just a bit, you know, so it kind of drools a little because I think maybe it likes them. I like the way it feels."

He found himself trying to adjust his seat belt across his hips.

The third stoplight arrived and she pulled her dress up over her hips.

"One more stoplight," said Olivia, as the light turned green, "and I might be able to get to my underwear."

He went to the next block and slowed the car to an idle waiting for a yellow light to turn red. Olivia giggled as a car honked his horn and swerved around them. She pushed her underwear down around her thighs. The wisps of red hair peeking at him between the fabric and her skin made his breathing uneven.

One more stop light and the panties were down around her knees.

"Almost home," said Olivia.

He brought the car to a screeching halt in his parking spot and Olivia stripped off her underwear and handed it to him. Then she pushed down her skirt and exited the car.

He managed to hold on to his self-control until he got inside the condo, but the second the door shut, he grabbed Olivia by the waist, pulling her back to him. He unzipped her dress in on smooth gesture and shoved the straps off her shoulders. The dress fell to the floor with a whisper of fabric as he plunged his fingers downward, pushing between her thighs.

She was wet and moaned as he circled her clit, feeling it plump and ready beneath his touch. He unsnapped her bra and removed it.

She was moaning his name as he cupped her breast, feeling the nipple harden in his hand. He pinched it just a little and she bucked against him, gasping. He spun her around and buried his face in her tits. He used his teeth how she wanted and she seemed to melt a little in his arms.

"Evan, sugar, upstairs, upstairs." She tried to pull away from him.

"Couch is closer," he said, unwilling to let her go. She had her back to him again and he returned his hand to her sex, while he used the other to unbuckle his belt. She was breathing hard as he continued to work her clit. Abruptly she broke free and spun around, kissing him, and yanking at the buttons on his shirt. He stripped out of his jacket, tossed it on the floor, and unzipped his pants. She finished with his shirt and pushed it off of him.

"Upstairs," she said backing up.

He followed her, his cock swinging, heavy and painful. He caught her in the hall, pinning her against the wall, kissing her, lifting her, fucking her. She wrapped her legs around him, arching back, making cries of pleasure at each thrust. Her fingernails were digging into his shoulders, a tiny, breathless bit of pain that only highlighted the pleasure of her body.

"Evan, oh God, Evan!" Her face contorted as she got closer, and her body began to clench, tightening around his cock. He knew he would come when she did. He thrust into her harder, the impact of their bodies rattling the walls. She screamed his name as she came, her body shuddering in orgasm. Then she curled into him and bit him on the thick muscle of his neck and he came inside her with a white-hot jet of pleasure.

"Liv," he murmured. "Olivia." He kissed her neck, wanting to sing her name, wanting to shout it from the rooftops. She lifted her head, and he kissed her lips, tasting the salt of her sweat. She let go with her legs and tried to set her feet on the floor. But she wobbled, Bambi legged, and he had to put his arms around her.

"Evan," she whispered and then laughed. "Evan, how do you do that to me? I can't even walk when you're done with me."

"But I'm not done with you," he said and pulled her toward the bedroom.

Olivia – Tokyo Gifts

Olivia pulled off her hat as she entered the hotel lobby.

"Good afternoon, Dr. West," said the concierge with a smile. "How was your tour this afternoon?"

"Fantastic, Aiko! And delicious! I think I ate my weight in monja-yaki."

The concierge, a fifty-ish woman who managed to combine sophisticated polish with a warm mom vibe, laughed. "That's easy to do. I'm glad you enjoyed it! Did you want me to book the sake house tour for tomorrow?"

"Mm. Not yet. I was going to see if Evan wanted to come with me for that one. Is he back yet?"

"No, I don't believe so."

"Well, I'll call down once I get a chance to talk to him."

"Of course," said Aiko with a small bow.

Olivia went up to the penthouse suite. After five days of living the hotel life, she was unsurprised to find that the flowers had been replaced and everything but her notes tidied away. She was wildly enjoying her trip to Tokyo, and she was not oblivious to the fact that it was partially because Evan was spending gobs of money.

She tried to discern if she should be concerned about that, but so far everyone at the hotel acted like his behavior was standard for all of his previous visits. Evan himself appeared to spend without a second thought. In fact, he'd been more than a little concerned that he couldn't send her out on her daily adventures with his credit card. They had actually argued about it. He'd been adorably frustrated at her refusal to take his money and they ended up compromising on her booking all of her tours through the hotel so he could pay for them. Olivia was not at all sure how this was a compromise and thought that he had used unfair negotiating techniques, mainly his lips on various parts of her, to get her to agree.

It was disconcerting because she couldn't tell if she was his princess or his pretty woman. She was trying not to think of it in general. Because thinking about it might ruin it.

She went to stand in front of her wall of notes.

Besides Evan seemed to enjoy spoiling her.

Which was one of the reasons she was sticking to their arrangement. She was very afraid that she was giving Evan a bad name. The day after she'd arrived, she had been facedown in the spa getting a hot stone massage when she'd come up with the best idea for her research. She'd gone sprinting into the lobby clutching her towel and demanding paper and a writing utensil. And now her notes were taped up on the sitting room wall.

Evan probably deserved to get his way now that his reputation included a crazy girlfriend. Of course, Evan had only been amused and said not to worry about it, but she couldn't help but think her eccentric behavior reflected badly on him.

She took off her shoes and started to change as she stared at the wall, going over her math. She picked up her pencil and began to noodle through an equation, while the rest of her brain pondered the problem with Evan. Because there was a part of her that thought that Evan should always get his way. When he smiled at her, her heart did backflips. When he kissed her, she went a little woobly in the knees. And when they made love, there was literally nothing she could do to stop herself from saying his name.

The night of his office party, the night he'd confirmed her theory about Fetish, was the last night she'd had any doubts about him. She supposed that would have sent other people running for the door. But she got it. Locking himself into a place he hated, so that other people would be safe was twisted, and maybe it was the wrong decision, but she got it. How long had she stayed in Georgia with Clark because she wanted to make her family happy? It had taken Clark's blatant infidelity and one sleepless night to make her realize that she couldn't make up for what her mom had done and she couldn't keep punishing herself for not being able to save her mother. So she'd left. She'd left her cage and so had Evan.

The night of the office party was also the night that he'd fucked her in the hallway, making her come so hard she couldn't stand upright. Even a week later she still touched herself when she thought of it. She had shot down Clark on multiple occasions for lacking a condom. The idea of accidentally getting pregnant had disgusted her. Or maybe it was Clark who had disgusted her. But there in the hallway, Evan had come inside of her and she'd wanted it, loved it. It had felt so complete. He had switched back to condoms with an apology after that, but she hadn't been able to stop thinking about it.

"God, I love science!" exclaimed Evan, walking in.

She blinked at him and then looked down at herself, realizing that she'd forgotten to finish changing and she was still in her underwear.

"Hi. You're home!"

He looked so handsome in his suit that Olivia couldn't help feeling a pang of smugness that he belonged to her.

"I mean," she said, replaying her own words, "back. I guess home isn't the right term."

"You're here," he said, stepping in to kiss her. "You're mostly naked. Feels like home to me." Olivia leaned into him, purposefully pressing her boobs against him. His arms went around her waist and the kiss became deeper. "Mmm, science is the best."

"Support women in STEM fields," she whispered in his ear, and he laughed.

"I think you're using your powers for good," he said. "We've got that casino thing tonight. Are you going to be ready or do you need more time alone with your math?"

She laughed. "No, I was going to get changed. I just got distracted."

"Can I distract you?" he asked, reaching into his pocket and pulling out a long velvet box.

"Evan! That better not be jewelry."

"And what if it is?" he asked, opening the box and she couldn't stop herself from making a little *ooh* noise. The necklace was large and sparkly and looked like diamonds. She didn't even want to think about how much that cost if it was real.

"You keep buying me stuff. You can't keep buying me stuff!"

"Why not?" he asked, sliding the necklace out of the box. "I like buying you stuff." He slipped the necklace around her neck, reaching under her hair to work the clasp. The pendant hung, heavy and cold against her chest, but quickly warmed to her skin.

"Because…" She tried to think of an argument she hadn't already deployed.

"It's Christmas," he said.

"And I haven't gotten you anything but wine that I forgot at home."

"What kind?" he asked, looking interested.

"Something that you don't have, but I think you'll like."

"Excellent," he said. "I'm looking forward to it."

"Well, but you've already bought me like three Christmas

presents—" She cut off, catching his expression. "It's more, isn't it? There's more, isn't there?"

He grinned sheepishly. "It's vacation. Presents are like calories when you're on vacation, they don't count."

"You're making me uncomfortable," she said, and his face shifted to a serious expression.

"I'll stop," he said. "I don't want to make you uncomfortable. I just like buying you things."

"And I start thinking about how much you're spending, and I have a panic attack."

"Ah," he said. "Speaking of that."

"Oh dear," said Olivia.

"Tonight I'm going to spend a fuck ton of money."

"Would you care to define fuck ton?"

"No, you'd probably go hide in the bathroom. But—and look at me, I'm very serious—this is all budgeted for, you don't need to panic." He held her eye as if looking for confirmed understanding. She nodded. "Also, as part of… the appearance of things, I need you to look as if you're not even thinking about panicking. Ordinarily, I wouldn't ask. I don't think you should ever have to change your behavior for me. But tonight, I was hoping to look…"

"Cool?"

"Yes," he said.

She fingered the necklace. "So I should look hot?"

"You always look hot."

"And I should look like we totally do this all the time and we don't spend the majority of our time just making out and drinking wine. In other words, like we're fancy people."

He looked as though he were trying not to laugh. "Think of it as your alter ego."

She caught sight of herself in the mirror and sighed. The

pendant was just the right length and glittered with a subtle, but still impressive sparkle. She liked how it looked against her skin. She didn't want to take it off. She looked back up at Evan and bit her lip. God, why did she always want to fuck him after he gave her things?

Evan – Kake Casino

The limo pulled away from the curb and Olivia looked around the interior and then frowned. She scooted across the seat to snuggle next to him, holding his hand and resting her head on his shoulder. "You were way over there," she said by way of explanation.

"Clearly a problem," he said. He was smiling. No, he knew he was beaming like an idiot.

Evan was under no illusions why he had started buying her more presents. He wanted her to love him. He wanted her to love him with the overriding passion that he felt for her. He just didn't know how else to accomplish that.

"I'm sorry I've been making you feel uncomfortable," he said.

She sighed. "I'm sorry I keep harping on the money. You don't need me to tell you what to spend. Especially if you've got it in your budget."

"It's Christmas," said Evan again, sensing an opening. "And vacation. I'll stop once when we get home."

"It's just that..."

"That what?" he prompted when she didn't continue.

"I actually love every single thing you've gotten me. And I love everything we've done this vacation. Honestly, it's the best vacation of my entire life. But when I was growing up there was a whole list of things that good girls didn't do. And admittedly, I've crossed quite a few of those off the list, but when you buy me things I feel like maybe my grandfather was right about me. Maybe I am a... wanton harlot." She laughed, but it was hollow, like she didn't really think it was funny.

Evan felt a tightness in his chest that appeared every time she mentioned her family.

"I can't fix that," he blurted out.

"I don't need you to fix it. Just… hear it."

"I don't want to hear it," he said. "The idea that someone would say that about you infuriates me."

"It's kind of true," she said reflectively.

"Olivia West!" he said, sitting upright and turning to look at her in the seat.

"Rose," she said.

"What?"

"If you're going to use my full name and be that mad, then you need to use the middle name too. It's Rose. Olivia Rose West. That's how it's done."

"All right. Correction noted. Now you note this: Olivia Rose West, that is not true."

"No, it is actually. Frequently after you buy me things I want to… um…" She was blushing. She rarely blushed about sex. It was one of the things he liked about her. But in this instance, he found it adorable.

"You want to throw me down on the bed and fuck my brains out?" he suggested.

"Kind of a lot."

"Well, I don't want to fix that," he said leaning back in his seat, feeling smug.

She laughed. "I shouldn't have told you. You're going to take advantage of me."

"I reiterate: repeatedly and as often as I can. Mine's Alexander, by the way. In case you need to be mad at me at some point."

"I generally don't," said Olivia, smiling at him, before putting her head back on his shoulder. "That's the problem. I never want to be mad at you, and I want to give you everything you want."

"I just want you," he said.

"You've already got that," she said.

He squeezed her hand and hoped she was right.

They entered the Kake Casino through an archway of glass illuminated in blue light. The archway became a tunnel, and the further they progressed the more strange lights moved behind the glass.

Eizo was waiting for them at the casino. Shorter than Evan, with long, purposefully deviant hair that he frequently tied up like a samurai, Eizo enjoyed, and took advantage of, a reputation as one of the most eligible bachelors in Tokyo. He had taken the news that Evan was traveling with a companion in bemusement.

Evan had known Eizo for the better part of a decade, and on every trip to Tokyo, Eizo had done his best to throw a party that would get Evan in some sort of trouble. Girls, drugs, that one time with the Yakuza that cost him fifty thousand dollars—Eizo always tried to push Evan's boundaries in some way. Evan was not sure what Eizo had planned for the night, but he hoped that Eizo had taken the note that due to the presence of Olivia West, the party had better be a notch down from the usual mayhem.

"Eizo Matsuda, this is—"

Olivia shrieked.

"Evan, they're *Vampyroteuthis infernalis*!"

So much for looking cool.

She ran to the glass, a sight to watch in her low-cut dress, and peered into the interior of the glass and Evan realized that it was an enormous aquarium and the lights were bioluminescent fish.

Evan went to join her and looked at the collection of vampire squid. They were about a foot in length and velvety black. One drifted away from him, showing an interior lined with hundreds of spiky barbs. "That's a lot more teeth than I was expecting," he said.

"Look at him, flashing his photophores," cooed Olivia, as the spots on the squid lit up. Then she paused and seemed to realize that she was not behaving like her cool person alter ego. She grimaced at him and it was all Evan could do to stop himself from laughing.

"I'm so sorry," she said, standing up and turning to Eizo. "Olivia West," she shook his hand. "Please forgive my rudeness. I don't often get to see living vampire squid, and I was very excited."

Eizo looked surprised, but in the best of the Japanese tradition of manners, covered it up.

"You like fish? Then you will love this casino. It is essentially a very large aquarium."

There were others waiting for them inside. Evan guessed that most of their girlfriends were paid for in some way, but he wasn't sure if Olivia noticed. The girls flocked and did what they were told, and Olivia allowed herself to be bossed around as well, which he could tell she was finding slightly hilarious, but also annoying.

"Why don't we let the girls go gamble?" suggested Eizo, which was essentially code for getting down to business. Eizo always wanted to hammer out negotiation terms over drinks.

Evan glanced at Olivia, who looked around. "I don't have any chips," she said, eyeing the girl-pets who were getting handfuls of chips from their owners. Evan grabbed a stack out of the carousel he'd collected when they'd entered and handed it to her. He knew it was probably about twenty-thousand. He could tell that Eizo knew that's how much it was. What he couldn't tell was whether or not Olivia knew. He'd told her not to look like she was panicking, but there was something blissfully unaware in her smile as she accepted the chips.

"Thanks," she said, kissing him on the cheek.

"What do you think she'll do with that?" asked Eizo. Eizo had appeared to add up the boobs and Southern accent and come up with stupid. It was annoying, but trying to tell him otherwise would only backfire.

"No clue," said Evan.

"Hello, good evening," said a casino host, coming into their room. "Is there anything I can help you with?"

On the other hand, perhaps proof could be offered without sounding like bragging?

Evan waved the host over. "You have someone managing the aquarium?" he asked, and the host nodded. "My girlfriend would like a behind-the-scenes tour."

The host beautifully showed no shock or dismay. "Of course, sir. I will inquire."

The host disappeared and Evan settled down to the work of arguing with Eizo. Thirty minutes later the host returned with a gray-haired man and a younger employee.

"Dr. Onishi would be happy to show your friend around, sir," said the host.

"Great," said Evan. "She's the redhead on the floor. Can you get someone to find her?"

"Of course, sir."

Five minutes later, Olivia appeared, following the host.

"Did you want me?" she asked smiling up at him.

Evan beckoned to Dr. Onishi. "Dr. Onishi is in charge of the aquarium and has volunteered to give you a behind-the-scenes tour."

She looked surprised and pleased.

Evan switched to Japanese and turned to Dr. Onisihi. "This is Dr. Olivia West. She is—"

Dr. Onishi's face immediately lit up in recognition.

"Phosphorescence in the Vampyroteuthis infernalis!" His next words were a tumble of Japanese and English that Evan had to struggle to wade through.

Olivia looked at Evan and he did his best to translate.

"He read your most recent article in *Scientific American*. He's very excited to meet you and would like to show you his fish."

"Oh, that's so lovely," said Olivia, blushing slightly, and looking demure. "I'm very pleased to meet you as well. Thank you for taking the time to show me around." The attendant casino host rapidly translated. Dr. Onishi beamed and gestured toward the door, but Olivia paused and looked around. "Evan, I had chips. Someone said they were bringing them?" She flapped her hands as if expecting them to appear.

"Yes, miss," said the host, touching her lightly on the arm and pointing to the door where an employee was toting two trays of chips.

"Oh, good. Evan, do I do something?"

"I'll take care of it," said Evan, and she smiled.

"Thank you, sugar." Then she turned to Dr. Onishi and followed him.

Evan gestured to the table where his carousel of chips sat. The employee gravely set down the chips and Evan tipped him with one of the smaller denominations. Then he sat back down and took a sip of his drink.

"Your girlfriend is a doctor who has recently been published in *Scientific American*?" asked Eizo.

"Yes," said Evan. "Double Ph.D.'s actually."

"And she went away for a half-hour and came back with…" Eizo checked the stacks. "Seventy-five thousand dollars?"

Evan looked the stacks over himself. "Closer to eighty-five I think, but yes."

Eizo sat back and glared at him. "How American of you."

"I beg your pardon?"

"You always take the best."

"What else would I want?" asked Evan.

An hour later, Olivia returned, all smiles, and leaned against him, while he continued to sit. Her ass was distractingly near his face, but he pretended he didn't notice as he wrapped his arm around her waist.

"Did you have a good time?" he asked. "I was starting to think that we lost you to the fish."

"Well, you very nearly did," she said, taking a piece of sushi off his plate with delicate fingers.

"What do you mean?" asked Eizo, eyeing her with a sort of skeptical amusement.

"Well," she said, putting her hand over her mouth as she finished chewing, "we went to look in a tank and we were using one of those industrial step-ladders, you know the kind made of diamond-plate? And my heel got stuck in one of the holes, and I just about pitched headfirst into the fish tank. I think I gave Dr. Onishi a heart attack. I don't know if it was because he thought I was going to drown or because he thought I was going to crash his tank, but either way, he may wish to consult a doctor."

"You didn't end up in the tank, though?" asked Evan, laughing.

"No, no, don't laugh yet. That's not the funny part. Just as I was thinking, *holy crap I'm going to get squid in my hair*, the little translator guy caught me. Only I look down and he's got just a whole hand full of boob."

Eizo began to laugh.

"Which I suppose I could have been offended about, but considering that he just saved me from a close encounter of the squid kind, I was inclined to let it go. But then he blushed. And I mean, blu-u-shed. I haven't seen a blush that red on someone who wasn't a redhead since, well, never. Anyway, the poor kid goes red like a cherry tomato. So, and this is totally unkind, and I'll probably go to hell for it, I said, *and he's safe at second base.* Poor kid nearly dropped me."

Evan found himself laughing, which set Eizo off on another round.

"Yes, I'm a terrible person," she agreed. "And I plan to feel bad about that later after it stops being funny."

"So never, then?" asked Eizo.

"We'll see," she said. "Are these my chips?"

"Yes," said Evan.

"Well, I guess they were starting to crowd the Blackjack table a bit," she said, looking doubtful, "but, my, they did stack up." She picked up one of the chips and flipped it from one knuckle to the next. "I do like this place better than Vegas. These days in Vegas, they just give you that stupid plastic card. Who wants a credit card? No one. You don't feel like you've won anything!" She paused and flipped the chip in the air and caught it. "Although, you also don't feel like you've lost anything, so I suppose that's why they do it." She put the chip back in the stack. "But chips are so much more fun."

"Also, harder to carry," said Evan, and she sighed.

"Stop being smart," she said, leaning down to kiss him.

"I leave that to you," he agreed, and she grinned at him.

"Anyway," she said, looking around the table, "was I interrupting? Should I go off and see about that backgammon game? I think I can ace that."

"No," said Evan. "We were done. I'll come with you."

Olivia — Doors

Olivia walked under the arched glass of the entrance and felt that the evening had ended up a success. It hadn't started out that way. She had blown the entry and Eizo had kind of been a dick. She wasn't sure Evan had noticed, but Eizo had spent the start of the evening speaking mostly in Japanese and being very dismissive. And not just dismissive, but oddly jealous, always angling Evan away from her or stepping between them. It was as if he was intentionally trying to show Olivia that she didn't belong at their party. But after she had returned from her trip through the aquarium, he'd switched to mostly English and suddenly bothered to become charming. She wasn't sure if Evan had said something to him, or if Dr. Onishi's excited recognition of her name had impressed him, but it had been a definite shift. Evan had watched his friend's efforts to charm her with a skeptical air but hadn't said anything. She got the impression that had she shown Eizo the slightest bit of actual interest that Evan would not have been so hands-off, but it didn't matter. There wasn't anyone who could turn her head from Evan.

She glanced back over her shoulder at him, and his eyes flicked up to meet hers. She smiled. She was certain that he'd trying to take her panties off in the limo. She was equally certain that she was going to let him. She'd never done the limo thing for prom. It seemed like a good time to check it off her bucket list.

She stepped out into the chilly Tokyo night and someone grabbed her by the arm, hauling her forward off her feet. She stumbled, trying to remain upright, and failed. Behind her, Evan was shouting.

She let go of her purse and grabbed at the hand holding her.

The man was young, early twenties, and pulling her across the parking lot. She turned her head and bit his hand. He yelled and let go. Olivia scrambled away from him. She turned, preparing to run back to Evan.

Evan had his own problems. A crowd of men stood around Evan and Eizo. As she watched, one of them swung a long stick at Evan. She tried to scream but found herself seized from behind.

"You just get to watch," hissed the man, seizing her by the back of the neck. She looked down at the gun he pressed into her side.

Evan took the hit from the stick, but he didn't seem to feel the impact. Instead, it was as if he became sticky. He took the bat, wrenching it out of his attacker's grasp. Then seized the man, pulling him in, before shoving him at one of the others. Evan spun the stick around and struck out with it. The other two men launched themselves at Evan, but Evan didn't flinch. He appeared to have no sense of fear or self-presentation. What he did have was blind fury. Behind him, Eizo punched one of the men, but to Olivia, it appeared that he was not backing Evan as he should have been. Evan grabbed the third person and threw him to the ground, kicking out with a sharp vicious kick.

The man holding her began to back up. It was becoming clear that Evan was not going to be stopped.

Evan struck out at the last man standing in cruel, punishing punches and stepped over his body, walking toward them.

The man dragged her backward. She didn't blame him. The Evan coming toward them was no Evan that she recognized. He was furious—rage personified. He advanced with the inevitability of an avalanche.

The man pulled the gun away from Olivia and pointed it at Evan, lifting it to his face.

"I will shoot," said the man.

Evan stared past the barrel into his eyes.

"Go ahead."

Olivia's heart stopped. He was absolutely serious. His face was empty, devoid of emotion. And in that moment, she knew that Evan had not been merely miserable in his twenties.

The man holding the gun shifted nervously. Then he yanked Olivia in front of him. He pulled off her necklace and shoved her at Evan. She heard him sprinting away as she clung to Evan.

An hour later she was still sitting in a private room of the casino being fussed over by paramedics and watching as Evan continued to rage, but this time at the police. His anger had hardened into a cold fury. She had never seen him so autocratic, so dismissive, so contemptuous. Eizo came into the room. He looked amused at Evan's behavior and drifted to stand next to her.

"Enjoying your evening?" he asked, and Olivia stared at him. She couldn't decide if he meant his comment to be amusing or mocking. She decided it didn't matter.

"Eizo, would you be so kind as to fetch Evan for me?"

"You want me to fetch *The Deveraux*? There are a few problems with that. I don't fetch and Deverauxes don't come when called. Particularly not, I think, at the moment."

"Never mind," said Olivia, pinning him with a stare that she hoped expressed how useless she found him. "I'll do it myself."

She got up, collecting her purse, but shedding gauze and paramedics. They followed her, bowing. Evan noticed her movement and turned toward her as she approached.

"Evan," she said, realizing even as his name left her mouth that she was sounding her most Southern, but unable to do anything about it, "I would like to go home now."

Silence seemed to ripple outward as everyone in the room turned to see what would happen next.

"Of course," said Evan. He turned to someone in a casino uniform and snapped something in Japanese. Moments later, she and Evan were being escorted by police and security out to a waiting limo.

The hotel had obviously been alerted to the situation, and they were greeted with a cadre of people who offered ice packs, sympathy, and waves of sucking up. Evan ignored all of them, and Olivia couldn't tell if she was supposed to do the same. Considering that she did not think that Evan had permitted himself to be looked over by paramedics, she decided to take the ice packs and wave off everything else.

Once they were alone in the room, everything seemed uncannily silent.

"I'm going to take a shower," she said, handing him an icepack.

She stood under the hot water and felt it sting in every scrape and scratch along her legs. She tried to think about the evening in some coherent, linear fashion, but her thoughts kept coming back to Evan staring down the gun.

He was laying on the bed naked, an icepack on his ribs when she came out wrapped in a towel. She sat down on the bed, her back to him.

"Are you mad at me?" he asked, his voice hoarse.

"Yes," she said. "I'm furious."

"What did I do wrong?" he asked.

She turned and scrambled across the bed to him. "You told him to go ahead and shoot."

"He had to believe that I didn't care," he said. "He had to be scared of me."

She found her hand raised to slap him. He watched the hand but didn't move. She put her hand down gently on his chest.

"My mother committed suicide," she whispered. "I know what that looks like. Don't lie to me. You wanted it."

"No," he said, his voice was firm and he met her eyes easily.

"You're telling me that you have never tried…" She couldn't even finish the sentence because his eyes flicked away from hers. "Answer me."

"Once," he said, his voice strained. "I got therapy. I got help. That isn't… I'm not there anymore."

"You were there tonight!"

"No," he said. "No, I swear. It's a door. It's a scary door and I opened it. I needed that man to be scared. He had you, and I needed him to be scared. It was just the right answer at the time."

"It's not an answer!" Olivia was shaking and furious and scared, so very scared. She grabbed him on either side of his face, wanting to make him hear her. "I love you and that can't ever be the answer."

Evan stared up at her as if processing her words, then he moved. He flipped her over onto her back and then he was on her, kissing her, tugging at her towel, ripping it off. His hands were rough and urgent, but his mouth moved with a gentleness that set her skin on fire. He moved down her body until he was between her thighs. His hands pushed her legs apart and his tongue darted inward, circling her clit. She grasped his hair as she found herself building toward orgasm. She moaned his name as she got closer. She was right on the brink when he abruptly pulled away. She blinked up at him and found that all that could come out of her mouth was an inquisitive noise. He leaned up and kissed her breast, taking the nipple into his mouth. It was lovely, but it was not what she wanted. She pushed him back down and he went. This time was faster. He had her on the point of coming when, again, he broke away.

This time she was angry, but he wouldn't go down on her again when she pushed him. Frustrated, she reached down to finish the job herself. He grabbed her hand and held it. She stared at him in disbelief. He seemed to count to ten and then he dipped his head, keeping his eyes on her, began again. The pressure this time was unbelievable. She found herself murmuring his name in an endless begging loop.

"Please Evan, please Evan, please Evan."

Olivia gasped, her hands clenching in the sheets as she began to come, his tongue moved faster. Her body throbbed, pulsing as she came in wave upon wave. His every touch extended her orgasm, and she came again and again. She was writhing on the bed as she continued to come uncontrollably. He finally pulled away standing up, his cock proud before him, and he reached for the condoms in the bedside drawer.

"No," gasped Olivia. He hesitated. "No, just you. I just want you. I want you to come inside me."

He breathed out in a ragged gasp and came to her. He seized her by the hips and pulled her to him, thrusting into her. She reached up and brought his head down to hers, kissing his mouth, letting her tongue explore his.

He broke away, kissing her neck as he murmured her name. She wrapped a leg around him and ran her hand down his side. His skin was warm and she luxuriated in each thrust as he took her back upward toward orgasm. This one bloomed like a hothouse flower, sensuous and slow without peaks and valleys, and left her feeling rung out.

He pulled away from her and she realized that he hadn't come yet.

"No," she said, sitting up, trying to lure him back with kisses. "No, you promised. You said." She was not oblivious to the fact that his lips hadn't spoken, but his body had committed.

"I will," he whispered between her kisses. "I will. I'll fuck you like you like. I promise," he said, pushing at her. "Turn over."

She did as he commanded and he took her from behind, one hand on her clit like the first night they had been together. Her body was nearing the end of its strength. The adrenaline, the fear, and now Evan, combined to leave her trembling as he drove into her again and again. She quaked as she neared the peak.

"Evan! Evan!" she screamed, sobbing into the mattress as she came again, her entire body shuddering.

"Olivia," he gasped and came into her, with one final violent thrust and they collapsed together onto the bed.

An hour later, they were still spooned together on the bed and Olivia realized that she could not remember a single thing that she had thought in that time. Had she been asleep? Had he seriously fucked all of her thoughts out of her head?

"I did that wrong," said Evan, his voice breaking the silence of the penthouse.

"No, you really didn't," said Olivia.

He moved so that she rolled into him and he was over her. "You said I love you," he said. "I was supposed to say it back. I'm not sure what happened."

She wanted to laugh at him. He looked confused and worried. And sweet. His hair was still wet with sweat and sticking up on the side where he'd been laying. She smoothed it down with one hand.

"Evan Alexander Deveraux," she whispered, "I love you."

He smiled, beaming. "Olivia Rose West, I love you back."

He lay back down snuggling in close to her. "Although," said

Olivia, "I wasn't confused. Somewhere around the fifteenth orgasm, I got the message."

"Sometimes words are not my thing," he admitted sleepily.

"That's OK," said Olivia. "I like the way you talk."

Evan – Christmas Gifts

At five, Evan left Olivia sleeping and began to make some calls. The call with Jackson did not go well. Unable to mention Olivia, he found himself unable to express why he was so angry. Next, he called the insurance company to report the theft of the necklace. The police report made it easy and they said they would courier over a replacement immediately. After that, he made a call to one Mr. Tanazashi.

Mr. Tanazashi was not a nice person. But he was exactly the sort of person who would be able to find the thug who had put a gun to Olivia. Mr. Tanazashi had helped him out of his little problem with the Yakuza and Evan hoped that he would be able to perform similar miracles here.

The replacement necklace arrived just as Olivia emerged for breakfast. He took it from the courier and handed it to her, but she closed the box and handed it back. "I'm sorry," she said, "but that one's not mine. I wanted the one you gave me. It's just… not the same."

The necklaces were the same. In another girl, Evan knew he would have been impatient and angry. He also realized that rules he had applied to other women no longer applied to Olivia. So he kissed her. "That's fine," he said.

Somewhere between breakfast and lunch, Eizo dropped in. He brought flowers for Olivia, and Olivia smiled and said thank you, but something had shifted in her demeanor toward him. It took Evan a moment to place the difference. She was being gracious at him.

It was a distinctly Southern manner that said everything polite and proper while negating any attempts at an actual connection. Olivia no longer found Eizo amusing. It was surprisingly Japanese of her and he could see that Eizo understood exactly the degree to which he had been marked down. He could also see that Eizo found it galling, which amused Evan.

"You don't like Eizo?" he asked after the door shut.

"He should have helped you more last night," she said.

"Eizo doesn't really help people," said Evan.

"And that's why I don't like him," she replied.

She was making some notes on her wall and tiredly rubbing her neck when the front desk called.

"Good afternoon, Mr. Deveraux. This is Aiko. I was recently apprised of the horrible events of last night. I was wondering if Mrs. Deveraux would care to come down for a private soak in the spa."

"That is a thoughtful idea, thank you. I'm sure she would love that. I'll send her down."

It wasn't until after he hung up the phone that he realized that they'd referred to Olivia as his wife. It was a strange thought. And he turned it over in his head like the novelty it was. Even if they were married she probably wouldn't change her name—Dr. West was her career. Also, he had always assumed that he wouldn't get married. His father never had. His mother, a Ukrainian model with fabulous cheekbones, had essentially been Owen's chosen egg donor. He'd dismissed her by the time Evan was two. Evan saw her every once in a while. They usually stared at each other in mutual distrust and confusion. He shook his head and sent Olivia to the spa.

He was asleep when she returned. Legs kicked out in front of him in a chair in the bedroom. He'd sat down to take off his shoes, fully intending to get up again in a minute, but not quite making it. He woke up when Olivia began to unbutton his shirt.

"You need to take a nap," she said.

"No, I've got a little more work to do," he said. "Then we've got reservations tonight."

"Nap," she said, kneeling in front of him, continuing to un-button. She wriggled to get between his legs and then kissed his chest as she unbuttoned. She rested her boobs on his cock, letting the weight of them rub back and forth as she kissed.

"That's not going to lead to a nap," he said.

To his disappointment, she pulled back and began to unbuckle his belt. "Hips," she said, tapping his hip bone. He lifted a little and she tugged his pants off onto the floor. "Evan, you rebel, you're not wearing any underwear."

"Seemed like too much work this morning," he said honestly.

"Mmm, I know the feeling." She tilted her head and blew gen-tly on his dick, which brought him jerking more upright. His cock did the same. She licked the tip and then blew again. He shivered at the difference between her warm tongue and the cold air. Slow-ly, gently, she licked the entire length of him from the tip to the base. Then, instead of blowing, she opened her mouth and breathed along the path of her tongue, her breath was warm and wet against his shaft. She took him in her mouth and pulled gently with her lips, leaving him breathing heavily. She worked in and out and he buried his hands in her hair. "Liv," he groaned. He was getting close. She went faster, her tongue working in concert with her mouth, and he came with a gasp, his hand clenching at her shoulder. She swallowed and stood up.

"Nap," she said.

He did as he was told, and when he woke up the sitting room

was illuminated only by the glow of the city outside the window, the fireplace, and candles on the table that was set for dinner.

"I thought we had reservations?" he asked. She was wearing his favorite outfit besides naked—short shorts and one of his button-ups.

"I had them bring the food to us," she said.

It was a three-star Michelin-rated restaurant. They did not do take-out.

"How did you manage that?"

"I may have thrown your name around. Evan," she paused, one hand on the back of the dining chair, "you're very rich, aren't you?"

"I don't know about *very*," he said.

"But you don't need to work if you don't want to?"

"Not really," he said.

"One of the girls last night was going on and on about Eizo. And then said, *well, you know, you already got a Deveraux*. And Eizo called you *The Deveraux*." Evan snorted. "Are Deverauxes a... a thing?"

"We're a bit of a thing," he admitted.

"That necklace was real diamonds, wasn't it?"

"Yes."

She rubbed her nose. "Do you really like the wine I pick out?"

"Yes! What kind of question is that?"

"I don't know. I always pictured rich people as learning about wine at birth or something. What if all this time I've been yapping about something you know more about?"

"You're one of the most educated oenophiles I know," he said. "Hardly anyone brings me a bottle I like and you knock it out of the park every time."

She looked pleased.

"OK. Well. Then I hope you liked what I picked out for dinner."

"I'm sure I will," he said, smiling.

They were mid-way through dessert when there was a soft knock on the door. Evan opened it and looked at Mr. Tanazashi.

"The item you requested," said Mr. Tanazashi, not bothering to cross the threshold. He handed Evan Olivia's necklace. Evan rubbed the spot of blood off the center diamond. "One thing though," said Mr. Tanazahi, "this was not an accident. He didn't have a name, but the money came in this." He handed Evan an Absolex envelope.

"I thought as much," said Evan, tucking it into his pocket. "Thanks. The money will be in your account by the time you reach the lobby."

Mr. Tanazashi nodded and left.

Evan hit send on the wire transfer and went back to the table. Olivia was sipping her wine and watching him. Evan slid the pendent across the table to her. She made the same *ooh* noise she'd made the first time he'd given it to her and seized it off the table.

"How did you…" She looked from him to the door.

"Mr. Tanazashi specializes in retrieving things," said Evan. "I thought he'd move faster than the police."

She flung herself at him and, unprepared, he ended up catching her, but toppling onto the rug in front of the fireplace. She kissed him, the pendant clutched in one hand and he kissed her back and began to unbutton the shirt she was wearing. He realized part of the way through that matters were going to be hampered if she continued to hold the necklace in her hand.

"Hold on," he said getting up. He took the chain off the pendant from the insurance company and strung it on hers, discarding the broken chain.

Her breasts peeked from the shirt as he knelt down to slide the necklace around her neck. "Thought you might want to wear it." She sucked in a little air as the necklace made contact with her skin and he saw her nipples visibly rise.

"It's cold," she said.

"I'm warm," he offered and she giggled and then tackled him again. Eventually, she stopped kissing him. Straddling him, she reached up to the table for the bottle of wine while he finished the unbuttoning process. The pendant hung above her breasts, twinkling in the firelight as she drank straight from the bottle. A little wine trickled from the bottle and onto her breast, and he sat up to lick it off. As he did, he caught sight of the rejected pendant on his desk.

He lay back down and looked at his Dark Phoenix, perched on his stomach.

She wasn't turned on by gifts. Money didn't matter to her.

She was turned on by giving. She was turned on by him. She liked it when *he* gave her things. Evan laughed, and she looked down at him with a questioning expression.

"By the way, what are you going to do with all your money?" he asked.

"What money?"

"The hundred thousand dollars you won at the casino."

She choked on the wine and a large blob dropped down on his chest.

"What?"

"They issued you a cashier's check. You put it in your purse."

"It's still in my purse," she said, looking pale. "It's in Yen. I didn't bother to look at it."

"Yeah, but at the current market exchange rate, it's about a hundred thousand US."

"Holy shit, Evan. How much were those chips worth?"

"The green ones were a thousand each."

"Holy shit. I just thought… You said not to think about money. So I just played Blackjack because I'm good at it."

"And you cleaned up at backgammon too. Nice job."

"Fuck me. Can I even put that much money in my account? How do you cash something that big? I don't even have an investment person."

He raised his hand. "I can probably help with that."

She laughed. "Shoot. This boyfriend thing really is coming in handy." She looked up, squinting at the clock on the wall, then smiled down at him with a wicked grin and leaned down and licked the wine off his chest. "Merry Christmas, Mr. Deveraux."

Evan – Christmas Re-Do

Evan bounced up the stairs to Deveraux House and as usual, Theo managed to open the door before he could either knock or reach for his key.

"Good morning, Mr. Deveraux," said Theo.

"Good morning, Theo! Is everyone here?"

"No, sir, I believe that you are the first to arrive."

"What about Grandma?" he asked taking his bag toward the study.

"Early meeting with the DNC," said Theo, following him and trying to remove his jacket.

Evan opened the door and looked in disappointment at the room.

"Where's the tree?"

"Sorry, sir, Mrs. Deveraux had me take the tree down," said Theo.

"But it's only the twenty-seventh," said Evan. His grandmother had never, in his recollection, removed the Christmas décor before the first of the year.

"Yes, sir," said Theo, looking awkward. "There may be a small tree left up in the upstairs window. I'll bring that down."

Evan set his bag down with a frown. He was trying not to take this personally, but the lack of a tree felt targeted.

Theo returned with a two-foot-tall tree that he placed on the bar and whisked Evan's coat away. With careful fingers, Evan put his grandmother's present under the tiny tree. Then he flopped down on the couch and waited for his cousins to arrive. He kicked off his shoes and put his feet on the couch. His grandmother would yell at him if she caught him, but if she could take his tree then he could damn well besmirch her couch.

He was just starting to be nervous that his entire family had stood him up when he heard the front door slam open.

"We're here, we're here," called Dominique, hurrying into the room.

"What took you so long?" he demanded. "I was about to start eating your mochi balls."

"Oh, I asked Aiden to give me a ride," said Dominique tossing off her scarf and jacket at Theo. "But then his car wouldn't start."

"I haven't driven it in a month," said Aiden coming in after her. "Because of Evan's damn Nazis."

"They're not my Nazis," objected Evan.

"And then they had to call me for a ride," said Jackson bringing up the rear.

Jackson did not look especially pleased to see him, and Evan felt a twinge of guilt. Possibly if Jackson had known Olivia was going with him, he might have recommended different security arrangements. Evan hadn't even thought about it. He'd just assumed he'd be safe in Tokyo.

"Well, hurry up and sit down," said Evan. "Theo's got cocoa going and I want to give out my presents."

"Irish cocoa?" asked Aiden hopefully.

"As Irish as you like, Mr. Aiden," said Theo.

"Aren't we waiting for Grandma?" asked Dominique, sitting down.

"No, I'm afraid not," said Theo. "Early meeting at the DNC."

"Oh," said Aiden, looking affronted. "Well, all right. I guess it's four cocoas and bring on the presents."

Evan waited until they were settled and then began to pass out his presents.

Dominique ooh'd over the gloves that he'd picked out and promptly by-passed them in favor of the mochi balls in their own cooler. Aiden laughed at his box of giant pocky. And Jackson looked surprised that he had a present at all.

"I didn't ask for anything," he said, taking the box from Evan.

"Amazing thought," said Evan, "but it occurred to me that you might want something anyway."

Jackson opened the box and laughed. "You're right," he said, taking the short samurai sword out of the box. "I do want this."

"There's some candy in there too," said Evan. "I didn't want you to feel left out in the weird edible department." Jackson chuckled as he pulled out the seaweed candies.

"I will fight you," said Aiden pulling out one of his giant pocky and waving it like a sword. Jackson took out the short sword and sliced the pocky in half, nearly burying the point into the arm of the chair. Dominique choked on a mochi ball from laughing so hard. Evan collapsed back onto the couch feeling successful.

"Speaking of Tokyo," said Aiden, pulling his own bag of presents forward and beginning to distribute. "Funny story: I ran into Bradley Kingsley yesterday."

Evan stared blankly at him. He had no idea who Bradley Kingsley was.

"He said he bumped into you in Tokyo," continued Aiden, handing him a present.

"Shit," said Evan sitting up. "That's where I know him from."

"From being friends with me? Yes. He said you must have been in a good mood because you actually chatted for over thirty seconds and introduced him to your girlfriend."

"Busted!" crowed Dominique around a mochi ball.

"Goddamn it, Evan!" yelled Jackson, throwing down the sword and standing up. Aiden and Dominique exchanged confused glances. Jackson stomped to the window and stood staring out at the back garden, hands on his hips in a way that reminded Evan distinctly of his father. "I can't keep doing this," he said turning around, raking them all with an angry glare. "I can't keep compensating for things you don't tell me. If I had known you were taking someone, I would have been a lot more insistent about your security."

"Yes," said Evan. "Sorry. I thought of that after I hung up."

Jackson threw his hands in the air in frustration, then took a deep breath. "Is she OK?"

"OK? What do you mean, *is she OK*? What happened to Olivia?" demanded Dominique.

"Nothing," said Evan. "She's fine. I'm fine. It's just that it almost wasn't fine. Granger took another run at me. This time, one of them had a gun. He pointed it at Olivia. And really," he said, turning to Jackson, "I cannot have that happening again."

"I'm starting to think…," said Dominique. She paused, rubbing her eyebrow with a very Grandma-type gesture. For the first time, Evan also remembered that it was something that his father had also done. "Something is going to have to be done," she said at last and smiled the picture-perfect Deveraux smile.

Evan stared at Dominique. "Like what?" he asked, torn between horror and fascination.

"Oh, I'm sure I don't know," she said. "But I guess I will have to come up with something."

"No squashing Deverauxes?" asked Evan.

"Precisely."

Evan looked back at Jackson. He wasn't sure what to do with a

Dominique who came up with things to do to her enemies. Jackson shrugged.

"Yes, you're the Godfather," said Aiden, turning to his sister. "I'm sure we all sleep better at night knowing you're on our side. Meanwhile, what do you mean, *is Olivia OK?* Brad didn't mention her name, so I know I sure as hell didn't." Dominique took a hasty gulp of her coco, as Aiden focused on her with an intensity that he usually reserved for court. "You knew?"

"That Evan was dating the very lovely Dr. Olivia West? Yes, I did."

"When did you meet her?" demanded Jackson, his eyes narrowing at Dominique.

"A month ago," said Dominique. "Mochi ball anyone?"

"I'll take one," said Evan.

"That's like an entire ice age in Evan dating time. How long have you been dating her?" demanded Aiden, turning to Evan.

"Since Halloween," said Evan around a mouthful of ice cream.

"Let me guess," said Jackson, "long red hair?"

"Why doesn't anyone tell me anything?" demanded Aiden.

"This one's on you," said Dominique, looking pointedly at Evan.

"I didn't tell anyone because I didn't want all of you to scare the crap out of her."

"We wouldn't do that!" exclaimed Aiden. "Well, maybe Jackson and Grandma might, but Nika and I are nice!"

"Hey!" said Jackson. "Look, I might run a background check or something, but what did you think I was going to go do? Go over and give her the third degree? I thought we…" He glared at Evan, clearly biting his tongue, but not pulling out the autopsy report or the storage unit.

"I know," said Evan, fighting a surge of guilt. "I was going to tell you, but then I thought this was something that you would have to report to Grandma. And lately, she has not seemed very…"

"She's been a fucking bitch," said Aiden. "And you're getting the pointy end of that fork."

"I don't know what her problem is," said Dominique. "But she needs to stop."

"I just wish I could figure out what I did to piss her off," said Evan, feeling awkward. He wasn't sure what was worse—thinking that his cousins hadn't noticed, or knowing that they had.

"I don't think you did anything," said Jackson. "Or rather, I think you got sober, and I'm not sure she knows how to deal with you when you're healthy."

"Oh," said Evan. That was even more awkward. "Well, there's nothing I can do about that."

"Well, maybe give it a bit more time and see if she comes around," said Aiden, sounding like even he didn't buy that.

"We'll see," said Dominique, but she glanced up at the picture of Henry Deveraux.

Three hours later Evan was lying in front of the fireplace, Aiden was face down on the couch and Dominique and Jackson occupied respective wing chairs.

"And what has happened here?" asked Eleanor, coming in and inspecting the carnage.

"We won, Grandma," said Evan.

"I demand a rematch," said Jackson, opening one eye.

"I ate too many marshmallows," groaned Aiden with his face still in the pillow.

"Serves you right. You cheated," said Dominique. "I don't know how, but I'm sure you and Evan could not have outshot us."

"We had more ammunition," said Aiden.

"Why is Evan wearing oven mitts?" asked Eleanor.

"They're my Christmas present from Dominique," said Evan.

"He needed bigger oven mitts," said Dominique with a snicker.

"Your present is under the tree," said Evan, waving an oven mitted hand toward the bar. Reluctantly, Eleanor picked her way across the paper-strewn floor and opened the box. Evan watched her from the floor. She opened the box and smiled. She removed the delicate blue teacup from the velvet box. It was a perfect match to the Wedgwood set that sat behind glass in the dining room—the set was almost complete, missing only one teacup. A teacup that he remembered his father smashing at a family dinner twenty years earlier.

"How did you find it?" she asked.

"The internet is a big place," he said.

"You're a sweet boy," she said.

Olivia – Tyler

Olivia picked up the phone with a smile.

"Hey, Ty!"

"Hey, Liv! Am I bugging you at work or anything? I can call back later."

"No, I just got back from vacation. I'm only trying to sort through my email and catch up before I come in for actual work tomorrow."

"You went on vacation? Who are you? Do I even know anymore?"

Olivia chuckled. "Yeah, I figured if I wasn't going to go home then I sure as hell wasn't going to sit alone in my apartment and mope. And also, um, Evan invited me to go on a work trip with him."

"Oh, Evan invited you. Hmm."

"Shut up," said Olivia, grinning at her brother's salacious tone.

He laughed. "Where'd you guys go?"

"Tokyo! It was awesome!"

"Seriously?"

"Yes! I bought you some interesting sake. But I still have to make it to the post office to ship it to you."

"Cool! I just can't believe you finally got out of the country. You went on like a twenty-minute rant about that last time we were drunk."

"I know! They almost didn't stamp my passport, but I made them do it. Evan kind of laughed at me."

Tyler laughed. "So you and this guy are having a good time?"

"Um, yeah. We really are," said Olivia. Olivia didn't know

what else to say about Evan without going into a Hamlet's worth of a soliloquy, so she cut it short.

Tyler was silent. "You're kind of serious about him, aren't you?"

"Yes," she said. "I am. Why?" She changed her grip on her phone and prayed to the God she didn't believe in that Tyler wasn't going to say something horrible. He was the only family member she had that was on her side right now. She couldn't lose him too.

"Nothing. Just jealous."

Olivia breathed out a sigh of relief. She was pondering about how to ask about the sad note in Tyler's voice, but he continued before she could formulate words. "Hey, speaking of Evan, did you give him the Reserve I sent you home with?"

"We split it last Naked Tuesday before our trip. It was great."

"Yeah, apparently he thought so too. A phone order came through today for an entire case from Evan Deveraux. Considering, that it doesn't go to our online retailers until the first of the year, I figured it was your guy."

"Yes, that's him. It was really good."

"Yeah, except that it's three hundred dollars a bottle."

"Oh. I wish you would tell me these things before I drink them."

"It spoils your judgment," he said.

"I suppose. Anyway, Evan can afford it," said Olivia with a shrug.

"What does he do, work for Amazon?"

"What?"

"Sorry, maybe that's a Washington thing. Isn't Deveraux the name of that woman that Pops hates?"

"What woman?"

"I don't know. I wasn't paying attention. The one he hates at work."

"No clue," said Olivia. "You know I tune him out whenever possible."

"Completely reasonable. But hey, speaking of Pops, did you talk to Sofia?"

"No, I haven't talked to her since the hospital. I called Dad a couple of times, but that's it. Why?"

"I spent an hour on the phone with her last night. She was a weepy mess. She kept going on about how you don't respect her because she never finished college. Which then sort of segued into how she has no job skills and no future."

"Well, maybe she should have finished school," said Olivia.

"Liv, you hyper-educated freak, not everyone is meant for college. And as far as job skills, she's been managing Grams and Pops farm for years. If she came out here I could get her a job in like twenty minutes."

Olivia sighed. "It doesn't matter," she said. "Sofia won't ever leave. She's going to end up married to some asshole who pats waitresses on the butt and thinks that's OK."

"She feels stuck and abandoned, Liv."

"Yeah, I'm familiar with the feeling," snapped Olivia. "That's why I left. And as I recall, when I said I was leaving she told me I was never going to do better than Clark and I was being stubborn, standing too much on principle and buying into the myth of the modern woman."

Tyler groaned. "We've got to get her out of there."

"I tried! I told her to come with me. She wouldn't leave. And now she won't even talk to me."

"I'll work on her," said Tyler. "Just maybe next time you talk to her try not to be so condescending."

"Maybe she shouldn't call me a whore every time I turn around."

"You know that's Pops talking."

"Ty, do you ever wonder if Mom would be alive today if she had just fucking moved away from Pops?"

Tyler was silent. "Yeah," he said. "Yeah, I have wondered that. But if she had, then chances are we wouldn't be here."

"So that's the trade-off? Us for her?"

"No. It's just… When people die we always picture the happiest possible outcome if only they had lived. I'm just saying, that's not how it works."

Olivia sighed. "Yeah, you're right. But the longer I'm away, the more I see I should have left sooner. Do you know, Evan announces my title every time he introduces me? He's proud of me. He thinks I'm cool. Which is obviously a mistake on his part. But my point is that it makes me realize how, I don't know, shut off, I guess, that Mom was. She supposedly had all this family, but she was really on her own. She didn't have enough people who liked who she was. Or at least she didn't feel that way."

"I see a therapist once a week," Tyler blurted out.

Olivia took a second. "Good for you," she said.

"OK," he said.

"Is there anything we should talk about?"

"I'm jealous of the fact that you're with Mr. Normal and I have a hard time making normal conversation with anyone."

"Don't be," she said. "He's as fucked up as we are. Really, in a very similar way."

"I feel like Mom's death overshadow's and defines my life."

"Yes," agreed Olivia. "I'm working hard not to let it. But yes."

"I'm really angry at her."

"Yes," said Olivia again. "But also, I miss her."

"Yes," he said. He cleared his throat. "OK, good chat."

"Tyler," she said, with a laugh, "I love you."

"I love you too," he said and it sounded wistful. "Next Christmas… even if we don't go home, maybe you and I can I don't know, go see Dad or get together or something. I don't want the Ralph Taggert Christmas extravaganza, but I miss my family."

"I miss you too," she agreed. "Next Christmas we'll figure something out. I know I screwed the pooch on this Christmas—"

"It wasn't you."

"Next Christmas we'll figure something out. Promise."

Evan – Painted Blackmail

Sunday dinner had been moved to Sunday brunch so that everyone could get on with their New Year's Plans. Evan was looking forward to New Year's this year. He and Liv were going to go see some fireworks from the Deveraux boat, yacht, whatever thing it was that floated in the water that Evan forgot about ninety percent of the year. He thought that she'd like the champagne he'd picked out too.

But first, he had to tell Eleanor about Olivia.

Evan blew out all of his air in a big breath, straightened his tie, and climbed the stairs to Deveraux House. Christmas repeat day had gone well—Jackson's minor explosion over Japan aside—Grandma had been nice and there had been hugs and smiles all the way around. He shouldn't be this nervous. All he had to say was: *Grandma, I have a girlfriend and I'd like you to meet her.* Jackson was on board. Dominique liked her. Aiden just seemed happy that Evan was happy. Everything should be fine.

Then why was he so nervous?

Why couldn't he shake the sense of impending doom?

"Good morning, Mr. Deveraux," said Theo. "I believe Mr. Jackson and Mrs. Deveraux are in the study."

Was that a worried look on Theo's face?

Evan went to the study and felt a tightness in his chest the second he crossed the threshold.

"You're not giving me enough time," Jackson was saying as

Evan entered. Evan looked at Jackson's expression and knew it was bad news.

"There is no time," said Eleanor. "Evan, good, you're here. It's time we talked."

"Talked?" Evan had the feeling of a trap closing around him. He looked at Jackson, who looked away. "About what?"

"This… girl you've been seeing." Eleanor sneered around the word *girl*.

Evan looked at Jackson again, this time he grimaced and shook his head. Evan wasn't sure what that meant.

"Olivia," said Evan. "Her name is Olivia."

"It doesn't matter," said Eleanor. "You'll stop seeing her."

Evan stared at his grandmother and thought about all the ways to respond to her.

"No," he said, deciding that his therapist was right, simple direct communication was usually the most effective.

"Evan, loyalty is a virtue, but she lied to you. And now you've gotten us, me, into a very bad position."

"Olivia doesn't lie," said Evan.

Eleanor reached into her briefcase and pulled out a sheaf of paper. "She's a honey pot," said Eleanor and handed him the paper.

Evan found that his hands were icy and he had to blink a few times to focus on the printed material in front of him. The top sheet was an email. From Ralph Taggert. He had to read it twice to make it make sense. It finally came clear when he realized that the granddaughter Ralph Taggert was going on about was Olivia.

He thought of all the times he'd wanted to strangle her grandfather and all the times he'd met Ralph Taggert in person and wanted to punch him in the face. In some ways, it was nice to narrow the field of his hate to a single person.

He thought of Olivia standing in the hotel room in Tokyo. *Are*

Deverauxes a… a thing? There was no way she'd known that, for the Deverauxes, Taggerts were a thing.

"Yes?" he said looking up.

"Next one," snapped Eleanor.

He read the next email and then pulled out the page after it, which featured a photo of him and a girl whose name he honestly didn't remember if he had known it at all. It was exactly the kind of photo that Fetish was supposed to guarantee never existed. Their policy was anonymity at all costs. Apparently, their policies had failed. He went back to the email.

OLIVIA WILL BE RETURNED TO GEORGIA AND YOU WILL CEASE TO CHAMPION THE HEALTHCARE BILL.

"I see," said Evan. "What are you going to do?"

"Do?" repeated Eleanor. "It's really about what you're going to do. You're going to break up with Olivia."

Evan thought about that. If the goal was to make him break up with Olivia, then that negated his grandmother's first statement—Olivia had not entrapped him. This was all Ralph Taggert.

"And you're going to stop your work on the bill?" Evan was skeptical.

"Don't be ridiculous," said Eleanor. "As always in politics, it's about negotiation and compromise."

"There would seem to not be a lot of leverage with which to negotiate," said Evan.

"Leverage exists where you create it," said Eleanor. She reached in her bag and pulled out an envelope and handed it to him. "You will break up with Olivia. Ralph will get something that he wants. And I will continue to work on the bill."

He opened the envelope and pulled out three photos. This time the girl with him in the photos was Olivia. The Photoshop job was impeccable—it truly looked like her. His fingers jerked spasmodically and he dropped the photos.

"You did this?"

"Leverage," she said. "If he releases his, I'll release mine."

"That doesn't accomplish anything!" Evan was sweating. His heart was hammering in his chest. "All it does is hurt her."

"Yes, particularly when I have them sent to her work. Possibly to her university. I'm sure I could get them distributed to her alumnus listserv."

He found his hands were curled into fists and Eleanor was watching his hands with interest.

"People can say what they like about modern times, but that level of kink will still shock ninety percent of the population. And maybe you can ride it out in your profession, but it will sink her career."

He found himself staring at his grandmother in furious, impotent rage.

"Break up with her, Evan," said Eleanor. "You don't have any other choices. It's you or her."

Evan turned around and walked out of the door.

"Hey!" said Dominique, coming in the front door, as he came out into the hall. "Where are you going?"

"To break up with Olivia," he said.

"Wait, what?"

He walked past Dominique, ignoring her attempts to slow him down. He had to do this now before he lost his nerve. The anger at his grandmother would carry him through. He'd done worse things for stupider reasons. Pain didn't matter much to him anyway. He just had to keep Olivia safe.

Jackson – At Dominique's

"What the fuck happened?" demanded Aiden, slamming the door on Dominique's condo. Dominique had unlocked the door when Aiden had buzzed her from the lobby. Jackson was amused to see that Max had vastly improved the quality of the front door and the front door lock.

Dominique came out of the kitchen. She was wearing her after-work outfit of leggings and one of Max's t-shirts. She had a plate full of what looked like snacks and a bottle of wine under one arm.

"Everything was fine for Christmas do-over," continued Aiden, angrily yanking off his jacket. "Ella and I go skiing and I come back and everything is in the shitter. What the fuck happened?"

"Grandma," said Dominique, as if it explained everything. She handed the wine bottle to Jackson and set down the plate on her coffee table. "And do we really have to pretend you went skiing? Can't you just say that you went out of the country for a fight?"

"What?" Aiden froze, halfway into the living room. Then glared at Jackson.

"What?" repeated Jackson, investigating the wine bottle and wondering how he was supposed to open it without a corkscrew. "I didn't tell her. I assume she talked to Ella."

"Of course, I talked to Ella," said Dominique. "She's a teeny-tiny bruiser and you turn up with bruises. It raises questions."

Jackson bit back a laugh, and Aiden whacked him in the arm.

"My girlfriend is not beating me up! And that's a screw top."

"It could happen," said Dominique, going back into the kitchen. "I don't know why people get weird about it."

"Well, she's not!" Aiden yelled after her.

"Well, obviously not. But I don't know why we have to wander around pretending you don't do illegal fighting. It's annoying."

"Because I don't want to talk about it!" snapped Aiden.

"I'm not saying talk about it, I'm saying just don't lie about it. I think this family needs to work on not lying to each other."

"It would be nice," muttered Jackson, finally stripping off the wrapping and unscrewing the wine.

"OK, fine. Can we move on to whatever Grandma did now?"

"I'd like to," said Dominique, returning with glasses. "I don't know why we're talking about this in the first place."

Aiden gaped at his sister in furious astonishment, then turned to Jackson for support.

"I hear you," said Jackson to the look that spoke volumes, "but there's nothing I can do about it."

"I give up," said Aiden, throwing his coat down on a chair. "Yes, let's talk about Grandma. What'd she do?"

"There was no early meeting at the DNC," said Jackson. "I believe Eleanor ditched me to take a meeting with Ralph Taggert in which the two of them negotiated away Evan and Olivia's future."

"That bitch," burst out Dominique and both men turned to look at her. "She was nice," said Dominque, looking like she was going to cry. "She was nice to him at Christmas do-over, and she knew the whole time… I actually thought she might have started to come around. But no, she was just setting him up."

Aiden took the glasses out of her hand and set them on the coffee table and hugged her.

"But setting him up for what?" demanded Aiden looking at Jackson. "What did she do?"

"Ralph has some unsavory photos of Evan. He wants Eleanor to back off the health care bill and he wants Olivia and Evan to break up. Guess which one Eleanor agreed to?"

"Why would Taggert care if they break up?" demanded Dominique, sniffing and pulling free of Aiden.

"Well, if anyone had mentioned Olivia to me, and let me run a background check, we might have known that Olivia is Taggert's granddaughter."

"Ohhhhh, God," said Aiden, and he dropped down onto Dominique's couch. He spread out, shoes on the sofa cushion, and Jackson watched Dominique struggle not to say anything. "Did she know?" Aiden demanded, sitting upright again. "If this Olivia woman thinks she's going to take advantage of Evan, I swear to God I will figure out a way to sue the shit out of her."

"I don't think she did," said Dominique, picking up a glass and waving it at Jackson. "I met her. She's in love with him. She looks at him, and you can just tell that she thinks he's amazing."

"Awww," said Aiden, obviously melting on Evan's behalf.

"And," added Dominique, "when I asked him about her before Christmas, he said that they met at a party and that she had no idea who he was or that he even had money."

"I hate Grandma!" yelled Aiden, yanking off his shoes and flinging them in the general direction of the shoe rack by the door. "Why is she trying to ruin this? And why is Evan caving? He can't really be that scared of Grandma."

"No," said Jackson, pouring the wine. "He's not, and she prepared for that. She used a particularly talented and unethical Photoshop expert to insert Olivia into Evan's photos. Then she told Evan that if he didn't break up with Olivia that she would send those photos to Olivia's workplace and her school mailing list."

Dominique and Aiden stared at him in disbelief.

"She can't," said Dominique as Aiden stood up and stomped across the floor and stood staring out the French doors onto Dominique's balcony. "That's… She can't do that. Olivia hasn't done anything wrong. And Evan… She can't do that."

"That only gets her halfway home," Aiden said.

"I think," said Jackson before hesitating. "I think it's enough. The pictures with Olivia in them are double blackmail. They make Evan and Olivia break up, that's a win for Taggert and if he threatens to go public with the photos, she can counter with her photos. I think Eleanor believes that will be enough to keep Taggert off her about the healthcare bill and that Evan will go back to being how he was and everything will be back to normal."

"I don't fucking want normal!" bellowed Aiden.

"Breathe, Aiden," said Dominique. In response, Aiden made an inarticulate growl and turned back to the window.

"How bad are they? The photos, I mean," asked Dominique.

"From my perspective, not that bad. But for the average member of the public, S & M is not generally acceptable."

"God, I didn't want to know that," said Aiden.

Dominique sighed. "Poor Evan. I really did not understand how badly his father screwed him up."

"S & M is not screwed up," objected Jackson. "Some people enjoy that and there's nothing wrong with it."

"Is there something we need to know about you?" asked Aiden, and Jackson exhaled in frustration.

"I'm just saying that S & M is not an automatic problem—unless you're Evan and you're using it to punish yourself. Anyway, Evan used to go to a club. He quit going a couple of years ago, and these pictures appear to be from that time frame."

"No," said Aiden, taking an angry lap around the couch. "Just no. I have known Grandma all my life. There's no way she would be caving to Taggert. She has to have something up her sleeve. And how did whoever took these photos know about Ralph Taggert anyway? Why go to him? Why not go directly to Grandma? If you've got photos of Evan, you go blackmail his wealthy and powerful family. You don't go to his girlfriend or his girlfriend's family. Something is wrong with this whole setup."

"You got there really fast," said Jackson, impressed.

Both Dominique and Aiden exchanged glances. "Meaning that you're there ahead of us?" demanded Aiden.

"Yes, but it took me several hours," said Jackson. "In my defense, I was trying to talk to Grandma, and Evan, and text Pete at the same time. But yeah, I'm slow."

"Jacks," said Dominique, looking at him sternly. "What do you know?"

"Lots of things. I know that I'm a very suspicious bastard and I know that Eleanor should never have invited me to be in charge of security if she thought that she was ever going to try and go around me. I pulled her phone records. I pulled her cash expenditures and last, but not least, I pulled the GPS off her car."

"What did she do?" demanded Aiden.

"Are you acting as my lawyer right now, Aiden?" asked Jackson.

"Fuck," said Aiden. He closed his eyes and then opened them again. "Yes. Yes, of course, I am."

"OK, then tell me when Evan asked you about public records requests."

Aiden stared at him for a long moment. "Um… November? I don't remember. Um, yeah. It was before Thanksgiving. Why?"

"We have all noticed that Evan has been somewhat distant this year. The truth is that Evan has been avoiding us because of something troubling that he found in the storage unit."

"Oh, shit on a shingle," said Dominique. "I don't know what

it is, but I swear to God, I will dig up Randall and Owen and kill them all over again."

"Funny you should say dig up." Jackson cleared his throat and looked at his cousins.

"Don't keep us waiting," said Aiden. "I'm about to start drinking straight from the bottle out of anxiety."

"Randall had Henry dug up and autopsied because he thought Eleanor offed him."

"Oh," said Aiden. "Oh, whew. I thought it was going to be something horrible."

"That *is* generally considered horrible," said Dominique.

"Well, so was Grandpa. Who cares?"

"Pretty sure you once told me that there's no statute of limitations on murder," said Dominique, glaring at her brother.

"Well, yeah, but Grandma didn't get caught and Evan and Jackson aren't going to let her get caught and besides, even at this late date, I can put together a bang-up defense. I mean it would be a bit sucky for her career, but she's got to retire at some point anyway."

"You're either an idiot or amazingly confident," said Dominique. "However, regardless of your thoughts on the subject, I can see that Grandma wouldn't want that to come out."

"I don't think she knows about it," said Jackson. "However, as Evan was digging through the storage unit he found an email from Randall to Genevieve saying that they needed to talk. It was dated three days before their vacations."

"Right before the plane crash," said Aiden. "Evan thinks they were going to tell Mom about it?"

"It was right when Grandma was planning her first campaign," said Dominique. "They might have decided to bring it up."

"Maybe," said Aiden with a shrug. "I'm not sure it matters."

"Yeah, well Evan couldn't find anything else, so he put in a public records request at the FAA. I'm guessing in November because right before Thanksgiving she got a call from someone at the FAA."

"Shit," said Aiden. "I told Evan that no one could tell if he'd made a public records request. I didn't count on Grandma having fucking spies in place."

"Next up," said Jackson, "Christmas. That's when she gets a call from a pre-paid phone that I can't trace. She exchanges calls with that phone number and then she withdraws five thousand in cash and I have no idea what she spent it on. She gets out another three shortly thereafter and I'm ninety-eight percent certain that went to the photographer in mid-town."

"That would be the doctored photos of Olivia," said Aiden slowly, trying to follow the breadcrumbs.

"You think Grandma is targeting Evan for looking into the plane crash," said Dominique.

"I think she's very uncomfortable with his sobriety. I think she's freaked out that he's looking into the plane crash, and I think when someone approached her with blackmail on Evan, she sent that person to Ralph Taggert so that she could blame everything on him, and at the same time she created the photos of Olivia to make sure she wouldn't lose the healthcare bill. It's chess and she only has to sacrifice Evan to win."

"This cannot be permitted," said Dominique. "We have to stop her."

"I intend to," said Jackson. "But I need to get both sets of photos. If I can get Eleanor and Taggert's photos then they're both back at square one. I know who Eleanor used for hers. I can get those, but I'm not sure what to do about Taggert's copies. I'm also not sure where he got them. Which makes me worry that there are more to be found."

Dominique's phone chirped and she dashed off a quick reply. "That was Max's thirty-minute warning. So be prepared to be normal in a half-hour. Aiden, do you need to borrow some sweats and take a jog to calm down?"

"I'm not seventeen," barked Aiden. He was silent for a moment then shrugged. "Yeah, maybe."

"I'll get them in a moment. Meanwhile, Jackson, I think you need to talk to Olivia. She did not strike me as someone who took a… parochial approach to sexuality. I'm not anxious to discuss Evan's past sex life with her, but we need an ally in the Taggert camp and I think she will have some insight."

"Maybe you should do it," suggested Aiden. "Girl-to-girl kind of thing."

Dominique nodded. "Ordinarily, I would agree. However, if we pull this off, Olivia and Evan will be back together. And it is my distinct impression that Evan would be a bit distressed that I knew about his club thing."

"Mm," said Jackson, nodding.

"That doesn't deal with the plane crash situation," said Aiden.

"I'm also working on that," said Jackson. "Evan found two of Randall's old hard drives from DevEntier, but they're encrypted. I'm having my people work on them. It could be something or there may be absolutely nothing."

"It would be better if there were nothing," said Dominique. "What are we going to learn that would help any of us?"

"It might be nothing. It might be something. Whatever it is, we'll know where we stand once and for all," said Jackson. "We'll tackle Eleanor on that topic once I can get Olivia and Evan sorted."

"And we're just going to never mention the murdering her husband thing?" asked Dominique, looking at both of them.

"You seem happy enough to have Jackson put a bullet in Granger," said Aiden. "You're going to quibble over our horrible grandfather?"

"Well, I don't mind it. I was just thinking maybe… therapy or something? I don't know. It seems like the kind of thing that other people care about."

Jackson choked on a surprised laugh. "And Pete wonders why I still have cravings for cigarettes. You two are enough to drive me to bad habits."

"Sorry," said Dominique, looking genuinely sympathetic. "We don't mean to."

Aiden sighed and scrubbed his hand through his hair. "I can't believe Grandma did this. And even if we fix it… What's to stop her from doing it again?"

"Nothing," said Jackson.

"Well," said Dominique, sounding calm, "then we are going to have to explain it to her."

"Agreed," said Jackson. "But not until I've got the pictures in hand. We can't give her a chance to fight back."

Olivia – Baking

Olivia stared at the wall and waited for the cookies to finish baking.

One week.

She kept waiting to cry. Because Evan had broken up with her. He'd been very clear about that. And that ought to result in tears. But instead, she kept baking and obsessively re-running the conversation in her head. It hadn't been much of a conversation, more of a soliloquy. She couldn't figure out what the hell had happened.

He'd stood in the hall. His arms down at his sides, his face ashen, and he'd said he couldn't see her anymore. And she hadn't said anything because she kept waiting for him to say something that would make that statement make sense. She'd literally blurted that out at him.

"That makes no sense, Evan."

His hands had twitched like he wanted to reach out for her. But his mouth had just repeated its nonsense. It was as if all the parts didn't match up. Like she'd forgotten to carry the one or cross-multiply or something. So she went over it again. Trying to figure out where it had gone wrong.

"You love me, Evan."

He'd stared at a point above her head and said, "No. I lied."

That had made her cry at the time. Why would he say something so hurtful? He couldn't just say that it wasn't her, it was him, or whatever bullshit, people said these days. He had to say that?

Then he'd left. He'd turned around and walked away. She'd

followed him to the elevator and stared at him as he got in. She probably looked like a lost dog, but at the time, all she could think was: *that makes no sense.*

Logically, it did *not* work. She went over it again, looking for more nuance. She was starting to hate herself for obsessing. She kept trying to solve it like an equation, to make the conversation come up with a different answer. She looked down at her hands. They weren't doing anything. They needed to be doing something. Did she have yarn somewhere? She could try knitting.

Sooner or later, she was going to realize that there was only one answer to the equation. She'd probably cry then.

Her phone chirped with a text message. Her grandmother had started texting recently. There had been invitations to come home for a visit. And a job listing in Atlanta that was actually applicable to her field.

Olivia ignored the phone and flipped on the TV. It was on PBS, of course. A woman was talking to the camera. Olivia could tell the woman was an expert in her field because she was horribly dressed in a jolly fleece vest. Nerds who didn't have an Evan could never get dressed appropriately. The caption said the woman was an Occupational Therapist.

"Body language is the second form of communication that humans use to express their wants and emotions. As with speech, the autistic child has difficulty, or no skill at all, deciphering what a person is saying with facial expressions or body language. If you want someone to come closer you wave to them. If you want somebody to know you're angry, you usually have a scowl on your face. If you are sad or happy, you can see the emotion in your facial expression and how you move your body. We work with high-functioning autistic individuals to get them to recognize these cues. The interesting thing is that once they reach a level of proficiency, they frequently become frustrated. They find that the body cues of happy, angry, sad, don't necessarily match up with the verbal cues. Like this."

The woman frowned heavily. "I'm very happy." She relaxed her face. "Other cues, like crossing your arms, standing too far away, or turning away from someone—those are blocking signals, no matter what words are coming out of their mouth. It can be very confusing for those on the spectrum to be getting these mixed signals. Or… basically… lies."

Olivia stood up with an *eep* of excitement and took a step toward the door.

Evan had been lying. He loved her. His body said so. No matter what his stupid mouth said.

She stopped, breathing heavily. Then she sat back down again. Why?

Why had he been lying? What could make him do that?

The woman on TV was still talking, and impatiently, Olivia turned off the TV. She could look up the program later. She should also probably make another donation to PBS. Their programing *did* enrich her life.

She couldn't just go ask him. Could she? If he'd wanted her to know the truth, he would have just said it the first time.

She looked at the kitchen table that contained a cake, two pies, and the first sheet of cookies. Possibly run a bake sale at work and do a matching donation?

Why, why, why, why, why. Why would Evan do that?

There was a knock on the door and Olivia jumped in surprise. She checked the peephole and saw a dark-haired man in a suit.

Jehovah's Witness?

She did enjoy arguing sometimes, but she didn't have time to convert Jehovah's Witnesses today.

She opened the door and found herself staring into the wary

blue eyes of someone who did not look like a Jehovah's Witness. He looked… Evan-ish. Why was that? Was his suit expensive? She could never tell. She checked his shoes. Those were expensive. Maybe that was it.

"Dr. West?"

"Yes."

"I'm…" he glanced down the hall at Mrs. Roberson who was eyeing them from her door. "Jackson Deveraux." He looked at Mrs. Roberson again, clearly uncomfortable.

"It's my boyfriend's cousin, Mrs. Roberson," Olivia yelled. "You can go put that in your log."

Mrs. Roberson sniffed and went into her apartment with an air of injured dignity. Olivia looked back at Jackson. "She thinks she's the neighborhood watch. Would you like to come in?"

"Yes," said Jackson. "Thank you."

He entered the apartment and she was aware that he was scrutinizing everything. "I would like to discuss Evan," he said, still eyeing the table full of baked goods.

"OK," said Olivia. "Would you like to discuss what all ya'll did to make him break up with me?"

He hesitated, looking startled. "Yes," he said.

"OK," said Olivia.

He stared at her.

"That was your cue to start talking," she added.

"Did you and Evan ever discuss your grandfather?"

"Weird place to start. Um, sure."

"So Evan knew?"

"Knew what?"

They stared at each other. Jackson itched his ear. "Did Evan know that your grandfather is Ralph Taggert?"

"Well, sure…" Olivia trailed off. She distinctly remembered

turning off the TV the last time a clip of her grandfather had been playing. She hadn't wanted Evan to know that she was related to Ralph Taggert. "No, he didn't."

"And did you ever mention Evan's name to your grandfather?"

"I think… just his first name," said Olivia.

Jackson nodded. "Did Evan ever mention our grandmother?"

"Sure." Olivia kept waiting for this to go somewhere. Jackson looked as if he was waiting for her to get whatever coded message he was trying to send.

"Specifically that she is Eleanor Deveraux, the senator?"

Olivia closed her eyes, blinded by realization. "Oh, shit on a shingle. Your grandmother is Evil Eleanor?"

"That may be taking it a bit far," said Jackson, looking a little offended as she did a frustration-based lap around the couch.

"That's just what he calls her. Oh, for the love of mercy. Please tell me this isn't why Evan broke up? Because I swear to God, I'm sorry my grandfather's an asshole, but there's nothing I can do about it. It is not my fault."

Jackson grinned in a way that was disturbingly Evan-like. "No. At least, not exactly."

He glanced down at the table of cookies again.

"I'm sorry. Where are my manners? Would you care for a cookie?" She held up the plate of cookies and he took one. The alarm went off for batch number two and Olivia went into the kitchen.

"Do you think there's any way your grandfather knew you were dating Evan?" asked Jackson as she shoveled cookies onto the cooling rack. "This is a really good cookie."

"Thank you," she said, smiling at him. "And no, I don't see how. My brother is, I think, the only one who knows his last name and he didn't know it until last week when Evan ordered wine."

"Right," said Jackson. "Tyler. In Washington State."

"Yes," said Olivia, eyeing Jackson. He seemed overly familiar with Tyler's location. Olivia pondered the direction of Jackson's questions. He was angling at something, but what? It was like trying to work out the problem from the answers. "Are you saying Pops had something to do with this?" she asked, reaching for the mixing bowl and starting to load more dough onto the tray.

Jackson looked like he was trying to swallow the cookie with a dry mouth. She opened the fridge and poured him a glass of iced tea. He looked at the tea and smiled.

"Thank you," he said, taking a sip. "Um, yes. I'm sorry. This next part is awkward and I'm not sure where to start."

"Well, you'd better just say it, then. No sense in going the long way when you can cut straight through the field."

"Your grandfather sent us pictures of Evan, and he threatened to release those photos to the press. He wanted Evan to break up with you and my grandmother to drop her healthcare bill."

Olivia picked up the cake and hurled it against the wall. It hit with a splat and an explosion of crumbs. She realized that she was probably going to regret that later. And now there was an awkward point where her guest knew that she had icing on the carpet. Olivia decided to pretend it wasn't there. She turned to Jackson with a smile. "Pictures, you say?"

Jackson looked from where the cake was slowly sliding down the wall and back to Olivia. "Pictures from several years ago, that paint him in a less-than-flattering light." Jackson took a hasty gulp of tea.

She stared at him, trying to read the subtext. What had Evan been doing several years ago that was less than flattering?

"Oh! They're from that damn club, aren't they?"

"Yes," said Jackson, looking both relieved and a little startled.

"Let me see them," said Olivia, wiping her hands on a tea towel.

"I'm not sure…" said Jackson. Olivia held out an impatient hand. Jackson reluctantly took an envelope out of his jacket. Olivia suddenly realized that she was remiss in her hostessing duties.

"Jackson, honey, take your coat off and sit," she said. "It's a thousand degrees in here with all the baking I've been doing." She took the envelope over to the couch and opened it. The photos were not particularly pleasant, but they didn't show any of his bits, which was a relief. He did not look happy, or even particularly turned on, which was also nice. The girl in the photo looked like she was having a very good time, which Olivia did not particularly care for. She stared at the photos and then at Jackson. He was putting his coat on the back of the kitchen chair and looking like he was thinking about another cookie.

Olivia stood up and held up the photo. Jackson looked uncomfortable as she looked from him to the photo. Olivia moved the photo trying to line up the angle and distance from which it had been taken. She took a step closer and then another. She frowned at Jackson.

"It's a body cam. It's got to be. No one holds a camera, here." She pointed to the center of her chest. "See, part of Evan's head is cut off in this one." She looked back at the photo. "And this one is from a different distance, but the same angle. That means it was a third person in the room."

She pondered what she knew of Evan and Fetish.

"I'm going to kill her," she said at last.

"Kill who?"

"Leona Meade. Evan's ex… whatever. We ran into her last month at a party. She was very upset that I would no longer let

Evan come out to play, if you take my meaning. I bet these are her photos."

Jackson smiled at her. "That's very useful, thank you."

"But did Evan really cave to this? I mean it's embarrassing, and I would not care at all for this dirty laundry being aired, but…" she shrugged. "Pops shouldn't be allowed to get away with this."

Jackson's expression changed to pained embarrassment. "No. He caved to our grandmother. When she received the photos, she did something that… Evan is not pleased about but he knows enough to take her seriously."

"What did she do?" she demanded.

"Don't throw the pie," said Jackson. "But she made a second set of photos. She told Evan that if he did not break up with you, she would release these." He reached into his pocket and handed her another photo—it looked similar to the first, but this time the girl in the photo was Olivia.

"Oh!" exclaimed Olivia, startled. "Well, that's not something you see every day."

"No," said Jackson. "I suppose not."

"So essentially he's being blackmailed into going along with blackmail because he doesn't want to besmirch my good name?"

"Um, yes," said Jackson. "That would be the basic gist."

"Well, that's very sweet of him, but I don't think we can let him do that."

"I can control the Eleanor half of the equation," said Jackson. "But the Ralph Taggert side… I was hoping you could help with that."

"Oh," said Olivia. She thought about her mother and her sister and her brother. They had all worked out plans around the idea that they should get out and away from Ralph Taggert. Because Ralph

Taggert was a powerful man, a bully, and a terrifying force. Who could win against someone like Ralph Taggert?

But what had Evan said?

You have all the power. You have what he wants and he has no leverage to make you do it.

Well, this time Pops had found the leverage to make her do what he wanted.

A man could move a mountain with the right leverage. The thing that people didn't remember about leverage was that it could go both ways. Sometimes a mountain could move a man.

"Yes," said Olivia, "I will."

Evan – Checkboxes

"Too much partying?" asked Devonte, looming over him on Monday morning.

Evan looked up and tried to remember how to talk.

"Move your bag," ordered Devonte. Evan did as he was told and Devonte sat down. "You said a week. It's been a month. I was starting to get worried your family had kidnapped you or something."

Evan laughed, then stopped, and shook his head.

"You doing OK, man?"

"No," said Evan. "Not really."

Devonte stared at him appraisingly. "But you're going to go to work?"

Evan pulled himself together and tried to remember how to be a Deveraux. "What else would I do?" He managed to nail the Evan Deveraux tone just right: two parts condescension, one part arrogance.

"Sure," said Devonte. "Because that's what you do when shit goes in the shitter. Check the boxes and keep moving."

Evan stared at him in frustration. "Can you not be sympathetic right now?" he asked.

"Sure," said Devonte with a shrug. "We can just sit here."

Evan's shoulders sagged and he looked out the window into the dark of the tunnel. Olivia was there too, just like when he closed his eyes. Her green eyes big, confused, and hurt. At stop four they both got up to make room for Lucinda and her kids.

"See you tomorrow," said Devonte as Evan got off. Evan almost turned but didn't. He just nodded and kept moving.

Work was eight hours of torture. At the end, he took a cab home.

"Hello, Evan," said Isabelle Elliot as he entered the building. She was wearing yoga pants that were more mesh and straps than fabric.

"Go away, Isabelle," said Evan. "I don't like you."

She made a shocked noise and stopped dead in her tracks. He kept walking and made it to the elevator before she recovered. Once inside, he dropped his bag and coat on the floor and took a bottle of scotch into the living room. Everywhere he looked was something attached to a memory of Olivia. Finally, he just poured scotch down himself and tried to fall asleep on the couch.

On Tuesday after work, Dominique found him in front of his building, trying to work up the courage to go inside.

"Let's go get dinner," she said. He'd gone, but he didn't eat anything. Then she'd taken him over to Aiden's. He'd passed out on Aiden's couch.

On Wednesday, he'd borrowed Aiden's clothes and gone to work because that's what you did when shit went in the shitter.

Jackson picked him up after work and took him to an appointment with his therapist that he hadn't made. Dr. Nicholas helped. She always did. But all the same, he'd gone home and drank until he'd passed out on his couch.

Thursday he was back on the train with Devonte.

"You going to make it, man?" asked Devonte when Evan had swayed the wrong direction from the train and bumped into him.

"Yes," said Evan. "There isn't any other answer."

Olivia loved him and there couldn't be another answer.

And then he'd made it all the way to Friday. Saturday, he thought would be a problem, so he went back to Aiden's.

"Did you talk to Jackson?" whispered Dominique.

"Yes," said Aiden.

Evan stared at the upholstery of Aiden's couch and pretended to be asleep. He wanted to be asleep. If he was asleep then he wouldn't be awake. When he was awake he had to think about things. Aiden had offered him a guest room, but Evan thought that was too alone, so he'd just gone back to the couch.

"Did he say anything?" demanded Dominique.

"Just that he was working on it and to get Evan there on Sunday."

Evan thought about rolling over and asking what Jackson was working on. There wasn't anything to work on. Eleanor had made that pretty clear.

"He didn't say anything else?" asked Dominique, sounding impatient.

"You know how cagey he is, and I didn't want to ask with Evan in the room."

"Will Evan even want to go on Sunday?" asked Dominique.

"Right now, Evan doesn't *want* anything," said Aiden. "I think it will be OK as long as we're with him. I cannot believe she did this."

"You keep saying that," said Dominique. "I can't figure out why not. It's got Eleanor Deveraux written all over it."

"Yes, but she's not supposed to do that to *us*!"

"I think she does it to anyone she thinks is a threat."

"Since when is Evan a threat?"

"Well," Dominique hesitated, and Evan flinched. "He kind of used to be, didn't he?"

"Yes, OK, he was not particularly good to be around growing up. But you can't tell me hasn't changed," said Aiden.

"Don't whitewash, Aiden," commanded Dominique, and Evan heard the snarl in her voice. "I love him, but he was abusive."

Aiden was silent for a long moment. "Sorry. Yeah, he was. I know. But he's not... He's better now, right?"

"Yes," said Dominique. "He is. He's genuinely better. And Grandma needs to recognize that."

"I don't think she's going to," said Aiden. "I want her to, but... well... I'm just saying."

Evan wanted to roll over and agree with Aiden. He appreciated Dominique's faith in him, but Aiden was right: Grandma wasn't going to change her mind. He closed his eyes and willed himself back to sleep.

Olivia – The Taggert's

"Olivia," said her grandmother as she came out of the office with Jackson in tow, "I don't know what you're doing, but I don't think you're supposed to be doing it."

"Go back to your coffee and stories, Gran," said Olivia. "And I'll bring you a nice piece of pie."

Olivia and her grandmother stared at each other.

"Pops will be home soon," said Gran.

"I'm counting on it," said Olivia. "I need to talk to him."

That seemed to settle the matter for Gran. "All right then." She turned and went back into the den where her bourbon-laced coffee sat next to her ever-growing afghan.

Olivia went into the kitchen and stared down at the pie she'd brought from home. Jackson had flown her to Georgia in a private jet. That was convenient. Rich people really did have the best stuff.

It was mostly dark in the kitchen, just the light on over the stove. She had spent many evenings in this kitchen. She didn't need the lights on to know where everything was.

"Are you going to be OK with this?" asked Jackson, going over to look out the window.

"We'll find out," said Olivia.

"I'm sorry," said Jackson.

"For what?" she asked.

"Making you do this, I guess," he said.

"You're not making me do anything," said Olivia. "This has been coming for a while. You're just the catalyst. Besides," she said, looking up at him with a smile, "Evan's worth it."

"I'm not sure he agrees with you," said Jackson.

"I know," she agreed. "He's very kind-hearted toward everyone but himself."

Jackson laughed. "Ninety-nine percent of the world would not agree with you."

"I know," agreed Olivia again. "He goes a long way to make sure no one knows."

"All the Deveraux's do it. They keep the shields way, way up," said Jackson, sounding tired.

"Self-defense," said Olivia, and Jackson nodded.

"Car in the driveway," he said.

"Let me do the talking," said Olivia. "Don't pitch in unless I ask for it."

He nodded his understanding and leaned against the wall arms folded. She went to the oven and turned it on. Then she went back to the table and took the lid off the pie container.

The door opened and Pops stood a long moment in the doorway. Olivia didn't need to look up to know that he'd be wearing dark suit pants with suspenders and a white and blue pinstripe shirt covering the expanse of his belly.

"Well, good evening Olivia Rose," he said. "This is a surprise."

"Is it? I cannot imagine why," said Olivia with a smile. "Would you care for a piece of pie, Pops? I'm just putting some together for Gran."

"Well, now I think I would like that," he said. "I do miss all the baking you used to do."

"Oh yes, I did use to bake a lot, didn't I? Do you remember that cake I did for mama's funeral? My, that was grandiose."

He shifted uncomfortably. "It was very nice. I'm sure she would have liked it."

"No, I don't think so," said Olivia. "She hated fondant. But she might have thought it was pretty."

Ralph was silent as he settled himself at the table. Olivia cut two slices of apple pie and put them on a plate.

"You want a drink, Pops?"

"Well, I wouldn't mind some tea," he said.

"Oh, I meant a real drink," said Olivia.

"Olivia, you know I don't keep liquor in this house," said Ralph sternly.

"Jackson, be a love. Reach up there behind the *Joy of Cooking* and pull down the bourbon for me, will you?" Jackson did as he was asked as Olivia slid the pie slices into the oven. He set the half-empty bottle down on the table with a soft, but judgmental thump then retreated to the wall.

"You want to explain to me what he's doing here?" demanded Ralph, but with only half a growl. She could tell that he was trying to figure out what she was up to.

"Don't worry about him," said Olivia, going to the cupboard and pulling out two glasses.

"I am worried about him. You've brought a damn Deveraux into my house. Now, you answer the question for me, young lady—what's he doing here?" He added more bite this time. She set the glasses down on the table and opened the bottle.

"A little bit of fetch, a little bit of carry, a little bit of holding up the wall. Don't worry about him." She smiled at Ralph and poured out a measure into each glass. "Ice cubes or neat?"

"Ice," he said, glaring at her.

She dropped the cubes into the glasses and sat down across from him. "Well, Pops," she said, taking a sip, "you've been a busy boy."

"I don't know what you mean," he said, sitting back and adjusting his suspenders.

"Blackmail. It takes a while to arrange. All that moving of cash around and whatnot. How did Leona find you by the way?"

"How does anyone find anyone these days?" His smile was warm, but his eyes were cold, as they assessed her. She smiled at him and he sighed gustily, shaking his head. "I suppose he told you about it. He shouldn't have done that. And I suppose you're mad. But Olivia Rose, you've got to listen to me now, it's for your own good."

"Hm. We seem to have different ideas of what's good for me."

"Olivia Rose, Evan Deveraux, he's a dangerous man."

"Yes, he is," said Olivia, and Pops stopped mid-breath. "Do you know I once saw him kick a man in the face? He punched him first, knocked him down, kicked him in the face, and then stepped over him like he wasn't even there."

Against the wall, Jackson made a soft movement that Olivia thought might have been surprise.

"There was a fellow hanging onto me at the time. Evan did *not* care for that," she said, by way of explanation. "I have to tell you, it was one of the sexiest things I've ever seen."

"I—" said Pops and then stopped and shook his head. She could tell he didn't know what to do with any of the information she'd just forced into his brain. "Well, that is as may be, but what I meant was that Evan Deveraux is dangerous to *you*. You may not know this, but he's got some nasty habits. I'm sure he didn't show you these photos, but if I showed them to you, you would be shocked."

"I saw them," said Olivia, taking another sip. She felt the bourbon leave a trail of warmth down her throat. "I suppose they were shocking. Although, I thought he looked a little bored in them, to tell the truth."

"He didn't show them to you," said Pops, smiling at her knowingly. "You know he didn't."

"No, he didn't. I don't suppose he would have liked that. But Jackson did. And it's a good thing for you he did."

"A good thing for *me*?" asked Pops, sitting back, his expression surprised and wary.

"Oh, indeed, yes, Pops. A very good thing for you. I was able to come down here and take them off your computer and delete your emails. Now no one will know that you tried to do such a bad thing."

She smiled at him and went to the oven. "Do you want ice cream on your pie?" she asked, pulling on the oven mitts.

"No, no ice cream," said Pops, smiling wolfishly. "Olivia Rose, I appreciate your spunk, but I've got those pictures on a thumb drive."

"I'm sure that you do," said Olivia. She set the plate down and lifted the slice of pie carefully onto a cool plate. "Cool whip?" He nodded his head and she dutifully spooned some out of the blue tub. "But you're going to give it to me."

"No, I most certainly am not. And your wall sitter there had better not get any fancy ideas either."

She set the plate down in front of him. "I do not know how you get ahead in politics, Pops. Ya slow."

For the first time, he looked uncertain. "Now," she said going back to the oven and putting her grandmother's pie on a cool plate, "I do not care if you and Eleanor Deveraux fist-fight it out on the senate floor. I would say that it is probably not in your best interest, but you're welcome to go at it as far as I'm concerned. But Evan Deveraux is mine. If you lift a finger in his direction, you're going to regret it."

"Oh, and how are you going to accomplish that?" demanded Pops, booming out a jovial laugh.

She waited until he was done. Waited until he was silent and looking at her. "I know where you keep the bourbon, Pops."

His eyes flicked to the bottle on the table.

"I know where you keep *all* the bourbon."

"Olivia Rose," he said uncomfortably, his voice carrying just the hint of a whine, "what are you doing? This isn't like you. You're a good girl. Stop behaving like this."

"You're going to give me that thumb drive," said Olivia, ignoring his commentary. "And you're going to keep your damn mouth shut. You're a busy man, Pops, and sometimes you just get ahead of yourself. Think of this as me keeping you out of trouble."

He stared at her, his eyes glittering in the light from the stove, the shadows carving his face into jowly jack-o-lantern shapes. Finally, he picked up his glass and drank it down.

"I keep my mouth shut, and you do the same?" he asked.

"That is the general idea," said Olivia. He lifted his briefcase onto the table and opened it. He produced a flash drive and slid it across the table to her.

"That's a good boy," said Olivia. "Now, be a lamb and go take Grams her pie. I'm sure she'll be happy to see you."

He accepted the plate and glared at Jackson. "Get him out of here, Olivia Rose. I won't have any Deverauxes in this house. And I think, after tonight, you'd better not come back either."

"See you at your funeral then," said Olivia.

His eyes flicked back to her, hard and angry.

"I'll bake you a real nice cake."

"I'll just bet you will," he said and walked out of the kitchen.

Evan – Deveraux House

"Oh, for fucks sake, Grandma!" snapped Dominique.

Evan sat on the couch between Aiden and Dominique. He had not wanted to come to Sunday dinner. He had not wanted to go into Deveraux House. He hadn't wanted to see Eleanor. He hadn't wanted any of it. But Aiden and Dominique had pushed and pushed and he hadn't had the energy to fight. And now they were in the study and they hadn't left him once. It was as if he had his own bodyguards.

Eleanor had been angry about it. He could see it in the way her eyes flicked between the cousins and the tightness of her mouth.

"Do you have to use that kind of language?" said Eleanor. "Your mother never did."

"Why do you think she does it?" muttered Aiden.

Evan abruptly stood up and went to the bar. He wasn't even sure what they were arguing about. He hadn't been following the conversation.

"I have some more inappropriate language," said Dominique. "Want to hear it?"

"No, I do not," said Eleanor crisply.

"Well, why should I care what you want?" demanded Dominique. "You don't seem to care about what we want. You certainly don't care about what Evan wants."

Evan found his eyes going from family member to family member. He felt disoriented and confused. Everything was off. He couldn't understand what he'd done. Was this his fault? His grandmother wasn't like this. Aiden and Dominique weren't like this. He looked again at his cousins. Sweet, ridiculous Aiden was wearing a bitter, fuming expression that Evan felt intimately familiar with—he'd worn it often enough himself. Light-hearted Dominique was eyeing Eleanor with a hard stare, a look he'd only ever seen coming *from* Eleanor.

"Don't be ridiculous, Dominique," snapped Eleanor. "Stop pretending to like Evan. You know what kind of person he is. Don't be so naïve to think that love conquers all and he'll suddenly become someone different."

"Lucinda Ramierz," said Aiden. "Every Monday Evan saves a seat for a woman with two kids who he's never even talked to. That's who Evan is."

"Comic book and a coke," said Dominique. "Dad used to buy Aiden a comic book and a coke on his birthday and now Evan does it."

"I thought that was you," said Aiden looking surprised.

"That's who Evan is," said Dominique smugly.

"Heh," said Aiden. "Genevieve Foundation."

"What?" Eleanor was looking from Aiden to Dominique in confusion.

"Dominique wanted to start that scholarship foundation in mom's name, but you shot her down. We didn't have any money of our own, but Evan had just inherited, so he wrote me a check and said to say it came from me."

"It was a foolish idea," said Eleanor dismissively. "We already have a Deveraux giving fund."

"It seemed like a good idea," said Evan weakly. "Why should we always have to be remembered as Deverauxes?"

"You're always a Deveraux," sneered Eleanor, and Evan felt like she'd slapped him.

"I can't," said Evan, backing up and looking at Aiden and Dominique in desperation. "I can't do this. It's all wrong and I can't be here."

He stumbled out into the hall.

"Ah, Mr. Deveraux," said Theo. "Did you want to be at the head of the table? Or should I put in another leaf?"

"What?" asked Evan.

"Mr. Jackson just phoned and said he was bringing a guest."

Evan tried to focus. "No, it will be five. I'm not staying."

"You will stay, Evan Deveraux," said his grandmother, coming out of the study.

"Alexander," Evan blurted out.

"What?"

"If you're mad, you're supposed to use the full name."

Eleanor marched forward and grabbed him by the arm, pulling him into the dining room. "We do not discuss family business in front of the staff," she said, shutting the door behind her. He blinked in surprise. He didn't think he'd ever heard Theo referred to as staff. "You will stay. You will stay and do as you're told."

The dining room doors slammed open. "Middle names, Ev?" asked Dominique. "That's how it's done?"

"That's what Olivia says."

"Eleanor Madeline Hicks Deveraux," said Dominique, "you are going to stop treating Evan like this."

"Dominique's right, Grandma," said Aiden, coming in after Dominique. "It's got to stop. Makes dinners awkward, and I don't like wanting to kick my Grandma in the shins."

Evan barked out a laugh and walked away from his grandmother. He stood at one end of the table and looked at the three of them. What was he supposed to do? His therapist would say talk. Share feelings. That didn't seem like a Deveraux thing to do.

He didn't even know how to start. Everyone was so angry. He just didn't understand why Eleanor was so angry at him.

"Aiden, Dominique, you're being childish. I decide what's best for this family. I always have and I won't have you questioning me." Eleanor was using her mother-knows-best voice.

"And I won't have you treating Evan like this," hissed Dominique, who clearly didn't like Eleanor's tone any better than Evan.

"I'll treat O—Evan however I want!" barked Eleanor.

Silence fell in the dining room. They all heard the tell-tale wrong vowel sound in front of his name and Evan felt a click of recognition. Eleanor wasn't angry at him. She was scared. And Eleanor Deveraux did not get scared, she got even.

"You almost slipped, Grandma," said Evan, standing up straighter. "Want to try that again?"

"Stop being childish," snapped Eleanor.

"Childish? You want childish?" demanded Dominique. She yanked open the glass case on the far side of the table. It housed the antique Wedgewood tea set.

"What are you doing?" Eleanor took a step forward.

"Who is he, Grandma?" yelled Dominique.

"This is ridiculous!"

Dominique dropped a cup on the floor. The white and blue pieces burst outward in a starburst on the floor. Evan stared at her in shock.

"Who is he?"

Eleanor was silent and Dominique threw two more cups on the floor.

"Answer the question!" Dominique swept an entire armful onto the floor.

"Genevieve! Stop that, this instant!"

Dominique grabbed the last cup and hurled it at the wall

behind Eleanor. "I'm not Genevieve!" Dominique screamed, and Eleanor stared at her in horror. "And he's not Owen," Dominique gasped, breathing hard.

"Well," said Aiden, "as long as we're breaking things. Here's what I want to break." He grabbed the portrait of Henry off the wall and put it down on the floor, then he kicked it, his foot splintering through the braces on the back and sailing through Henry's chin.

Theo appeared in the open doorway. "Mr. Jackson and Dr. Olivia West."

Aiden looked up one foot stuck through the painting, and Dominique paused, a plate in one hand. Eleanor and Evan stared at the new arrivals from opposite ends of the table.

Evan burst out laughing. He couldn't stop. He clutched the edge of the table, nearly doubling over. He tried to straighten up, almost made it, and then laughed again.

"You OK, there, sugar?" asked Olivia, looking doubtful. "Need to take a lap and walk it off?"

"No, no, I've got this." He stared into the light fixture, took a deep breath, and looked back at Olivia. God, she was beautiful. "Olivia, have you met my cousin Aiden? He currently has his foot stuck in my grandfather."

"Would you like some help with that?" asked Olivia, looking with concern at Aiden.

"Yes," Aiden said, "but maybe just from Jackson?"

"I got you," said Jackson, coming around Olivia, to help remove Henry Deveraux's face from Aiden's foot. There was a tricky moment of balance and then Aiden was extricated.

Evan took a deep breath. He knew what the problem was now and it was a problem he'd spent several years working on. It was probably the only one of his grandmother's problems that he actually could fix. He smiled at Olivia. She looked worried.

"Theo," said Evan, pointing to the painting, as Jackson freed it, "could you dispose of that for us?"

Theo glanced at Eleanor and then back at Evan. "Yes, Mr. Deveraux. I'd be happy to."

"And also the one in the study, I think. Aiden says it gives him gas."

"Yes, Mr. Deveraux," said Theo, taking the painting from Jackson. Then he looked around in disapproval. "The young mister and miss have made a mess. Dinner will be delayed while it is cleaned."

"Of course," said Evan. "We'll be in the library."

"Very good, sir," said Theo.

Evan stepped around the table and offered his arm to Olivia. "It was so nice of you to join us for dinner."

"Evan," said Eleanor, warningly, "I won't have Taggerts in this house."

"She's a West, Grandma," said Evan, as he led the way out of the room.

"Hi," he said, smiling at her as they walked across the hall.

"Hi," Olivia said, smiling back.

"I have had a terrible week," he said.

"Well, mine wasn't very pleasant either," she said. "My boyfriend tried to break up with me! Can you imagine?"

"No," said Evan. "What an idiot." He opened the door to the library and flipped on the light.

"I like this room," said Aiden, coming in behind them. "Why do we never come in here?"

"Uh…" said Dominique and jerked her thumb at the wedding photo of their grandparents on the wall.

"It's like he's everywhere," complained Aiden.

"I've got this one," said Jackson, he hooked a chair with one hand and climbed up on it, to take the photo off the wall. "Theo! We've got another one! I'm putting it in the hall!"

"Right you are, Mr. Jackson," said Theo peering from the dining room. "I'll collect it in a minute."

Eleanor entered last and eyed the photo, but didn't comment.

"Do we have booze in this room?" asked Aiden, looking around.

"We have booze in every room," said Dominique. "It's Deveraux House."

"The bar is over here pretending to be a bookcase," said Jackson, going behind what appeared to be a low bookcase in front of the window. "I'm pouring. Who wants what? Ev, Olivia Rose, what's your pleasure?"

"Just water, please," said Evan, sitting down on a yellow brocade couch that looked as though it dated from the 1870s. Olivia sat down next to him.

"Oh, I don't know, Jackson," said Olivia, leaning into him as he put his arm around her shoulders. "I don't think I need anything."

"No bourbon?" asked Jackson, his eyes twinkling.

"Don't get smart," said Olivia.

Evan looked from Olivia to Jackson. They had been up to something.

"Stop it!" barked Eleanor, coming in after them. "Stop it, all of you. I will not stand for this!"

"Yes, you will," said Jackson, pouring scotch out into glasses on the bar top.

There was silence in the room.

"Olivia and I collected the photos that Ralph Taggert had in his possession," said Jackson, putting the thumb drive on the bar next to the glasses. "Now, where are yours? Hand them over."

"I beg your pardon?" asked Eleanor, raising an eyebrow.

"I've already been to your Photoshop friend and collected them off his hard drive. Where are the originals? The one's you got from Leona Meade?"

"I don't know what you're talking about," said Eleanor. It was almost flawless, but Evan had seen her do it one too many times to be fooled.

"Leona Meade hates Evan. If she was going to blackmail someone, she'd come to you first," said Jackson. "She wouldn't go to Taggert. How would she know to approach Taggert unless someone told her? Unless *you* told her."

The silence in the room stretched out to an unbearable length.

"That is unacceptable, Grandma," said Dominique quietly, and Evan heard the hard note that so frequently defined Eleanor's speech.

"Grandma," said Aiden, "why would you do that?"

"It's for the best," said Eleanor. "Don't question me."

"I will question you," said Aiden, sounding unexpectedly firm. "Why did you do that?"

"I've told you," snapped Eleanor, looking around the circle of her grandchildren, desperation creeping into her tone. "He's a Deveraux. He's not ever going to…"

They stared at her, waiting for her to finish.

"She thinks he'll beat me," said Olivia, finally filling in the blank.

"Like Henry did to her," said Dominique.

"Like Owen did to Evan," said Olivia.

Eleanor rounded on Olivia, but Jackson stepped in front of her, blocking her view.

"Or maybe it's because Evan called the FAA," he said, handing Eleanor a drink. Eleanor looked like she didn't know what to do with either the statement or the drink. Jackson kept moving, heading back to the bar.

"What's wrong with looking into the plane crash, Grandma?" asked Aiden, sounding oddly older. Evan realized that it was the tone that Aiden usually reserved for court.

Eleanor rounded on Aiden. "Leave the plane crash alone!" she snapped. "It has nothing to do with anything."

"Really?" asked Dominique. "Then why did someone from the FAA call you after Evan put in the public records request?"

Eleanor turned to Jackson angrily. "What did you do?" she snarled.

"What you have always asked that I do," said Jackson. "I protected my family. Answer their questions."

"You shouldn't have to think about the plane crash," said Eleanor. "I don't want you thinking about it."

"Three days before they all went on vacation, Randall emailed Genevieve," said Evan. "He said they needed to talk."

"Where did you find out about that?" demanded Eleanor, angrily. "It has nothing to do with anything. Randall wanted to talk about Genevieve's DevEntier shares. It doesn't mean anything."

"So you knew about it?" asked Aiden. "Why didn't you mention it to us before?"

Eleanor spun again, trying to focus on Aiden as he walked around the room. Dominique had moved to stand by the window. Evan could see Eleanor's increasing frustration as she couldn't get his cousins to hold still. It was like fighting a bee swarm. He could also see that his cousins were doing it on purpose.

"There was nothing to mention," snapped Eleanor, finally looking at the drink in her hand and taking a gulp.

"Or maybe they wanted to talk to her about Henry," said Jackson.

"Get out," said Eleanor. She took an angry step toward Jackson. "We don't talk about him. Get out. Get out, right now."

"No, Grandma," said Evan softly. "No, we have to talk about Henry."

Eleanor's hands were shaking.

"They knew, Grandma," said Evan. He thought it was probably the cruelest moment of his life, and he took his arm from around Olivia's shoulders. He couldn't look at her right now. She was about to know all of the family's dirty secrets, but after everything they'd put her through he thought she deserved to know the truth even if it sent her running from the room.

"Randall had Henry exhumed and ran an autopsy report," continued Evan.

Eleanor's eyes filled with tears and none of the cousins moved. They had never seen their grandmother this vulnerable.

"I had to," she gasped as if the words had been squeezed out. "I had to. He was going to make Owen… I couldn't… I couldn't… I failed them so many times. I couldn't let him."

She dropped down into the nearest chair as if her knees had given out, tears trickling down her cheeks.

"What was Henry going to do?"

"He was getting better, and the stronger he got the more he started back into all of his old tricks. He said he'd let things slide. Jack wasn't good enough for Genevieve. Randall was spending too much time in Chicago. And Owen…"

"What about Dad?" asked Evan.

"He always targeted him. Randall tried to protect him. But Henry…" Eleanor shook her head and blinked tears away. "He'd always hated that Owen wasn't… Owen wasn't ever going to be… Owen had you. He had a son. I thought that would be enough. But Henry hated Owen for being…" Eleanor couldn't even say it.

"Gay?" blurted out Dominque, as if she had just put the pieces together and Evan hung his head in exasperation.

"Nice," muttered Aiden.

"Dad was bisexual," said Evan.

"It didn't matter what he was," said Eleanor.

"Yes, it does," said Evan. "People are always trying to force bi people to pick a box to lock themselves in."

"I mean it doesn't matter what he was because he wasn't straight and Henry hated it. I know this doesn't seem like much, but you don't understand. Henry would announce these things, and then somehow he would get his way. I can't prove it, but I swear he made your mother leave. And the healthier he got the more Henry started talking about how he was going to force the family to straighten up and act right. And I just couldn't..." Eleanor stroked Evan's face. "I couldn't protect them when they were young. I was a failure as a mother. I am aware of that. But I couldn't let him ruin their lives any more than he already had. I couldn't let him..." Her voice died away to a whisper and she swallowed hard.

"Couldn't what?" asked Jackson softly. "What was Henry going to do?"

"He was going to take Evan."

"Take me?" repeated Evan, stupidly.

"Owen loved you. He really did. You should have seen his face when you were born. And the idea of letting Henry do to you what he did to Owen and Randall... I couldn't face it. It would have broken Owen. I know he was a terrible father. I know, and I'm sorry I didn't stop him from hurting you, but he really did love you."

"I know," said Evan, because he did. It was the worst dichotomy of abuse. Reconciling the broken and warped puzzle pieces of his father still frequently seemed beyond him. On many days it required him to hold two very contradictory truths in his head at once, but he wanted both of those truths to be honored.

"He did love me, but respect me by stating the truth. Dad abused me." Evan glanced up at Dominique. "Don't whitewash the past."

Dominique smiled at him and for the first time, he felt all right with her forgiveness.

"I don't want to," said Eleanor, straightening up into a semblance of her usual poise. "But I don't see the point in dwelling on it. He isn't here now and you are."

"Yes, I am," said Evan in frustration. "So why are you treating me like the enemy?"

Eleanor stared at him, clearly at a loss for words.

"Because you changed," said Olivia. "And she's afraid you'll change back. A lot of times it's easier to just have things be bad than wait for them to go bad."

Eleanor turned to Olivia, her expression furious. "I don't want you here!"

"Then you don't want me here," said Evan. "You want me to leave."

"No! I want you to…" She trailed off clutching at his arm.

"You want me to what?" demanded Evan. "Be depressed and suicidal?"

"I just want everyone to be safe," said Eleanor, sounding desperate. Her hand was clenching and unclenching on his sleeve.

"Grandma," he said, tilting his head to catch her eye, trying to catch her eye. "I love you."

She looked up at him, clearly startled.

"I understand that you're scared, but I'm not Henry. I'm not Owen. I'm Evan. Remember me? You would whisk me away from

Dad's and bring me home and we would have tea parties in the parlor and you let me wear great grand-uncle Leon's top hat."

She put her hand up to his face. "You keep getting older," she said. "And you keep looking more and more…"

"But I'm not them," said Evan. "It took me a while and a very expensive therapist to figure how not to be them, but I'm not. I didn't do anything wrong and I won't be punished for what they did."

Eleanor's bottom lip trembled. "Dominique broke all the cups. She broke your cup."

"I will buy you lots more cups," said Evan, hugging her.

"We have a top hat?" demanded Aiden. "Where? Can I get a monocle too?"

"Nice," said Dominique, sarcastically.

"I could be Mr. Peanut for Halloween." Over his grandmother's shoulder, he saw Dominique glare at Aiden, and Evan tried not to laugh. "Well, I could be," Aiden muttered.

"I'm sorry about the cups, Grandma," said Dominique, crossing the room to Evan and Eleanor, to rub Eleanor's back through Evan's hug. "I'll replace them."

"I know you're not Genevieve," said Eleanor, wiping her eyes and standing up straight. "But there are a lot of you and sometimes I get the names wrong."

"That's true," agreed Aiden, casting himself down on the other couch. "I called Jacks Nika the other day. Couldn't look less alike."

"Aiden, feet off the furniture!" snapped Eleanor.

"But, Grandma," protested Aiden, "this couch is really old!"

"Yes, it's an antique," said Dominique.

Eleanor sighed in exasperation and took another sip of the drink in her hand.

"Well," said Jackson, "in case anyone's wondering how Randall and Owen felt about matters," he reached into his jacket pocket and pulling out a sheaf of papers, "Kerschel did crack the hard drives."

"Hard drives?" Eleanor looked around the circle of cousins. "What hard drives?"

"I found some hard drives of Randall's," said Evan. "I'm sure it's not important." He looked hopefully at Jackson.

"There is nothing to indicate that Randall and Owen were planning on flying with Genevieve and Sam," said Jackson. "But I did find some things about Henry." He flipped open the pages. "Here's Randall: *The autopsy report came in. Call me. I think Mom killed Dad.* Then Owen's response: *Really? Wow. Well… That's very proactive of her. I guess someone in this family finally ballsed up and did the right thing. Not sure what else to say. Evan is getting some sort of award at school tonight. We'll be home after eight. Come over then.*"

Eleanor pursed her lips, looking surprised. Evan was startled by how relieved he felt at Owen's response.

"See?" said Aiden, turning to Dominique. "I told you. Not that horrible."

"Randall replies," said Jackson, looking amused. "*No, seriously. I think she overdosed him on his medication and caused his death. The autopsy report said those levels are unlikely to be accidental.* To which Owen responds," Jackson paused to flip pages, "*I was serious. I don't think I've ever loved her more. Too bad she didn't do it twenty years ago. I'm ordering her flowers right now. She likes gardenias, right?*"

"I hate gardenias," said Eleanor tiredly.

"Randall replies," continued Jackson. "*Toss in some roses for me. Should we tell Gen? Your call.* To which Owen says: *Why? She'd just freak. See you tonight.*"

"I remember that," said Eleanor. "They sent me a bouquet and I found it deeply suspicious. I could never figure out what they were up to."

"And that's it," said Jackson, tossing the pages on the bar.

"Are you sure?" asked Eleanor, her lips pinching tight. They could all see the desperation in her face.

"There's nothing else. I looked over the plane crash stuff. But the best that I can tell is the same thing the investigators at the time said. I think Genevieve and Sam's flight got canceled and they wanted to get home, so they called Owen and they got on the plane. And that was it. Just a plane crash. No deep dark secrets. Just an accident."

"That seems so unlike us," said Aiden.

"Aiden!" snapped Dominique.

"Well, he's right," said Evan, standing up and turning back to Olivia. He cautiously met her eye and she gave him a sympathetic smile. He sat down next to her and she promptly leaned into him. He squeezed her shoulders, feeling an overwhelming sense of relief that she was still hanging with him.

"Doing OK?" he asked. "This isn't exactly the first impression of my family I was hoping for."

"Doing great," said Olivia. "You're making my family look practically normal."

"I suppose I will have to resign," said Eleanor.

"Why?" asked Dominique, and Eleanor gestured to Olivia.

"I expect Ralph Taggert is going to make me."

"I'm not telling Pops anything," said Olivia. "None of this has anything to do with him."

"Forgive me, my dear," said Eleanor condescendingly, "but I find that unlikely. I know Ralph. Twenty minutes after you leave this house, he's going to be on your phone asking for details. Even if you don't tell him anything, it still tells him something. He pushes. He always pushes."

"Yes," agreed Olivia, "he does. But after last night, I believe that he will not be calling me. I'm no longer welcome at my grandparent's house."

Evan looked at Oliva and then at Jackson, feeling a fresh sense of anxiety. "You're OK, though, right? What happened?"

"Your girlfriend took the screws to Ralph Taggert," said Jackson. "With a bourbon bottle and a pie. It was the nicest takedown I've ever seen."

"I didn't take him down," protested Olivia. "I just reminded him that maybe messing with people I care about is possibly not in his best interest considering all the dirt he gets up to. Just because I don't talk about the skeletons in his closet doesn't mean I *can't*. That's all."

Olivia looked at Eleanor and Eleanor's expression hardened for a moment and then her head tilted as if assessing.

"Oh," said Eleanor softly, "is that all?"

"But with pie," said Jackson. "And bourbon."

Evan glanced nervously at Olivia; she was still holding Eleanor's gaze.

"Well, I am Southern," said Olivia, smiling her sweetest most gracious smile. "I would have brought a cake today, but Jackson said not to, and, also, I threw it against the wall."

"You threw it?" Evan asked. He couldn't imagine Olivia getting that mad.

"I was very upset," said Olivia. "My boyfriend broke up with me, and my grandfather was blackmailing him."

"Well, anyone would be upset about that," said Aiden. "Perfectly reasonable response. Still, a terrible waste of cake though."

"Personally," said Dominique, "I think it's an opportunity."

"Well, if we've learned anything in the last twenty minutes," said Aiden, "it's that you like an opportunity to throw things."

"No, weirdo. I mean *Olivia* is an opportunity. This healthcare bill is family values, the opioid crisis, science, and religion all in one big fat package. And about half of those are Ralph Taggert specialties. But this gives us the opportunity to show that while he may discard his relatives, we welcome them. And isn't that just the perfect metaphor for the bill? He wants to cut people out of the family, but Deverauxes want to bring them in."

Evan glanced at Eleanor, who was looking thoughtful.

"No," said Evan. "We are not using my girlfriend as a talking point."

"You can if you want to—Pops always does," said Olivia. "As long as I don't have to talk to anyone, I'm OK with it. But if you do, you have to get my degrees right. Pops never does. And if you could figure out a way to plug my research at the same time, I'd appreciate it."

"I'll draft something up," said Dominique.

"I'm not sure—" began Eleanor, but she stopped as Theo came in.

"Dinner will be served in five minutes," said Theo. "I have put the portraits of the old Mr. Deveraux in the wine cellar."

"Really? With the wine?" asked Evan, feeling pained.

"Not to worry, Mr. Deveraux. I have turned him to the wall, so as not to make vinegar."

Aiden began to laugh and Dominique nudged him so hard he slipped off the brocade fabric of the couch and fell on the floor.

"Five minutes," repeated Theo, looking disapprovingly at Aiden, and shut the door.

Eleanor sighed and held the glass of scotch to her forehead. "I do not how I shall cope if Theo starts making jokes. I really don't."

"I'm not sure that was a joke," said Evan. "Well," he said looking around at his family, "shall we go into dinner?"

"Yes," said Olivia, smiling up at him, "I'm starved."

Olivia – All Along the Way

"How did it go with Leona?" asked Olivia. Evan grunted and chopped the vegetables faster. "That good?"

"It went fine. I told her that if she had any more clever ideas about blackmail and photographs that I'd burn her to Fetish. She told me to go fuck myself, but in the end, she agreed."

"You think she'll stick to it?"

"Yes," said Evan. "I do. She needs Fetish, and if they found out, they'd blackball her across the city and probably a lot of other places. I also reminded her that I know how she passes all her inside trading tips to Bob Degrossier, which gives me Bob's nuts in a vice as well as hers. She's not going to do anything if she wants to keep her money."

"I can't get used to the idea that…"

"That what?" he asked looking up.

"Well, that all of you Deverauxes are so… I mean, Aiden's so goofy, Dominique is so sweet, and Jackson tries to pretend like he's a grown-up, but he really isn't. I just can't get used to the idea that you're all such…"

"Conniving monsters?" supplied Evan.

"Well, those weren't the words I was going to use," said Olivia.

"And that is one of the things I love about you," said Evan. He put the vegetables in the pot and came around the kitchen island to kiss her and, because it was Naked Tuesday, feel her up.

"Am I safe at second base?" he asked, his eyes twinkling.

"You could probably make it to third," she said. "Assuming

you washed your hands after the onion." He laughed but didn't take the option. "Hey, speaking of awkward conversations. You'll never guess who I talked to today."

"With that as a lead-in, I'm scared to know," Evan said.

"The district attorney's office. They no longer need our testimony."

"What do you mean? I talked to them last month and they were still saying they were going to prosecute!" Evan was looking annoyed in a way that didn't bode well for Glen.

"They don't have to. They finally ran his DNA and it came back as a match for four open rape and assault cases. He ended up taking a plea deal and he's going to prison for like six years."

"Oh," said Evan, looking surprised. "That's good. I didn't want to have to buy his condo."

"Were you going to do that?" asked Olivia, surprised.

"Well, I didn't want to. But I can't have him around here. It seemed like one of the viable solutions."

Olivia was about to speak when they heard a knocking at the front door. They stared at each other.

"Olivia, are you in there?" yelled a female voice. "Can I come in? Um… After you put some clothes on?"

Olivia stared at the door in disbelief. "That's my sister."

"Want the oven mitts?" asked Evan.

"No!"

"Dominique got me new ones."

"Just go answer the door! I'll go put clothes on."

When she came back downstairs, Sofia was standing awkwardly in the dining area, watching Evan cook. Evan was ignoring her. Olivia was rather afraid that Evan's opinion of everyone in her family except Tyler was terribly low.

Olivia stared at her sister. Sofia was carrying the travel

backpack that Olivia had purchased for the non-existent Mexico trip with Clark, and she looked a little glassy-eyed, like she was thinking about crying. Her red curls were escaping from her ponytail like they always did when she was tired.

"Sofia Lynn," said Olivia.

"I went to your apartment," said Sofia. "But you weren't there and then I remembered that it was Tuesday. And then I called Tyler because I didn't know what to do and he said to come here and he gave me the address."

"OK," said Olivia. She wasn't sure what to do with that information. "Did you want to see me for something particular?"

If Sofia started in about wanton harlots again, Olivia was going to kick her straight out the door, no matter if the escaping curls said she needed a hug or not.

"I only had enough money for a bus ride to here," said Sofia. "Or I would have gone to Tyler."

"OK," said Olivia.

"He told me—" A tear escaped Sofia's eye and trickled down her face.

"He told you what?"

"Pops told me to go out with Clark," said Sofia in a tiny whisper of a voice.

Olivia felt an overwhelming sense of rage. She looked at Evan and found her hands clenched in angry fists by her face.

"We don't have any cakes," said Evan. "Go for the pillows in the living room."

"Agghhh!" yelled Olivia.

"Sofia, would you like some wine?" asked Evan.

Sofia looked from Olivia to Evan. "Yes, please?"

Olivia took Evan's advice and went into the living room and kicked a pillow across the room. Then she took a deep breath, counted to twenty, and kicked another pillow. Then she went back into the kitchen and hugged her sister. "I'm sorry, Sofs."

"I'm sorry," said Sofia with half a sob, pressing her face into Olivia's shoulder. "I shouldn't have said those things to you. It's just that ya'll keep leaving me. And that hurts."

"We're not leaving you, Sofia," said Olivia. "We're leaving Pops."

"Yeah, I figured that out right about the time he told me to go put on some lipstick and go talk to Clark."

"I hate Clark," said Evan, pouring stock into the pot of vegetables.

"So say we all," agreed Olivia. "OK, so you left. That's great."

"Is it?" asked Sofia, looking worried. "Liv, I don't even know what I'm going to do! I thought and thought the entire bus ride, but I don't know. How am I supposed to even get a job? All I'm good at is farm stuff."

"Well, Tyler says that he could get you a job in twenty minutes up in Washington," said Olivia. "He says your farm management skills would be in high demand."

"He said that to me too," said Sofia, looking doubtful. "But I don't know. What if he gets me a job and then I screw it up? What if I embarrass him?"

"If I have learned anything in the last week," said Evan, "it's that sometimes your siblings know best. Trust your brother."

Sofia looked from Evan back to Olivia. "He's nice," whispered Sofia. "Can we keep him?"

"I intend to," Olivia whispered back.

After they had sent Sofia back to Olivia's apartment with the keys, Olivia slipped back out of her clothes, brushed her teeth, and washed her face in the bathroom, getting ready for bed. When she was done, she stood up and stared at herself in the mirror. Evan was wandering around in the bedroom, doing whatever it was that he did to get ready for the next day. The familiarity of it was soothing.

She turned to the left and right examining her figure. She knew that, culturally speaking, there was a lot attached to breasts, and sometimes she could get into that, and sometimes she thought they were just some damn big boobies that got in her way both mentally and physically. She wondered what else in her life was the mental equivalent of society's fixation on breasts. Was there something she was attaching an unnatural significance to? She considered that.

The last few weeks had been a round-robin of dinners with Evan's family. She thought they were all delightful. Dominique had hugged her extra hard and Max had been welcoming with a few asides on the oddity of Deverauxes that were completely hilarious and on target. Aiden had been more cautious than his sister but had looked delighted every time she and Evan held hands. It was like he wanted to be level-headed, but seeing Evan happy put him over the moon. Olivia liked that. She had also liked it when Ella had simply put it out there that the Deveraux boys were modern-day Prince Charmings with a little bit of tarnish on their crowns. Olivia was relieved to find someone who validated her opinion. Dinner with Jackson was the easiest, of course. He didn't make them get dressed up or go anywhere. He simply dropped by with take-out after work one night and the three of them had spent the evening laughing.

Olivia had to admit that she'd been feeling a little bit guilty that she was having such a good time with the people who grandfather hated. She wondered when she'd be able to let go of that. She thought that now was the time to start considering how Pops had tried to pimp out Sofia.

Evan came to stand in the doorway. In the mirror, she watched him check out her and then raise an eyebrow at her expression.

"You like my boobs, don't you?" she asked without turning around.

He laughed. "Yes, you could say that."

"But when you think of me, do you think of my boobs first?"

"No," he said, grinning. "I think of the way you look when you get excited. I don't mean just sex kind of excited, but like when you get an idea, or you see a squid, or when…" He paused, blushing.

"When what?" she asked.

"When I come to pick you up at the airport and you finally spot me in the crowd."

"I was happy to see you," she said.

"And that makes *me* unbelievably happy," said Evan.

"I think I should move in with you," she said.

"Uh…" he said. "That sounds great. I've been missing you since we left Japan. I mean, I know there were some other issues there, but I like having you in the next room even when we're not doing things together."

Olivia nodded. That was how she felt as well. But Dominique had also pointed out that moving in with Evan would probably do more to reassure Eleanor than any words could. Olivia thought that meant that Evan would probably never ask her to move in because he wouldn't want to have a reason other than wanting her there.

"I'll check on my lease. I can always sublet if it's a thing."

Evan stepped forward and wrapped his arms around her from behind. "Liv, what's up?"

"Am I being weird?"

"I'm not sure." He kissed her shoulder. "That just seemed a little out of the blue."

"Evan, sugar," she paused to rotate around in his arms, "this is going to sound strange, but when we're old, even if we don't end up together, I think that I would like to live with you."

"What?" he asked, laughing.

She put her arms around his neck and tried to find the words for what she meant.

"I've decided that I don't want to waste any more time on people that want or expect me to be something I'm not. And after everything with your grandmother and Pops, well, I just can't imagine trying to be old, when I will have less energy and probably more problems, and still be trying to keep up appearances. You seem to enjoy me the most when I being the most me. That's what I want for my life. So, when we're old, promise me that we'll hang out and laugh at nerd jokes and do the crossword puzzle together."

"Do we have to wait until we're old?" he asked, smiling down at her. "Can't we just do that all along the way to old?"

"Well, yes," said Olivia, "and also sex."

"I was assuming that," he agreed, leaning down to kiss her.

"And also travel," said Olivia, pulling back at the last second. If he was agreeing to her list of demands, she might as well get them all out there.

"Nerd jokes," he promised, kissing her shoulder. "Crossword puzzles." He kissed her neck. "Sex." He nibbled her earlobe. "Travel." He kissed her temple. "And me cooking you dinner," he said and kissed her lips.

Olivia moaned and melted into him with an overwhelming sense of happiness. They had faced down their families, they had faced down their past and they were together. They had won.

Dominique Deveraux

Dominique waited until Theo had shut the door behind all of her grandmother's staff. Usually, Eleanor didn't have them at the house. Even her assistant was kept stringently to the office that Eleanor owned in mid-town. But today's meeting had been a last-minute hash of the health care bill strategy and the house had been the fastest meeting place. Dominique had weighed in on the public messaging and now she was about to step into the ring with Eleanor. Dominique had never tried to take on Eleanor directly before. She was feeling nervous. And also mad. She was glad Evan had forgiven their grandmother, but even with a few weeks of distance, Dominique found that she hadn't. If anything, she had gotten angrier. Dominique refilled her teacup from the teapot that Theo had provided and considered how to start.

Eleanor finished typing and shut her laptop. "Well," she said, frowning, "I think that will have to do. I don't think there's anything else we can do before we get to D.C."

"I think it will play all right. We'll just have to see how Taggert reacts."

"Jackson believes he won't say anything. He seems to place a great deal of trust in Olivia." Eleanor made a face that expressed that she didn't share Jackson's confidence.

"Olivia, yes," said Dominique. "Ralph, no. If he can find a way to weasel around Olivia I think he will. But if Jackson thinks it will be fine, then I'm sure it will be." She shrugged to indicate that she had no intention of speculating beyond that.

"And you believe whatever Jackson says?" asked Eleanor in what Dominique thought was an unnecessarily condescending tone.

Dominique gently itched the tip of her nose and considered how to reply.

"Yes," said at last. "I do. I also believe the things that Aiden and Evan tell me."

"Hm," said Eleanor, with a small disbelieving smile.

"I don't believe half the things that you tell me," said Dominique. "But that seems justified."

Eleanor's face froze.

"You lie to us, Grandma," said Dominique. "You spy on us, and you treat us like the enemy."

"That is not true," said Eleanor.

"It is. In many respects, we accept this as part of your job and the price of your love."

"The price…" Eleanor flinched a little and her lips tightened as if she had bitten into something sour.

"We understand that your life has not been easy and that you do not trust anyone." Dominique paused to consider. "Well, maybe Theo. But we understand that although you don't trust us, you still care about us."

Eleanor was breathing more heavily than she had been a moment before.

"It's disappointing, of course, but we understand. However," Dominique put her teacup down on the saucer and was pleased to see that her hand was steady. "What you did to Evan cannot happen again. Not to Evan and not any of the rest of us."

"Is that a threat?" demanded Eleanor.

"Yes," said Dominique. "It is."

"I would have thought you would have sent Jackson to make

threats," said Eleanor. Dominique admired her poise. Eleanor was quite good at this. Dominique was envious.

"It's not that kind of threat," said Dominique.

Eleanor's eyes narrowed. "Then what kind of threat is it?"

"If we were talking blackmail and who knows what, and what could we tell…" Dominique sighed. "Then I suppose we would have sent Jackson. But we would never do that to you. We love you."

A micro-expression crossed Eleanor's face and Dominique couldn't quite decipher it. Confusion, maybe. She had seen it when Evan had said *I love you* in the library. Dominique was now resolved to say it to all of her family on every reasonable occasion. Eleanor shouldn't be confused by love. That was wrong. But Eleanor was wrong about several things.

"This was your only free pass, Grandma. We are your family. If something like this happens again—if you treat us as less than your beloved grandchildren—we will stop associating with you. Evan will divest himself of your financial interests. Aiden will pass all his files to your actual lawyers. And I will stop helping your campaign. There will be no support at events. No Sunday dinners. No Christmases. Deveraux House will be empty."

Eleanor was silent. Dominique picked up her teacup and took a sip. She looked out at the garden. Theo had started redoing the brickwork.

"I think Max is going to ask me to marry him soon," she said when she felt like the silence had gone on long enough. She had selected to segue subject carefully. She wasn't sure he really would or not. They had discussed it. The timing was dependent on his application to law school. But the topic would underline just what would be missing from Deveraux House if Eleanor didn't keep herself in line.

"That is excellent," said Eleanor. "He's a darling boy who clearly worships you."

Dominique smiled involuntarily at the thought of Max. "The feeling is mutual," she said. "Although, I'm rather wondering if Aiden is going to beat him to it. He's been trying to convince Ella to move in with him. Not that she practically doesn't already, but I think her family disapproves of such modern conventions as cohabitating."

"I believe he will hold off," said Eleanor. "Her family would probably want children instantly, so as to get them out of the way before Ella takes the reins of Zhao Industries."

"Children? Eek! Aiden couldn't possibly be a parent."

"I think he might be a good father." Eleanor looked like she was trying the idea on for size.

"I'm not ready to be a mother, so he couldn't possibly be ready to be a father," said Dominique, attempting to quash the idea before it blossomed into something. Eleanor gave a soft laugh.

"I don't believe it works that way."

"You might be right," said Dominique. "But I am refusing to consider such nonsense."

"As you wish," said Eleanor. "Honestly, what do you think of Olivia?" Eleanor looked distressed by Olivia's existence. Dominique was going to have to stomp at that idea too.

"Max and I had dinner with Evan and Olivia last week. Fully clothed, of course. It was a Wednesday."

"Of course—what?" Eleanor frowned.

"Never mind," said Dominique. "What I was going to say, was that I like Olivia."

"She's a Taggert," said Eleanor grumpily.

"Well, if Evan plays his cards right, she'll be a Deveraux in a bit and then that will take care of that."

"I really never thought he would get married," said Eleanor, still frowning. "He never seemed to be interested in anyone long term."

Dominique sighed at her grandmother's lack of understanding. "It is very difficult to be interested in anyone long term when you think they might not like you if they found out who you really are. Abuse leaves a legacy of shame. And shame makes open and honest relationships difficult."

Eleanor blinked as if Dominique had grown three heads.

"It's fine," said Dominique. Eleanor wasn't there yet. "I'll send you some books. They're very insightful."

"What?"

"Evan and Olivia are wonderful together. She is brilliant and a good match for our family. I think she'll be an excellent asset."

Eleanor relaxed a fraction, clearly on firmer ground with this statement, although one eyebrow cocked upward skeptically.

"However," continued Dominique, "if we're going to comment on all my male relatives, what do we think the odds were of Evan finding someone before Jackson?"

"Not as bad as you might think," said Eleanor. "Jackson is very much *not* looking for love. I don't think he believes in it."

Dominique blew a small raspberry, and Eleanor blinked in surprise. "What does he know?"

"I thought you just said you believed all the things he said."

"I did. And I do. But he doesn't know everything. And he certainly doesn't know about love."

Eleanor smiled. "I'll leave that to you three then. I certainly never figured it out."

Dominique thought it was the first time she'd ever heard her grandmother admit to not knowing something.

"You're right," Dominique said. "I'll have to talk to the boys.

There must be something we can do. We obviously can't leave Jackson to his own devices."

Eleanor shook her head. "Leave the poor boy alone. Doesn't he have enough to contend with?"

"Nonsense, Grandma. We only want him to be happy."

Aiden Deveraux

Aiden's phone vibrated on the table and he picked it up. Evan was discussing wine with the sommelier. There were only two modes of discussion for sommeliers when faced with Evan—defeated or excited to have a fellow enthusiast to obsess with. This one was flailing the wine list in excitement.

OLIVIA IS SCARY SMART. SHE JUST DID A CHEMICAL BREAKDOWN ON THE BATHROOM SOAP OFF THE TOP OF HER HEAD.

Aiden saw Evan look his way when he laughed at the text message. The sommelier ran down Evan's list, and Evan nodded approvingly.

"That should take care of us," said Evan, leaning back in his chair as the sommelier left. Aiden thought Evan looked happier and more relaxed than he could ever remember him. "Funny message?"

"Ella says your girlfriend is scary smart."

"She is," agreed Evan.

"Yes, but that's coming from a woman who is both scary and smart herself. So I'm saying Olivia's smartness maybe sort of in the stratosphere."

"We like smart women," said Evan with a shrug. "And yes, she is that smart. Lord knows what she's doing with me. I think I may have bribed my way into her heart through cooking."

"That actually works?" asked Aiden. "Damn it. I don't want to learn how to cook."

"I think you got yours on lock by solving her father's murder," said Evan. "I think you're good."

"Oh. Good point. Whew."

Evan snorted and shook his head.

"Evan?"

"Yeah?"

Aiden hesitated and then shook his head. Why was he even trying to bring this up? They were having a perfectly nice evening. Why did he try to ruin everything? "Never mind."

"What?"

Aiden didn't want to say it, but he couldn't shake the thought. "I know we just got this all resolved and I don't want to open up any more trouble, but I can't help thinking…"

"Thinking what?" asked Evan.

"Why shouldn't we look at the plane crash files?" Evan didn't say anything, and Aiden fiddled with his water glass nervously. "You barely even dug into the plane crash. I mean, not really, and Grandma flipped the fuck out and went the nuclear route."

"That wasn't the only reason," said Evan.

"Yeah, yeah," Aiden agreed, nodding. "But… I can't help thinking that it seems odd. I'm not trying to start anything, but I just… If I were working on a case and something like this came up, I would tear into it. It would bug me and bug me until I did something about it."

"Well," said Evan, straightening his silverware, "fortunately, we have Jackson, so you don't have to."

"You already talked to Jackson?" asked Aiden.

Evan shrugged. "He also thought it was… an overreaction."

"Do you think it was?" asked Aiden, cautiously. He was fascinated to get an insight into Evan and Jackson disagreeing over something. Usually, they seemed to be on the same page.

Evan sighed. "I don't know. I think that Grandma only knows one way to fight and that's all in and to the death. If she gets scared, there are no half-measures. What she did to me may have been an overreaction, but I'm not sure that is something we can read into."

Aiden let out a long breath. "Yeah," he said. "Yeah. You're right. I just…" He shook his head, unable to put the niggling suspicion out of his head.

"Jackson agrees and that's why he's looking into it," said Evan.

"Well, if you don't agree, are you OK with that?" asked Aiden, and Evan threw up his hands in frustration.

"What am I supposed to argue with? Jackson looking out for us? Your very well-honed legal instincts? It doesn't matter if we agree or not. If I'm right then Jackson finds nothing. If I'm wrong, Jackson will keep us from being blind-sided in the future."

Aiden sat back in his chair. "That's very reassuring. I'm going to start complaining to you all the time. You make me feel better."

Evan snorted. "Please don't."

"Nope, too late," said Aiden, latching onto a way to annoy Evan. "I've already decided." He grinned at his older cousin, waiting for Evan's riposte.

"You're looking far too happy with yourself," said Evan, which didn't even rate on the Evan scale of sarcasm. Evan was apparently in the best mood of all time.

"I am. But, Evan," said Aiden, "if we're all getting along and happy… who the fuck are we? I'm not sure that's allowed for the Deveraux family."

"My therapist assures me that it *is* allowed. Although, are we all happy? Seems to me that Jackson has been doing nothing for the last six years, except running around cleaning up our messes. Wasn't he supposed to be living the cushy post-prison life?"

Aiden chuckled. "I'd say we should get him a girlfriend, but I have introduced him to lots of girls—society girls, waitresses, lawyers… I've thrown lots of girls at him. It never goes anywhere."

"Well, it frequently goes somewhere," said Evan.

"Yeah, it goes somewhere," agreed Aiden, "but only with the

ones that weren't interested in anything beyond the next couple of hours. If our cousin could carry a flashing neon sign that said *Does Not Want a Relationship* I'm pretty sure he would."

"Yeah," said Evan, "but I mean… he's been busy with us. And I don't know about you, but my general plan is to not have these kinds of problems in the future. If he's not looking after us, maybe he could look after himself."

"Hm," said Aiden, considering that idea. "I wonder what kind of girl he would like. I mean, other than pretty."

"A smart one," said Evan. "Naturally."

Aiden laughed. "Yeah, OK. We'll find him a smart one."

"Find who a smart one of what?" asked Olivia as she and Ella returned to the table.

"We're trying to pick out a girl for Jackson," said Evan, smiling up at her. Aiden couldn't stop himself from smiling like an echo. Evan looked so happy when he looked at Olivia.

"Ooh," said Olivia, sitting down. "Yes, she has to be smart."

"And tough," said Ella, returning to her chair. "She can't be one of these society cream puffs."

"No, a little bit of cream puff!" argued Olivia. "So he can rescue her."

"I'm not sure Jackson likes being a knight in shining armor," said Aiden with a laugh. "None of us do. It runs in the family."

Olivia looked at Ella, who made an expression that Aiden didn't quite catch.

"OK," said Olivia, in a beaming, hundred-watt lie of an agreement.

"I think maybe she could just not *want* to be rescued," said Ella, as if she were trying the argument on for size.

"That could work!" agreed Olivia.

Evan laughed. "So, we need a smart, tough, pretty girl who

needs to be rescued, but doesn't want to be? I'm sure we'll bump into one of those any minute."

Jackson Deveraux

Jackson got out of the car and waited for the rest of his crew to do the same. Pete stepped out and looked around the neighborhood critically. The streets were wide, clean, and at ten in the evening, empty. To Jackson, it seemed strange. Devonte got out of the SUV and jogged across the street to meet him.

"This place gives me the creeps."

"Same," said Jackson, looking suspiciously at the tall oak trees. He thought they were oak based on the leaf shape, but he wasn't completely sure.

"Yeah, but you probably aren't going to get shot for being here," said Devonte.

"I'm hoping we brought enough white dudes that won't happen," said Jackson.

"Not funny," said Pete, walking up behind Devonte with Kerschel in tow. She looked excited.

"I wasn't joking," said Jackson. "This is exactly the kind of neighborhood I would have been ripping off back in the day. I know what kind of private security and cops I had to bribe. I'm hoping Devonte wore a vest."

Devonte flipped open his jacket, revealing his vest. "Might be overkill, but my girl likes me to come home alive."

"Seems reasonable," said Jackson, wondering how everyone he knew had someone to go home to. He loved all of his cousin's significant others, but he was starting to feel like the odd man out.

"Here comes Garcia," said Pete. They all turned to watch the dark-haired man walk briskly down the sidewalk.

"I didn't see anyone," said Garcia without preamble. "But

some lights came on while I was watching. So someone has to be home."

"Are we sure about this?" asked Pete.

"Riley said bail would be revoked when she got the charges filed on Evan's Nazis. So as of…" Jackson checked his watch, "forty-five minutes ago, Granger is wanted by the police. Now probably, they're talking to his lawyers and expecting him to turn himself in, but I don't care what they want. I didn't go through the trouble of getting licensed in a bail bonds and recovery just so I could make our building's sign accurate. I want to haul Granger's ass back to prison personally."

Pete sighed. "All right. If you're set on this, then we are going to do it with the minimum amount of fuss and bother. Kerschel is going to cut the security system. Garcia and I go in the front. You and Devonte go in the back. We stay live on coms. No one fucking gets trigger happy. I want zero guns drawn. Once we have him, we signal Kerschel and she drives up to the front door and we leave nice and quiet."

They all looked at Jackson to see what he thought of the plan.

"Sounds great," said Jackson, giving an exaggerated thumbs up. Devonte snickered and Pete gave him a drop-dead look.

The team split up and he and Devonte walked along the back alley until they were behind Granger's house.

"So I talked to Evan this morning," said Devonte, as they waited for Kerschel's signal.

"Yeah?"

"He grows on you after a while."

Jackson chuckled. "Yeah."

"We usually talk about stock trading and stuff." Jackson squinted at Devonte, trying to assess where this was going. "Anyway, um, he said that if I was interested in taking the Series Seven, he could help me."

"What's a Series Seven?" asked Jackson.

"It's the test you have to pass to become a stockbroker. You have to be sponsored by a legit firm to even take the test. Evan said he could sponsor me if I wanted to get serious."

"Well, fuck, no," said Jackson. "You can't go work with him. I need you around to give Pete shit so that I don't have to."

Devonte laughed. "Is that my primary job function?"

"You may do a few other things," admitted Jackson. "Are you going to do it?"

"Are you going to freak if I do?" asked Devonte.

"A little bit," said Jackson. "I'm freaking out right now. Hiring people is hard. Who am I going to get to replace you?"

"I haven't made a decision. I'm still thinking. I mean, I can't do this forever. It's a career with a limited life span. I'm going to need a retirement job."

Jackson grunted. Devonte's logic made sense; it was just inconvenient for him personally.

"Well, I would prefer you to put it off a few years, but you have to do what's right for you," said Jackson after a minute.

"You're not even..." Devonte trailed off.

"What?"

"You don't think it's weird?"

"What's weird?"

"Me being a stockbroker?"

"Well, you're the only one who can get the math right on your expense reports," said Jackson. "Which probably isn't a pre-qualifier for stockbrokering, or whatever it's called, but it seems relevant. Plus, if Evan thinks you can do it, then I'm sure he's right."

"You don't think he'd shine me up due to the Nazi thing?" asked Devonte, and Jackson snorted.

"No."

"I wouldn't even have met Evan if it weren't for you."

"Yeah?" Jackson was lost.

"Some people might be mad about that," suggested Devonte.

Jackson still felt lost. "I don't know. It seems fine."

"You know," said Devonte, "you Deverauxes are like the chillest assholes I know."

"Aw, thanks," said Jackson, feeling genuinely complimented.

Jackson's earpiece chirped.

"Security is down," said Kerschel. "Good luck."

"Let's do this," said Jackson. He led the way to the back door. A few minutes with a lock-pick let them into the mudroom. They walked through the house until they met Pete and Garcia in the front hall. The light was on in the living room, but no one was there. Pete gestured them toward the stairs and they all followed the older man to the second floor. By the time they reached the well-lit bedroom Jackson had a bad feeling. The room, despite the light being on, looked empty. The bed was still made, but the dresser drawers had been pulled open, and a safe that would ordinarily be hidden behind a painting was exposed and open.

"I don't think he's here," said Devonte.

"I saw lights being turned off and on," said Garcia. "We can't have missed him by more—"

Before he could finish his sentence, the bedroom light went off. All four of them jumped. Jackson let out an angry growl and stomped over to the light switch and flipped the light back on.

"He's got one of those damn smart house integrations," Jackson said, tapping the display panel by the light switch. "They're either on a timer, or he's doing it on his phone. Devonte, go check the bathroom. Everyone else spread out tell me what you see."

The team scattered and Jackson went to check the safe. There was an empty gun-carrying box and suspicious powder residue. Granger had left with a gun, drugs—he leaned down to check the outlines in the dust—maybe papers of some kind.

"Shower is dry. Toothbrush is missing," Devonte yelled from the bathroom.

"His phone is in the next room on the desk," said Pete coming in from the hall.

"At least three pairs of shoes are missing," said Garcia, coming out of the walk-in closet.

"He split," said Pete.

"Maybe he turned himself in?" offered Garcia, looking like he wished he believed himself.

"Or maybe he knew what was coming down on him and he jumped bail," said Devonte.

"He's gone," said Jackson.

"Yeah, but…" Jackson turned to look at Pete, waiting for the *but* in the sentence to turn into something good. "His assets are frozen and he's got no cash. I don't think he can get that far. We can find him."

"We'd better," said Jackson. "He has a gun and he hates my family. I'm not going to wait around to find out what he can do. Reach out to every contact you have. I want him found."

Find out more at:

www.BethanyMaines.com

ABOUT THE AUTHOR

Bethany Maines is the award-winning author of action adventure and fantasy tales that focus on women who know when to apply lipstick and when to apply a foot to someone's hind end. When she's not traveling to exotic lands, or kicking some serious butt with her black belt in karate, she can be found chasing after her daughter, or glued to the computer working on her next novel.

OTHER WORKS BY BETHANY MAINES

CARRIE MAE MYSTERIES

Bulletproof Mascara
Compact With The Devil
High-Caliber Concealer
Glossed Cause

THE DEVERAUX LEGACY

The Lost Heir
A Deveraux Legacy Novella

The Second Shot
PNWA 2019 Literary Contest Award Winner

The Cinderella Secret
The Hardest Hit

GALACTIC DREAMS

When Stars Take Flight Vol. 1

The Seventh Swan Vol. 2
A Book Excellence Award Winner

The Beast of Arsu Vol. 3

SAN JUAN ISLANDS MURDER MYSTERIES

An Unseen Current
Against the Undertow
An Unfamiliar Sea

SHARK SANTOYO CRIME SERIES

Shark's Instinct
Shark's Bite
Shark's Hunt
Shark's Fin
Peregrine's Flight
Shark's Blood

Wild Waters
A Paranormal Romantic Suspense

BLUE ZEPHYR PRESS

Enjoy other books from Blue Zephyr Press!

THE FAARIAN CHRONICLES: EXILE
by Karen Harris Tully

Fifteen-year-old Sunny Price dreams of being an Olympic gymnast, but thanks to the worst custody agreement in the universe, she finds out she's half-alien and is exiled to her absentee-mother's home planet. She has to give up her friends and elite gymnastics career to live with a mother who only wants to give orders? This. Sucks.

THE CHRISTMAS SPIRIT
by J.M. Phillippe

In this award-winning dark comedy inspired by Charles Dickens A Christmas Carol, Charlene Dickenson's untimely death in a Christmas-related accident means she must do whatever it takes to become a Ghost of Christmas Past, Present, or Future or spend her after-life in chains. Can she learn to embrace the Christmas Spirit?